until him

CORA ROSE

credits

Editor: Angela O'Connell

Cover photography by Michelle Lancaster @lanefotograf

To my readers who said they'd read anything I wrote, including but not limited to, grocery lists, dog poo and beet farmers. This is for you.

I wrote this for me and then thought I'd share it with you.

one

LOGAN

"YOU NEED a tutor if you're going to pass this class." My chemistry professor's voice echoes in my head, and it's only overpowered by my coach's gruff one. *"If your GPA falls any lower, we'll have to bench you."*

Fuck me.

This is impossible. I run a hand through my damp, curly hair and sigh.

You would think I've made it this far at UC Berkeley because I'm smart. Nah, I'm only here because I was recruited to play on their competitive water polo team and I'm the motherfucking best at what I do. I can swim faster than all those assholes out there. I can chuck the ball across the entire pool. I can tread water for hours. I'm a winner. Winning is all I know how to do.

Except, when it comes to academics, I am drowning.

My head is barely above the water, and I am sinking fast. I need a life raft.

Case in point, as I stand in the grungy hallway and rap my knuckles against the apartment door in front of me. I need this. I need him, and only him. Theo Reign. The best science tutor on campus. It is said that he works miracles, and at this point, a goddamn miracle is the only thing that will save me.

If I fail chemistry, I lose my spot on the team, and then I have nothing left. I am nothing without water polo.

My phone buzzes in my pocket, and I quickly glance at it.

Shit, my mom. I'll call her later—if I work up the courage.

I hear the soft thud of footsteps make their way toward me, and the door is wrenched open. My eyes land on a tall, lanky guy with messy brown hair and pale blue eyes. He's not wearing a shirt, allowing me to take in the lean muscles of his abdomen and a large script tattoo that stretches across his entire right side.

"Who the fuck are you?" he rasps, irritation lining his voice. He shoves the pencil he's holding behind his ear and folds his arms across his chest. His sweatpants are hanging low on his narrow hips and they look like they're in danger of falling right off.

"Uh, hi there. I'm looking for Theo." I say, forcing my gaze up to his eyes.

"I'm Theo. What do you want?"

"Hey man," I say, plastering on a wide smile, trying my best to make a good first impression. "I'm Logan. I was told to come see you for tutoring and—"

He holds up a hand and shakes his head. "No. Nope. I don't have time to help you. You look like a lost cause. My schedule is full. I'm booked out through next year."

Slightly stunned, I huff out a breath and rub the back of my neck. I mean, no one ever says no to me. It's never happened and never will. I eventually get them all to come around.

I'm charming as hell, a motherfucking prince. I coyly peek up at him with a small smile.

"Yeah, man, I understand that. But you came highly recommended, and I can't fail this class. I can't drop it, either. It's past the withdrawal period. I don't think I have any other options."

I mean, I do have other tutoring options, but none are as good as this guy. He helped one of my teammates pass chemistry last year, and that guy was the real lost cause. Like incredibly lost—out to fucking sea with the sharks. I can still see the shore at least.

"The hell," he huffs, his light blue eyes inspecting mine, and for a moment, I think he's going to give in, but then he just arches an eyebrow at me. "That's not my problem, is it? Sometimes the weak just need to fail. It's a good life lesson for those of you who think you're invincible."

I frown at those words. I've heard that one too many times, but I'm not giving up yet. I'm not a quitter. This is my life on the line here. Water polo is everything to me. It's what I was born to do.

"Come on, name your price. Everyone has a price. I'll pay double. I'll pay anything."

He narrows his eyes and moistens his lips, his gaze

moving slowly from the top of my head all the way down to my toes. He's sizing me up, I realize, and my back straightens a bit under his scrutiny.

"I don't want your money."

I open my mouth to protest but then he says, "I'll agree to tutor you if you let me fuck you."

My jaw drops open and my muscles tense. He's smirking, his steely gaze boring into mine, a challenge twinkling in them.

"What the hell? I'm not even gay."

He just shrugs and leans against the doorjamb. "That's my price. One sexual favor for each lesson. Take it or leave it."

I eye his casual stance and wonder if he's actually serious. He could just be fucking with me. But what if he's not? Could I actually agree to this? I've never been with a guy before. I mean, yeah, there were some mutual jack-off sessions in high school with a couple of teammates, but we never touched each other's dicks. I may have discretely looked at them while beating my meat, but I've never actually *done* anything with a dude.

Don't get me wrong, I'm not completely repulsed by the idea. My dick is awesome, so I assume all dicks are awesome. I just don't know how I feel about pimping myself out to some random dude for good grades.

I really do need his help though. Fuck, I am in a bit of a pickle. I shift on my feet, gnawing on my lip, as I try to figure out this guy's angle.

"Are you for real? That's your price? You sure you don't

want money or, I dunno, fame? We could be friends, hang out publicly. I mean, I am *the* Logan Lewis."

I stick my thumb against my chest and tilt my head back a little, but Theo just rolls his eyes.

He rolls his fucking eyes at me!

"I have no idea who the hell you are, and even if I did, I couldn't give two shits about you. But I am in need of a good fucking, and I've been too busy this semester to put in the effort of going out and finding someone."

Well, he's entirely too honest.

I glance around the dim, empty hall warily. "You swear this isn't a joke? You're not just teasing me?"

He pulls the pencil out from behind his ear and flicks it between his fingers. "Bye."

The door starts to close in my face, but I quickly press my hand to it, holding it open. "Wait! Not so fast. I didn't say no."

I swallow, and Theo taps his bare foot on the floor impatiently. He's twirling the pencil around his fingers as he watches me.

Shit. If I don't take this deal, I could fail my class, and there goes my time in the water. I'll be kicked off the team, and I'll lose my scholarship and have to leave school.

Hell.

What would my parents think if they knew I was even considering this? My brother? My friends? It wouldn't be good, that's for sure. I could just say forget it and walk away now. But my heart rate triples and my stomach hurts from just the thought of losing my spot on the team. The fucked-up truth is I need him, desperately.

I can do this. I have to do this. And if I really think about it, whoring myself for tutoring isn't even the most embarrassing thing I've done. Probably doesn't even make the top five, if I'm really honest.

"Fine. Fine. I'll do whatever. Just help me out, man. I'm begging."

The pencil freezes in his hand and he cocks his head, eyes slightly widened. I've surprised him by agreeing, I know it, but that little reaction disappears the next second, and his mask of indifference snaps back into place.

"Fine. Come back tomorrow. Six o'clock. Bring your study shit with you. And a copy of negative test results."

I blink at him, speechless.

"I assume you have those."

"Yeah, but—"

The door slams in my face before I can finish my sentence, and I just blink at it. Well, that was interesting.

I look up and down the hallway, half-expecting to see video cameras hidden somewhere. Maybe my teammates are playing a practical joke on me, but when no one makes an appearance, I just move toward the rickety stairs that lead down to the parking lot. They groan and creak under my weight, but I barely notice.

Because, seriously, what the fuck did I just get myself into?

* * *

"I'm sorry, you did what?" my best friend, Finn, asks as I sink into the couch in the small living room we share. It's a small one-bedroom apartment off campus that's sparsely furnished. Not that we really spend much time here. I'm usually in class or in the water, and Finn spends every free second with his other best friend—my brother, Landon.

I groan and rub a hand down my face. Finn is never going to let me live this down. Hell, I don't even know if I will let myself live this down. I am selling my body for tutoring services. Is this a new low? Because it kind of feels like it. Although, I'm not as upset about it as I probably should be.

"You heard me the first time. Don't pretend like you didn't."

He sweeps a lock of his shaggy brown hair out of his eyes and then crosses his arms over his broad chest. The two of us play on the same team and have been friends since middle school. We've been inseparable for years, even choosing to be college roommates. So, he knows me, and it shouldn't surprise me how well he can read me.

"How the hell did you manage to get yourself into this?" he asks, cocking his head and watching me intently.

Take a good, hard look, buddy. I'm just as confused as you.

"I dunno, man. I'm desperate."

"So, let me get this straight—no pun intended—you're going over to some strange dude's place, and you're going to fuck around with him in hopes of maybe, hopefully passing a chemistry class?"

I sigh. "Yeah, it's the only way he'd help me."

Finn just eyes me like I've grown two heads. I probably have. I'm obviously not thinking clearly. Maybe neither of those heads have a brain.

"But you're not gay."

"Yeah, so? Sexuality is a squiggly line, right? Maybe I am a little gay or bi or whatever. I just don't know because I've never tried it. I have an open mind. Dicks are cool, and I'm willing to try anything. Hell, maybe I'll even enjoy it. He's not bad-looking, you know? His eyes are kind of...eerie, but he's sort of...hot?"

Finn blinks at me like he can't understand the words coming out of my mouth.

"Fuckin' hell," I mutter, growing just a bit frustrated at how dense he's being. If anyone is the dense one, it's me. Not him.

Stop pretending to be me, Finn.

"What else should I do, huh? There's no one else as good as him. Everyone's told me this. Even the TA for the class said, 'Logan, if you want a shot, you need Theo Reign'. Would you rather I sit out for the rest of the season? Because that's what will happen if I don't pass this class. My GPA is hanging on for dear life. Coach was yelling at me over it. He brought me to tears, man. I cried like a baby."

"Jesus, I don't want you to sit out, Logan, but what this guy is doing has gotta be illegal or some shit. He can't coerce you into sex. That's sexual harassment or something."

"Nah, I don't think it's illegal. His tutoring services aren't affiliated with the school, so I think he can do whatever he wants. He seems a little rogue anyway. But he's not coercing me and we're not exchanging money. We came to an agreement. Whatever we do, I'll be a willing participant."

Finn plops down next to me and eyes me. "What if you can't get it up or something? What then?"

"I dunno. I'm not going to worry about that until it happens."

I try to envision it, bending Theo's lithe body over and pushing my way inside his tight hole, and my dick twitches in my pants. And then, when I reverse the roles, and I'm the one bent over and taking it up the ass, my dick leaps to attention.

Oh, for fuck's sake.

I am so screwed.

We sit in silence. The only sound is the TV playing softly in the background. Finn fiddles with his phone, twirling it around and around in his hand.

"When do you go over?" he asks suddenly, and I jump. Shit, I'm nervous. If I think too hard about it, I start to sweat. It's not a good look.

"Tomorrow at six."

"Wow," Finn says, and then a small laugh bursts from him. "Hell, man, only this kind of stuff happens to you. I swear to God. You have the worst luck."

I rub a hand across my jaw. "It's the family curse. That's what this is."

He leans back and laughs loudly because he thinks it's a joke, but it's no joking matter. My family is fucking cursed. No one believes me, but it's a real thing. I'm like the kid in that book *Holes*. The cycle never ends.

Just look at my motherfucking luck. My virgin hole is going to get railed by some science nerd just so I can keep my spot on the water polo team. And then look at my brother...

Shit. *My brother.*

My heart clenches in my chest, and I rub at it. I need to

call him or text him or something. I can't keep avoiding him. It's been a year since the accident, and I've been acting all shifty, and he knows something's up.

"You should go see him. He misses you," Finn says, reading my mind.

Asshole's always doing that.

"I just saw him last month."

Finn nudges me, and I huff. My brother, Landon, and I used to be close. We talked almost every day before the accident, but the immense guilt has kept me from reaching out. Seeing him reminds me of *that day* and it's suffocating.

"Yeah, yeah. I'll call him. I will. I promise."

"He doesn't blame you."

I rub my chest again and then nod.

"Yeah, alright," I say, shutting the conversation down. I can't think about it too hard, or I get really sad.

"Okay, I'll let it go, but you have to keep me in the loop with this tutoring thing. Let me know how it goes," Finn says, slapping me roughly on the back of the head.

Shit, that hurts. Why does he have to be so rough with me? He isn't like this with my brother. I know that for a fact. We've all been best friends for ages and he's always been super gentle and thoughtful when it comes to Landon. He even brings Landon donuts, for fuck's sake. But do I get food? No, I get noogies and "playful" punches to the gut.

"Yeah, asshole, keep dreaming," I mutter.

No way I'm telling him shit.

I'll take what happens between me and Theo to the grave.

* * *

I show up at Theo's apartment five minutes early and debate waiting outside until the clock strikes six, but decide against it.

I just want to get this over with. I'm nervous as fuck, and in the past few hours, I've managed to really work myself up over this. My heart is pounding and my hands are clammy.

My knuckles rap on the door, and I experience a sense of déjà vu when it opens and I see Theo standing before me.

"You're early. When I said six, I meant *six*," he grumbles, the pencil hanging between his pink lips. He's wearing a pair of ragged grey jogger sweats, and once again, he's not wearing a shirt. What is his deal? Where are this guy's clothes? Maybe he's perpetually doing laundry.

His tattoo is on display, but the writing is small and in fancy cursive, so no matter how long I stare at it, I can't quite read what it says.

"Yeah, well, here I am. I didn't want to be late," I mutter.

He stares at me for a moment, and I half-expect him to make me wait in the hallway for another four minutes, but then he swings the door open further.

"Fine. Come in. We can get started."

I step inside his small studio apartment and take a look around. It's sparsely decorated with a murphy bed pulled out from the wall, a wooden desk and chair set shoved in the far corner, and a TV perched on a dresser. Directly to my right is a small kitchen with a microwave on the counter, and to my left is a closed door that I can only assume is a bathroom.

From the corner of my eye, I see a fluffy grey and white cat make its way out from underneath the bed.

"You have a cat," I say, smiling. For some reason, it makes him seem a little more relatable and less callous. I mean, you have to have some compassion to own a pet, right?

Theo eyes me like I'm an idiot for mentioning it. Whatever, I'm just trying to make small talk. I've got a serious case of nerves.

"What's its name?" I ask, holding my hand out and making little kissing noises toward it. The cat just stares at me like I've lost my mind.

Yeah, I kind of have, but what am I supposed to do, huh? Don't judge me, cat.

"Why the fuck do you care?" Theo asks sharply.

"Just want to know, is all."

He sighs loudly. "Her name is Curie."

"Oh...." I say, trying to figure out if this is like a play on words or something. I come up with nothing. Maybe he likes Indian food or some shit.

"Marie Curie was a female scientist." When my face registers that I still don't know what the hell he's talking about, he rolls his eyes. "Never mind."

I eye the cat once more and she suddenly turns and jumps onto the bed. She turns her neck to look back at me and flicks her tail as if proudly displaying her butthole.

Ok, maybe I was wrong about the cat. Maybe the cat is just as odd as Theo. Maybe they feed off of each other's strangeness.

"After services are rendered, we'll fuck," Theo says suddenly, and I flinch, my asshole clenching tightly.

Shit. Is this guy for real? He's more efficient than the local drug dealer back home...and that guy even has a website.

I wonder if Theo has one too.

Will tutor for anal.

I bob my head all casual, even though my heart thumps wildly in my chest. "Cool. Sounds good."

"We'll shake on it," he says and then holds out his hand. I stare at it before slipping mine inside of his. He has nice fucking hands—warm and strong with long fingers that curl around mine, and I suddenly wonder what they'd feel like wrapped around my dick.

He pumps our clasped hands twice, completely oblivious to where my mind has gone, thank God, and then gestures toward the floor.

"We'll sit here and work. Is that good enough for *the* Logan Lewis?"

Okay, I know when a dude is mocking me. But there's no need. Really, this kid can just chill.

"Yeah, it's cool," I say, trying not to sound irritated, because what else am I supposed to do? Complain? I have a feeling that wouldn't go down well.

I'm in this for the long haul; I'm committed.

I slide onto the floor and lean back against the edge of the bed. Then I extend my legs and set my laptop and chemistry book on my thighs. They're pretty thick thighs, if I do say so, like a nice little tabletop. It's from treading water all day long. Oh, and I can't forget those killer squats Coach makes us do.

He's a bit of a sadist, I think.

I wonder if Theo is impressed. The women I'm with

usually are, but what about this guy? What does he think when he looks at me?

I glance up and see him standing across the small room, his eyes on me, the pencil tapping against his lips. Fuck, he's unnerving. Why does he keep staring at me? I don't think he's checking me out, either. I think he's probably measuring my skin for lampshades.

Maybe he'll cook up my ass and eat it with a side of broccolini.

"Ready when you are," I tell him, gesturing to the space next to me.

Theo seems jolted out of whatever reverie he was in and moves to my side. He lowers himself next to me, grabbing onto a small whiteboard and marker on his way down. When he grabs the book off my lap, his hand grazes my leg, and I flinch a little.

Fuck, I'm tense, and we haven't even done anything yet.

But if he notices my nerves, he says nothing about it. He just calmly looks at me and says, "Tell me what you're struggling with, and we'll go from there."

The cat moves over to where we're sitting and splays across the floor in front of us, her yellow eyes slowly blinking at me.

Asshole cat...acting all nonchalant about this whole situation.

I wet my lips and then explain to Theo what I don't understand, which is basically everything. I don't even know if he can understand the shit flowing out of my mouth right now. I ramble on for a couple minutes and whatever I'm saying sounds like gibberish to even my own ears. I'm not sure I'm even speaking English.

"So—" he stops me mid-sentence, "you need help with pretty much everything," he mutters, running a hand through his hair. "I should have known. You better be really good with your mouth."

"I've never had any complaints," I reply. "One girl even said, 'Logan, your mouth was made in heaven.'"

He looks mildly disgusted. "Oh Jesus, no more, please."

"Yeah, yeah," I mutter.

Theo takes a deep breath and then delves right in. He doesn't even ask if I'm ready; he just starts talking and drawing on his board, and I'm left scrambling to write everything down. But once the initial panic wears off, what he's saying starts to actually make sense. The concepts that seemed so foreign to me in class sound completely logical with how he explains them. No wonder he came so highly recommended. No wonder he's booked out a year in advance. He's fucking amazing.

He also seems a hell of a lot more personable when he's teaching about chemical bonds and thermodynamics. His scathing attitude falls away and I get a small peek at the pleasant—dare I say happy?—side of Theo.

When the book closes with a thump an hour later, I lean back astonished. My hand is slightly cramped from all the writing I've done, and my brain feels a size too big for my skull, but I actually understand a hell of a lot more than I did when I arrived.

Maybe I won't sit on the bench for the rest of the season. Maybe I actually have a shot at this.

"Well shit, Theo," I mutter, watching as he sets the whiteboard and marker on the floor. The cat walks over and swats at it, rolling it right under the bed. "You're a genius."

He fiddles with the pencil tucked behind his ear. "Technically, I'm not."

"To me, you are," I murmur and then feel my cheeks begin to flush because I've just remembered that my tutoring session is over, and it's time for fucking. "Alright," I say, just wanting to get this over with. I run my sweaty hands over my thighs and exhale shakily. "What do we do now?"

Theo doesn't answer me right away. I look up at his face and he's just sitting a foot away, watching me, assessing me. His arctic blue eyes are unreadable, and I start to squirm. What the hell is he thinking?

He reminds me of a cat, actually. Maybe Curie is his spirit animal.

"You're making me nervous, man," I mutter, and he blinks slowly, almost as if coming out of some kind of trance.

"I need to see your test results."

Oh shit, yeah, I forgot all about them, and it's important. My hands tremble slightly as I pull them up on my phone and show him. He eyes my screen and then pulls his up on his phone.

The words swim and shift on the paper, but I see enough.

He's good to go.

So, as crazy as this is, we're not being reckless.

"Alright. Now, on the bed, shirt off, face up," he says.

My heartbeat is in my ears as I push myself off the floor and sink down on his bed. The mattress is a little lumpy and uncomfortable, and as I wrench my shirt off and lean back, I wonder how the hell he comfortably sleeps on this thing.

"All the way back," Theo says, and I flop the rest of the way down. My fingers clench the soft fabric of his comforter, and my eyes are fixed on the popcorn ceiling. Curie has hopped onto the bed and sits on the pillow directly next to my head, watching me intently.

Oh, fuck this.

Two sets of eyes on me are making me nervous, like I have to perform or something.

I'm *never* this nervous. I always perform so well under pressure, but for some reason, my entire body is thrumming with nerves now. This cat watching me is pushing me over the edge.

"Can you move the cat?" I ask. "It's just a little weird."

Theo tosses the pencil onto his desk. It clatters noisily against the tabletop as he moves toward me. He crawls up the bed and straddles my thighs.

"No."

"Shit," I mutter, trying to block Curie from my vision, but that puffball is all I can see. She's lying down now, purring. It's fucking distracting.

Shit on a stick.

What did I say about the family curse? It can't get any more terrible than this.

"Are you afraid of cats?"

"I'm not afraid...." I say, but my words come out choked as he plants himself right over my pelvis and sinks down against my soft, scared dick.

"You're shaking," he says, his eyes narrowed and his cheeks flushed. "Why are you shaking? Are you afraid?"

"I'm not afraid of anything," I mutter as I reach out and cup him.

Beneath my palm, I can feel his soft cock through his sweatpants, and I just press against it, not sure what else to do.

I mean, I should know what to do. I'm a dude. I jack off ritually. But I've never touched another guy's junk before. I don't know what he likes. This guy seems like he has standards, and I'm not sure I can live up to them.

"Well, come on then," Theo says, his hands fisted on his thighs. "Get me hard."

"You should be hard already," I say. "I'm Logan Lewis."

He huffs a humorless laugh and shakes his head. "Jesus, guys like you always think you're something special, but you're just ordinary."

Well, no one has ever told me that before, and it makes me feel a bit defensive.

"I'm not ordinary."

He eyes my bare chest and then grabs ahold of my hand and slides it against his dick. I feel it start to slowly lengthen and harden in his pants.

"The only thing not ordinary about you is your abs. They're ridiculously cut." He runs a hand across them, and I flex a little more so his fingertips bounce across them. When he reaches the waistband of my jeans, he stops.

"Pull me out," he says, his voice strained, and I freeze, my hand still cupping his dick over his pants and my other clutching onto the comforter for dear life.

He rolls his eyes when I don't move, hooks his thumbs into the waistband of his sweatpants, and tugs them down. They stretch across his thighs as his cock emerges long and thick before me.

I do absolutely nothing but stare at it.

It's humongous, and it's making eye contact with me.

"Go on," he says, and I wet my lips, my mouth feeling extremely dry.

My hand moves as if on autopilot, and I grasp onto him.

It feels so fucking *different.* Different from holding onto my own dick. Maybe because he's bigger than me, but damn. I'm holding another dude's cock in my hand. It's fucking with my mind.

"Come on. Jack me off. I have shit to do after this."

I give a clipped nod and pump my fist, watching as his tip emerges between my fingers. Jesus, it's saying hello, isn't it? Playing peekaboo.

"Tighter," he says, his cheeks flushed pink, his breath a little stuttered.

I do as he says, grasping him a little firmer. He's smooth as silk, and his dick almost throbs in my palm. A drop of precum beads at the tip and I swipe at it with my thumb. I wonder what this would feel like up my ass, stretching me out.

The visual makes my dick take notice, and it stirs in my pants, but my nerves keep it from hardening all the way.

Theo leans back a little, his hands still grasping onto his thighs, his eyes moving from where I'm holding onto him, to my abs, and then finally to my eyes.

"Faster," he mutters. "Why do you suck so much at this?"

My mouth turns down in a frown as I pump him more vigorously.

"I've never done this to another guy before," I retort, feeling defensive once again.

"I can tell," he grumbles and begins arching his hips a little, fucking himself into my fist. "You may owe me something else after this if I can't get off."

I narrow my eyes at him and squeeze him roughly. Asshole making up new rules. He can't change them now. I will get him off. I'll fucking make him come. I might not be a lot of things, but I am definitely determined.

I begin adding a little twist with my wrist at the end of each stroke, and oh yeah, he likes that. I can tell. A small moan slips from his mouth the first time, and he bites down on his bottom lip to keep them in, but I can tell he's close.

"Shit," he groans when I reach down and stroke his balls with my free hand. I've always liked when girls do this to me, so I just figure he'll like it too—and I'm not wrong. He likes it a lot.

"Shit. Shit. *Shit.*"

His chest is heaving, his mouth opens slightly, and I watch in fascination as his come shoots from his hole and splatters across my hand and my stomach.

Some even gets in my belly button.

Huh.

Never had another dude's come in my belly button before. It's like a tiny swimming pool. I should set up a small diving board or some shit.

"Let go of me," he says gruffly, his words sounding almost angry.

What the hell? I just gave him a fucking orgasm of epic proportions. He should be thanking me, not snapping my head off. It's like he's mad I went through with this.

Well, think again, fucker. I don't back down from anything. How do you think I got to where I am today? By giving up? Fuck no. I persevere.

I unwrap my hand from him, and he slides off of me, tucking himself back in his pants.

A box of tissues is tossed at me, and I grab onto it, wiping myself up as best I can.

Curie never moved from her spot on the bed, but now her leg is straight up in the air, and she's licking her butthole. She's probably just reminding me that soon my butthole is going to be wrecked by her human's monster dick.

Thanks, asshole cat.

"So that was good, yeah? We're even?" I ask, clutching the used wad of tissues in my hand and looking for a place to toss them. This guy came a lot. He has big balls or something.

Big balls. Big dick.

And, right now, I smell like his come, and I'm not sure how I feel about that.

"It was subpar, but we're even," Theo says, tossing me my shirt and then pointing to the trashcan.

"Subpar," I scoff. "I played with your balls."

"So?" he says, folding his arms across his chest.

"Prick," I mutter, tossing the trash into the can and pulling my shirt on. "Whatever." He can be a negative Nancy if he wants. I don't care. As long as I pass this class. That's all that matters. "When can we meet again?"

"Next week."

"Nah," I say. "I need to meet as often as you can squeeze me in because I have a test coming up."

"You do realize that just because you *think* you're important, doesn't mean I give two shits about you and your perceived needs."

What the hell is he talking about? How is this guy such a great teacher and yet, such a fucking jerk?

"Come on, man. Can you meet tomorrow?"

He runs a hand through his hair and sighs. "Fine. Tomorrow at six a.m."

My eyebrows rise at that. "Hell no."

"Take it or leave it. I have plans tomorrow night."

I rub a hand over my face and sigh. I guess I could get up a little earlier before practice and squeeze in a bit of studying. Hopefully, my brain works that early. Usually, it's mush until about four in the afternoon.

"Fine. And do we have to do that again?" I ask because I need to get my asshole in shape if he plans to stick anything inside it.

He shrugs. "Depends on what I feel like doing. Could be that, could be a blow job, could be me bending you over a desk."

My cheeks flush crimson at the image that pops into my head, and I avert my eyes. They land on Curie again.

That cat is everywhere, always judging.

I stick my tongue out at her and then mentally scold myself for letting a cat get to me.

"Fine. Whatever. See you tomorrow," I say.

Theo doesn't respond. He just turns around and sits on

his desk chair, his back to me, and I watch him for a few seconds before swiping up my stuff, turning on my heels, and leaving the apartment entirely.

When the door shuts behind me, I lean against the wall and breathe deeply.

That was fucking weird. The whole thing. Jacking off another guy, how cold he was afterward.

The cat.

Jesus. I rub a hand down my face. I really, really, for real, need to prepare myself for tomorrow morning. I don't want to go in blind.

two

LOGAN

I STUMBLE up the steps to Theo's apartment and pound on the door. My eyes are still bleary from lack of sleep because I've been replaying that hand job repeatedly in my head. I was obsessing over it. It kept me up until two in the morning.

And then I may have watched some gay porn too.

I didn't hate it. I watched quite a lot of it and got all sorts of ideas. At three a.m., I trudged into the kitchen to look for a cucumber I know we had—a cucumber that looked to be about the same size as Theo's dick—but Finn had eaten it. Who eats a whole fucking cucumber in one day? Finn, that's who. But it's probably a good thing he did; I was going to do awful things to it. The grocery man would see the guilt on my face and know when I went to buy veggies next time. They'd ban me from the produce

24

department, fearful of what I might do to a head of lettuce.

And honestly, what if my sphincter had sucked that thing right inside, and it disappeared entirely? I'd have to go to the ER, and Finn would never let me live it down. I'd end up on one of those reality TV shows where doctors laugh at you and call you an idiot.

I opted, instead, to order a dildo with a nice thick base to keep myself out of the hospital. It comes next week. I plan on using it often.

"You're late," Theo says as soon as he opens the door and sees me leaning, hands against the frame.

He's wearing nothing but a pair of boxer briefs, and the haze of fatigue slowly dissipates. Does this guy just get more and more naked each time I see him? Next time he answers the door, he'll just be wearing one sock.

Maybe he's just fucking with me or something. I don't think he likes me, so I wouldn't put it past him. He cackles about this when I leave and talks about it with his friends, I just know it.

"You look like shit," he says, and I mutter curses at him.

"I'm tired. I was up late." *Looking at dudes fucking each other and ordering sex toys.*

His eyes rove over me as he sips from a mug.

"Oh, fuck yeah. Coffee," I grumble incoherently. "Gimme."

"Did I say you could help yourself to my shit?" he asks, and I open my mouth to protest, but it's too early in the day to argue with someone this smart. I'll never win.

Like my mom always says, "It's better to ask forgiveness

than permission." So that's precisely what I do. I brush past him and catch the scent of soap wafting off of him. He smells clean and fresh, and I notice his hair is a bit damp.

Shit. I didn't take a shower this morning. I was planning to do it after practice later.

I hope that doesn't bother him.

In the kitchen, I pull open the two cupboards and fish out another mug. It has some sort of molecule on it. Or maybe it's an atom. I don't really know the difference, to be honest. It has a quote on it that must be funny or some shit but I don't get it. I just fill the mug to the brim until it sloshes out slightly and then lean down to slurp some out.

"Help yourself," Theo mutters bitterly.

His voice sounds like the taste of black coffee. Theo needs some creamer in his life to lighten up. I'll bring him some next time.

I don't have the mental capacity to deal with his negativity this early, so I just ignore him and make my way to where he's sitting on the ground. Theo already has my chemistry book sprawled across his lap and that notorious pencil behind his ear when I lower myself down next to him. He wears that thing like an accessory. What does he even write with it? Because he doesn't use it to write notes with me. He uses the whiteboard for that.

I wonder if he fished that marker out from under the bed.

I glance around the apartment and note that Curie is nowhere to be seen. It makes me feel a little wary. She's probably spying on me from some shadowed corner, plotting my murder.

"Okay, so let's start up where we left off..." Theo begins,

and once again, like magic, he explains everything so simply. He's brilliant, even at this ungodly hour. In between gulps of coffee, I'm writing as fast as I can. I interrupt occasionally to ask questions when I need more explanation, and he elaborates.

Theo is ridiculously good. He needs to start a YouTube channel so that chumps like me stand a chance in the real world.

When the book slams shut an hour later, I just blink at him in complete awe.

"You should be a professor," I blurt, and Theo eyes me.

"I'm going to be a pharmacologist."

My eyebrows meet. "Oh." Don't know what the fuck that is. I think it's kind of like a drug dealer, but fancier.

Theo watches me for a moment and then stands up, stretching his long limbs.

"Alright, on the bed again. On your side this time."

My hands start to sweat as I ask, "Shirt off?"

"No."

I bob my head as I push myself up and then lie down on the bed. I prop my head up with my hand, watching as Theo peels himself out of the boxers. His balls swing heavily between his legs as he crawls his way over to me, and then he lies down in front of me, his back pressed against my chest, his ass against my crotch.

"Jerk me off again," he says, and I lean a little closer, my knees knocking into the back of his as I reach over and cup his flaccid dick in my palm.

I wonder why he's never hard to begin with. Is he not attracted to me? He did say I was ordinary.

Maybe he doesn't like my face. Maybe that's why he's facing away from me this time.

For some reason, that kind of hurts my feelings. I mean, I think I'm kind of hot, and I have curly hair which chicks dig. But Theo isn't a chick. Maybe I'm just not his type.

I play with him a little and he gets hard, but it's a slow process and takes a lot of work. When he's fully erect, I begin pumping him feverishly like last time, and I make sure to add in that little twist at the end, my thumb brushing against his tip. I can tell he likes that because he presses his ass into me, and lets out a soft moan. I do it again, and he leans back further, his head falling against my bicep and I'm helpless to do anything but stare down at his face.

The more I look at him, the more I realize he's handsome, with a straight nose, a chiseled jawline, fair skin, and long dark eyelashes. And the pink flush to his cheeks as he pants through parted lips makes me want to...well, it kinda makes me want to kiss him or something.

He thrusts into my palm, and I move my gaze toward where our bodies connect.

It's so different doing this with him. He's all hard with sharp angles. There's nothing soft about him...except his dick before I start playing with it.

And maybe his balls.

Speaking of...I let go of his dick and roll his balls in my palm, and he inhales shakily. I tug on them like I know he likes, and he hisses, his eyes popping open.

"My dick only," he snaps, and I sigh, grabbing onto him again. Damn, he's so bossy and controlling. Does this guy even like to experiment, or does sex always have to be his way?

Theo's eyelids flutter closed again, and he nibbles on his bottom lip.

"Tighter," he adds, his tongue peeking out and wetting his lips.

I clasp him firmer in my grip, jerking him off with a purpose, and he groans.

His ass moves against my crotch over and over as he arches into my palm, and my dick rouses from all the friction. It's semi-hard now, and he must notice because his eyes snap open.

I stare down into those blue depths, my hand still pumping him.

He doesn't say anything, his eyes just flicker from mine down to my slightly open mouth and then back again, as he rolls his ass against me.

When he comes, my dick is fully hard in my pants—uncomfortably so—but he doesn't offer to help me out. Not that I really want him to.

And even if I did, I know that's not what this is. This is a transaction between two people. Sex for tutoring—and we both held up our end of the bargain.

It's done.

As I wash my hands in the kitchen sink, Theo moves to sit at his desk, his leg bouncing up and down as his pencil taps a nervous rhythm against an open book.

"Tomorrow?" I ask when he doesn't turn to look at me.

"Tomorrow. Six p.m."

I stare at his bare back. He still doesn't turn around. He's as cold as he ever was.

"Cool. See you then."

And then I let myself out.

* * *

My legs and arms burn from training today. Usually, we practice four days a week, but our coach threw in an extra one because we have a game coming up. I lean up against the wall of the shower to take some of the pressure off of me. Hot water sluices down my back as the heat soothes my aching muscles. My eyes close in exhaustion, but as soon as they do, my mind conjures up Theo pressed up against me yesterday morning.

Shit.

I look down at my dick, and it twitches between my legs.

After I left his apartment, I ended up sitting in my car having some kind of mini-identity crisis. I'd pressed my forehead against the steering wheel and took deep breaths through my nose because my dick was still as hard as a rock. So hard it hurt. When I couldn't get it to go down, I ended up jacking off right there in the parking lot while people made their way to work, throwing a discarded sweater I'd found in my back seat over my lap to hide my dirty deed.

And let me tell you…I came so quickly and so hard that I blacked out.

When I came to, I had a mini-anxiety attack because experiencing a shift in worldview is serious business.

Afterward, as I was sitting in my mess, my brother called

me. Needless to say, I didn't answer. I just couldn't handle it. Not right then. I'll call him later today. I gotta give myself a pep talk first, though.

Fuck, I'm losing my mind.

I force my eyes open, staring at the white tile in front of me, and then shut off the water. No time to dwell on it, I need to keep moving.

"You took a long ass shower," Finn says, eyeing me when I step out of the stall. My towel is wrapped tightly around my waist as I stride past him.

"I ache," I tell him, moving toward my locker and pulling it open.

"Nope, that's not it. Training this morning was normal. So, it's something else." He waits for me to tell him something, but I clamp my mouth shut.

Finn leans against the lockers and watches me. "You never told me how it's going with your tutoring."

I let my towel drop onto the floor and pull on a pair of athletic shorts. I don't even bother with underwear. Sometimes that shit is more work than it's worth.

"Nothing to tell. The tutor is good at explaining shit. I may have a real chance."

Finn leans a little closer to me and nudges me with his knuckles. "And you're still *paying* him, right?" His eyes widen as he says it, and I slam my locker shut.

"Yep."

He punches my arm when I don't give him more than that. "Come on, Logan. Tell me something."

"No," I say and push past him, pulling my backpack over my shoulders. I have to get to class. This is one of the easier ones too. The Rise of Digital Culture. My counselor said it would be a piece of cake, and they weren't wrong. I have a B in it. Not too bad, if you ask me. But still not good enough to bring my entire GPA up. My other two classes are C's. So, as it stands, I need a passing grade in chemistry to make sure I can still play.

"Hey, why all the secrets?" Finn asks jogging alongside me.

I stop abruptly and face my best friend. "Because, man, I'm processing shit...."

His eyebrows slam together, and all teasing slips off of his face. "Is it bad? Do you hate it? You know we can find other options...."

I shake my head and swallow roughly. I don't want to find someone else to tutor me, and to be honest, there's a small part of me that's looking forward to our next session.

And therein lies the problem.

I kind of like what Theo and I are doing. And so does my dick.

"You're making me nervous. Come on. Are you okay?" Finn asks.

"Yeah, I'm okay. I'm just processing shit, as I said. I have to go."

Finn reaches out and grabs onto my arm. "You can talk to me. No judgment. Remember that."

I give him a clipped nod. I *will* talk to him about it, but I need to make sense of it all in my head before I go spouting off.

I want what I say to make sense, so I need it to make sense to me first.

Sprinting to class, I barely make it in time. I slip into a seat in the back of the class and pull out my laptop, setting it on the desk. I open up a new document, and my fingers clack loudly on the keyboard as the professor begins to lecture, and I try to stay focused, I really do, but my mind wanders into dark alleys and lurks about mischievously.

I end up thinking about Theo—the shape of his hard body, the feel of his dick in my hand, that mysterious tattoo on his side, his smell—and about how I don't hate any of it.

When I finally shake my thoughts free of him, I glance around and realize my cheeks are burning.

Shit.

My dick is hard too.

I shift in my seat and stare intently at the computer screen. Focus, Logan. I need to keep my grade up in this class.

Easier said than done.

I'm sitting on the floor of Theo's apartment, my book in my lap as he explains a chemical formula I can't for the life of me make sense of—mainly because I keep thinking about his cock. I can't help it. All I can smell is him and it's making me horny.

I wonder what kind of deodorant he uses. Or maybe it's his soap. Or maybe it's just *him.*

He's wearing more clothes today than I've ever seen him in. Tight jeans and a checkered tank top that hangs loosely on his thin frame. At one point, he shifted, and I could see his nipple. It just peeked out and said hello.

I stared at it a little too long.

I wonder if he likes them sucked on? No one has ever done that to me. I wonder if I'd like it too?

Another guy was leaving Theo's apartment just as I arrived. Did he have his lips around Theo's nipples? Does Theo have other people jerk him off in exchange for tutoring?

The thought makes something unfurl deep inside of me.

"Does that make sense?" Theo asks, snapping my gaze up to his.

"Uh, um, no." None of this makes sense.

My eyes flick to the book in his lap and then back up to his eyes.

"You're not paying attention. You're wasting my time."

"Sorry, man," I say with a whine, running a hand over my face. "I'm so distracted."

You, Theo. You're my distraction.

He stares at me for a full minute, making me squirm, and then sets the book aside.

"Tell me why you're distracted so we can move on."

I swallow and look away from him. No way in hell I'm telling him shit. That is for my brain and my brain only.

"Nah, I'm sorry. I'll do better. Can you just explain it one more time?"

Theo studies me and fiddles with the bottom of his shirt, twisting it around his finger.

He opens his mouth to say something and then snaps it shut. Well, hell, now I'm curious. What was he going to say?

But I don't get a chance to ask because he just pulls the book back onto his lap and says, "Fine."

He explains the concept once more, and I try hard to understand it. Theo even writes it out on the whiteboard, but my mind is all jumbled up. All I can focus on is his mouth, where his soft pink lips are moving and his slick tongue peeks out as he talks. I keep picturing his tongue circling my nipples.

Fuck.

"Did that make sense now?"

I swallow and shake my head.

"Fuck, no. Sorry. I think I need a break."

I stand up and pace to the other side of the apartment and look inside the fridge. It's sparse; only a few cans of soda, a loaf of bread, and a jar of raspberry preserves are inside. This guy needs food, stat. How does he live like this? I would wilt and die. I probably eat more food in one meal than Theo has in his entire apartment.

"Can I have a soda?" I ask.

"Feeding you wasn't a part of the agreement."

"You're not feeding me. It's a drink. You gave me coffee yesterday."

He pulls his lips between his teeth and then nods. "Fine. One."

He holds up a finger as I swipe a can of Coke from the fridge and pop it open. It hisses in the quiet space between us, and I tilt the sugary goodness into my mouth.

I usually don't drink this stuff, but fuck if it isn't good. It burns my throat and makes my eyes water as I swallow it down.

A little burp escapes my mouth, and I set the can on the counter.

Theo is still sitting on the ground, the chem book on his lap. His eyes are on me, and I fidget nervously under his stare. What's he thinking? Does he know that I jacked off to thoughts of him last night? What I did with my fingers as I lay in bed?

"We can just take a break and come back to this tomorrow," he says after a moment of silence.

"No, man. I need to cram as much as I can into my head today. I need to bring my grade up soon. If I end up on academic probation, I'm fucked."

"Some days, it's best to just step away from something—"

"Can't do that. My grades are in the shitter already. There's a test coming up next week in this class, and I need to pass it. I gotta show my coach I'm bringing my GPA up, or he'll bench me."

And I can't let my team down like that. I have to stay focused, but Theo is making it fucking hard. He's making me hard. It's relentless.

Theo thumbs through the pages of my book, his eyes moving from the pages to me and then back again. "Just let me know when you're ready to start. But just know that I have plans in about an hour."

I take another sip of my soda.

"What plans?"

Fuck, here I am, trying to make small talk.

"None of your business," he mutters, and I sigh.

This guy is a fucking mystery.

"What do you like to do for fun?" I blurt.

He slams the book closed and folds his arms across his chest.

"Why the third degree?" he asks.

I run a hand through my hair and laugh a little. "This isn't the third degree. I'm not interrogating you. Fuck, I was just making small talk."

"I hate small talk. It's pointless and trivial. We're not friends, you don't get to know me."

I blink at him and then I finish off my drink, crumpling the can in my hand and tossing it into the garbage.

"What the fuck ever," I mutter, shaking my head. I start to move back to our spot on the floor when a cabinet door opens, and Curie pops out, leaping onto the counter in front of me. It scares the ever-loving shit out of me, and I let out a little squeal.

Theo chuckles, and the sound is so unexpected that I find myself smiling just a little.

Yeah, laugh it up, buddy. You need some smiles to cheer up that unhappy brain.

I skirt around Curie, back to where Theo sits, and lower myself onto the floor. The cat, of course, follows me, invading my space and plopping herself directly into my lap.

I can feel Theo's eyes on me as I grumble under my breath, trying to pretend like this cat isn't melting my heart as she headbutts my arm and silently demands I pet her.

I scratch behind her ear, and she tilts her head, a low purr flowing from her.

Alright, Curie. You're alright. Just don't watch so intently when we fuck around—freaks a man out.

"Hiking," Theo says, clearing his throat, his eyes straying to his cat, which is pressed against me. "I like to hike."

I open my laptop and peek over at Theo. "That wasn't so hard, was it?"

He huffs, "I feel splayed wide open."

I snort and feel my body relax. So maybe it isn't touching another dude's dick that's making me nervous. It's how impersonal this all is.

Or maybe it's a bit of both.

Dunno.

"What's your tattoo say?" I ask, pressing my luck because I am just that curious.

Theo glances at Curie and then says, *"Someone I loved once gave me a box full of darkness. It took me years to understand that this too, was a gift."*

I just stare at him. What the hell does that mean?

"Hold on, repeat that. I need to write it down," I mutter.

"Why?"

"Because I want to look it up."

Theo watches me carefully for a second and then repeats it slowly and I scribble it down. Most of it is unintelligible, but I'll manage. I have the gist of it anyway.

"Ready now? Or do you want to interrogate me some more?" he asks when my pencil stops scrawling on the paper.

I lean back with a major eye roll. "Yeah, yeah. I'm done. Go ahead."

He explains the chemistry concept once more, and I'm able to pay attention this time. When we're finished and he finally shuts the book and sets it down next to him thirty minutes later, I feel my nerves start up again. But it's more excitement than anything.

I close my laptop and set it over my crotch to hide the growing erection underneath it. God, why am I so horny for this? Maybe it's because this is new and exciting, or maybe it's because I haven't gotten laid in over a month.

"What do I owe you?" I ask, my voice embarrassingly squeaky.

He taps his pencil on his pursed lips and then sets it on the floor. He suddenly pushes himself up and stands in front of me, his fingers reaching out and brushing against my cheek, and my skin positively flames. I'm standing too close to the sun right now; I'm going to get burned.

The vein in my neck pulses violently, as does the one in my dick. It knows, positively knows, what's going to go down right now.

And I am so fucking ready.

Theo's thumb presses against my bottom lip, pulling it down slightly, and then he pulls away, unbuttoning and unzipping his pants. I'm practically panting as I watch him, but his face is impassive and expressionless. Either this dude has the best poker face I've ever seen, or he really doesn't like me. My stomach twists slightly at the thought.

He yanks down his pants, his cock jutting out right in front of my mouth, and I exhale shakily. Jesus, never have I ever done this before, and I am fucking tense. It doesn't help that Curie is sound asleep next to me and purring, loudly—damn cat sounds like a Corvette with a faulty muffler system.

I nudge her, but she doesn't wake up. So, I gently slide

her unconscious body under the bed. I don't want her watching my first time. I can just imagine her holding up tiny scorecards. *Four point five for effort, negative seven for technique.*

I glance up at Theo, our eyes clashing.

"Suck," he says.

"Go easy on me," I whisper, and he gives me a clipped nod.

My lips part and I lean forward, pressing them to the tip of him, then flicking my tongue out to trace his slit.

His breath stutters above me, and it spurs me on. I suck his entire head into my mouth and the taste of him explodes on my tongue—slightly salty, musty, and clean, like soap.

I shift a little closer, and his fingers thread through my hair as he pushes his cock further into me. My jaw aches from how wide I have to keep it open, and we've barely even started.

My hands reach up and clasp onto his hips, my fingertips digging into his skin as he continues to stretch my mouth around him. It goes on and on, and my eyes water as he bottoms out, my throat working around his thick length.

Apparently, I don't have a sensitive gag reflex, because he goes in quite nicely. Shit, who knew? He pulls back out slowly and his cock drags over my tongue until he's almost fully out and then he pushes his way *slowly* back inside, carefully entering my throat again.

I swallow around him again, and he moans, his fingers tightening in my hair, tugging roughly.

"Fuck," he whispers as he gently fucks into my mouth and throat. I'm drooling now, my jaw aching as I breathe through my nose. He bottoms out with every thrust, his balls hitting my chin, and I dig my fingers into his thighs as he softly rocks into me.

My eyes are drawn to his face, and when I look up, his eyes are on me. His pupils are blown out, his cheeks are pink and flushed, and his lips are swollen and red from biting down on them. It looks like he's the one who sucked cock.

"Look at you stuffed full of me," he says, one of his fingers tracing my upper lip.

He fucks down my throat again, and I swallow.

"Such a fucking cock slut," he mutters. "You don't even gag."

I hum around him, my dick happy from the praise, and his eyes roll back slightly in his head, his hips thrusting faster.

"I'm going to come," he says, and then he begins to fuck my face harder, the head of his cock hitting the back of my throat roughly. Suddenly, his thighs are flexing, and he sinks all the way down my throat, unloading straight into my stomach.

He trembles and jerks as I swallow his come, and then he sags slightly, his hands on my shoulders.

"God," he mutters, pulling himself out of me.

When my mouth is blessedly empty, I swipe at the mess on my chin, but it does nothing but smear it all across my skin.

A wad of tissues appears before me, and I grasp onto it, cleaning myself. I swipe at my eyes and sniff a little.

Damn, blow jobs are hard work. I realize I now owe several women nice thank-you cards, and maybe even apologies, because I was never as gentle as Theo was when I went at it.

"I need your number," Theo says suddenly, and I glance up at him from where I'm seated.

"Yeah, okay," my throat raspy and a little sore. I gulp and wince a little.

"Just in case we need to reach each other. Because I assume you will need my services until the end of the semester?"

"Yeah."

Fuck, six more weeks until this is over. Not sure how I feel about that.

My dick doesn't seem to mind because it's hard and pressed against my pants.

Yeah, I guess I know how I feel about it.

I adjust my cock and grab onto my laptop and chemistry book, standing on wobbly legs. My fingers press against my sore lips, and I massage my jaw.

"Are you okay?" he asks.

I nod. "Just sore."

He rolls his lips between his teeth and then holds out his hand.

"Give me your phone."

Reaching into my pocket, I pull it out, enter the code, and set it in his palm.

He peeks up at me after he enters his number and then hands it back to me.

"Only text me if you can't make it over. Do not text me for any other reason. We aren't friends."

My eyebrows narrow, and I shove my phone back into

my pocket. Why does he have to go and be rude? Especially after all I just did for him.

"Why the fuck would I want to text you?" I mutter, and Theo visibly flinches.

I'm surprised when I see it because it's the only clear sign of emotion I've ever seen from him. Now I feel like shit because maybe I hurt his feelings? I didn't mean to, but man, this guy is so frustrating. I just reacted without thinking.

He confuses me, and I don't know how to act around him.

"You can let yourself out," Theo says before I can say anything else.

Alright then. I zip my lips and leave the apartment without a word.

My phone burns a hole in my pocket the rest of the night.

three

LOGAN

Tutor: Opening today at 6 p.m.

Theo's text stares up at me, and I clench my jaw. The asshole didn't even put his actual name in my phone; just put *tutor*. I could just change it, but I don't.

Everything with him is so impersonal. It bothers me a little. I looked up his social media but his profiles are private, so I can't find out anything about him.

Maybe this guy should just stay a mystery...but I had his cock down my throat yesterday, and my dick gets hard when I think of him, so it's becoming a little personal on my end.

Last night, I looked up that poem he has on his side. It was by some lady named Mary Oliver. The poem is about overcoming intense hurt or grief and becoming stronger because of it. I'm scared to ask him more about it, though. I'm still surprised he told me what the tattoo said in the first place.

I think Theo likes to remain a mystery.

I grab the bag of takeout containers and walk out of the hole-in-the-wall Chinese restaurant near Theo's place. I bought a ton of food because I'm hungry, and this guy eats jelly for dinner, apparently. Maybe that's why he's so thin. I could probably lift him into my arms easily. I could wear him as a backpack.

I push those thoughts away as I drive to his place.

My phone rings from the cupholder, and I glance down at it.

Mom.

Fuck, I forgot to call her back.

I quickly fumble for the phone and press the green button.

"Hey, Mom," I say, and my heart jumps a little.

"Hey, Logan. I was just calling because it's been a while since we chatted and I miss you. And so does dad. You know how he is."

My ribs are going to snap with how tight my chest feels.

"Yeah, um, I've just been busy," I say.

"I know, I totally know. I just...I wanted to make sure you were okay."

I know what she's referring to, and no, I'm not okay. Not really. But I don't want to go there either. I've been avoiding my family for a reason.

"I'm fine. Doing really good," I say. "I'm actually on my way to meet my tutor for chemistry."

"Awesome. So glad to hear you found help."

"Yeah, me too."

"I just wanted you to know that I love you, and I would love for you to come home and visit if you want."

"Yeah, I would like that," I lie.

It just rings false to my ears, and she knows it too but neither of us addresses it. Avoidance must be another curse on the family.

We never like to bring up the stuff that makes us uncomfortable. We'd rather live our lives walking on eggshells. We love our fucking eggs. My parents even have chickens.

As soon as we hang up, I park in front of Theo's apartment complex, and then I'm striding into his apartment, feeling kind of dumb for bringing all this extra food with me. But whatever, this dude needs to eat.

I pull all the takeout boxes out of the bag, setting them on his counter in a nice little row.

"I had a long practice and was starving. Brought some for you too," I say, opening each of the drawers in his tiny kitchen before finding the forks.

"Why are you bringing me food?" he asks, seemingly offended that I brought something other than myself and my chem book.

I just roll my eyes. "So, you'll let me suck your dick and drink your come, but sharing a meal is too much?"

He blinks at me, the pencil stilling between his fingers. "Fine," he says in a clipped tone, grabbing a fork, opening one of the containers, and peering inside.

He seems to like what he sees because he stabs a piece of

meat and shoves it into his mouth. His eyelids flutter a bit, and I bite back a smirk.

The asshole was hungry, I knew it.

Curie walks over to me and brushes against my ankles, and I pull a toy mouse from my pocket. I chuck it onto the floor, but Curie just eyes it like it has an infectious disease.

"Go on," I say. "Play with it. It's yours."

She turns to me and gives me a look like I just insulted her mother and then struts away.

"Why the fuck are you buying my cat toys?"

I shrug. "Dunno. Wanted to win her over or something."

Theo devours another large bite and then mumbles, "Don't buy her stuff."

I shrug, feeling annoyed he's so prickly when I'm just trying to be nice.

I lean against the counter and try for something more positive. I'm not going to let him get me down.

"Wanna know something?"

He stares at me. "Probably not."

I roll my eyes, "My chem professor asked a question today, and I answered it. Correctly."

He stops chewing, and his eyes widen slightly.

"I was pretty fucking proud. I surprised that asshole too. He thinks I'm dumb. I mean, he's never said that, but I know he thinks it."

Theo resumes chewing.

I twirl my fork in some noodles and then shovel them into my mouth.

"So, maybe I actually have a shot at passing my upcoming test."

"Maybe," Theo says, stabbing another piece of orange chicken and chewing.

We eat in silence for a few minutes when I ask, "How old are you?"

Theo sets the box of food onto the counter and folds his arms across his chest. Oh, here he goes again, getting all defensive.

"Come on, man. It makes me uneasy to fuck around with you and not know anything about you. It might work for you, being all detached and shit, but it makes me feel weird."

He ponders that a moment and then says, "Twenty-four."

Ah, so he's a little older than me.

"You undergrad?"

"No, graduate."

Fuck, that's impressive. This dude is super smart. I mean, I knew that. But now I *know* that.

"I'm twenty-two. A super senior. Had to retake some classes because, as you can tell, school isn't my thing."

Plus, there was that one semester I was home with my brother, but I don't want to go there right now.

Theo doesn't notice my behavior change and picks up his food again, slowly chewing as he eyes me. Well, he isn't telling me to go to hell, so I decide it's his way of telling me to go ahead and ask more questions.

"What's your favorite color?" I ask.

He licks his lips. "Grey."

I roll my eyes and laugh softly. "Mine is yellow. Favorite food?"

"Cock," he says, and I choke a little on my food.

When I manage to clear my airways, I look up at him and see his lips twitching. Fucker. Thinks he's so funny.

"Come on, stop fucking with me...favorite food? Mine is pizza. Pepperoni, sausage, and pineapple."

He grimaces. "Waffles."

I beam. This guy is giving me a peek into his soul, and it makes me fucking ecstatic. But as he stares at me, his posture stiffens, and he sets the food down again.

"Alright, enough of this. Let's get to work."

I blink rapidly, confused at his sudden change. He almost looked like he was having fun for a second, and now he's all cold and distant.

Like I said, a mystery, this one. Where is Sherlock when I need him? Only he could solve the riddle that is Theo Reign.

I shove the leftover food into the fridge and walk over to where Theo sits with Curie on his lap.

Our legs knock as I lower myself next to him, and then I spend the next hour listening to him as he goes over the concepts in the chapter. I have to admit, I spend a little too much time watching the way his lips move and then have to ask him to repeat himself a few times. I think he's onto me.

When we're done, Curie is fast asleep on his lap and Theo leans back and rubs his temples.

"You okay?" I ask.

"Yes," he says, glancing at me.

"Want some Advil? I have some in my bag...."

"No, I'm fine. Just...get on the bed. Shirt off. I'm tired and want to make this quick."

"Hey, man. If you don't feel good, we don't have to...."

He narrows his gaze at me, and I lift my hands in surrender.

Fine, fine. He makes these transactions like they're life or death.

I whip off my shirt, lean back on the pillows, and Theo straddles me. My hands run up his thighs as he pulls his pants down, and because I'm getting the hang of this, I just reach out and grasp onto his semi-hard length.

His eyes flutter closed, and his nostrils flare as I pump his cock in my hand, but he doesn't really seem into it. If anything, he appears to be annoyed.

"Harder."

"Faster."

"Tighter."

Nothing seems to make his guy happy, and I'm starting to panic. What the hell am I doing wrong?

"Fuck this," he says suddenly, slapping my hand away and crawling up my chest.

"Open," he says, the tip of his cock hitting my mouth.

I open my mouth, and he slides himself inside. My hands move up to grasp onto his ass as he fucks himself in and out of me. He's rougher than he was the first time and I huff and gurgle around him as he pounds into me.

It's hard to breathe, but I still pull him into me each time. Maybe I'm into breath play or some shit because my hips hump the air as he slides in and out of my throat, and when I groan around his thick length, he explodes into my mouth. His orgasm goes on for ages, and when he slowly pulls out, he leans back, his chest heaving, and he swipes a hand across his sweaty forehead.

"Fuck," he says, tucking himself back inside his pants with shaking hands.

I massage my throat and lick my lips.

"You sure you're okay?" I ask, my throat raspy all over again. Gotta gargle with salt water or something. Finn will get suspicious if I keep talking like this.

"Yeah," he says, moving into the kitchen and grabbing a glass of water. He gulps it down as I tuck my hard cock under my waistband. Curie watches me as I make my way into the kitchen and narrows her eyes at me from her perch on the counter. I grab a paper towel and wipe up my come-smeared face, trying to ignore her.

But shit, she makes herself known, doesn't she?

Yeah, I know, Curie. I didn't manage to swallow all of it. Give me a break, this is only my second time.

"Tomorrow, same time?" he asks, and I nod, tossing the paper towel into the garbage.

Theo doesn't say another word. He just disappears into the bathroom, the door snicking shut behind him.

* * *

Tutor: Sick. Don't come over.

I eye my phone and then shove it into my back pocket. I knew he didn't look well yesterday. For a minute, I'd wondered if maybe he was just over me in general, but nah, he just wasn't feeling well. That's why it took him so long to come.

"Hey, Logan, I'm going to drive down to Santa Cruz and

chill with Landon," Finn tells me, slapping me on the back. "You want to come? We could watch a movie or something."

I pull my backpack over my shoulders and shake my head. Shit, I should go and see my brother, but the whole thing with Theo is bugging me. Some would say I'm using him as an excuse to avoid bigger issues. And yeah, maybe that's so.

"I can't. I have tutoring."

It's not just my younger brother I've been kind of, sort of avoiding. It's Finn too. I haven't told him what's going on with my dick. Or my brain. It's all a scrambled mess.

Last night, I caved and jacked off to thoughts of Theo standing over me, his dick down my throat. It couldn't be helped; my balls were aching.

I came so hard that I had to wash my sheets.

Then I did it again in the shower. I had one finger up my ass while I did it, too.

Finn's eyes narrow in concern. I really hope he can't read my thoughts right now. "Look, I'll tell Landon you're busy with school, but he won't buy that excuse forever. He knows you, Logan. And he knows you blame yourself. It wasn't your fault—"

"Yeah, but it was."

"Logan..." my best friend protests, but I just shake my head, my hand running across the back of my neck.

"I'll call him tomorrow and make a plan to go see him."

"You can't avoid this forever," he calls out to my retreating back.

Yeah, yeah, I know. I've lived with this for a year, and it's still hard as shit seeing him. I just don't want to think about it. Fuck. I just want to push all the bad shit to the back of my mind and check on Theo. He'll distract me.

So, thirty minutes later, here I am, cradling soup and crackers in one hand and a bag of medication dangling from the other.

After I knock and the door opens, I find a glowering Theo standing before me.

"Go the fuck away," he mutters, his cheeks flushed, and his hair a sweaty, unruly mess. He's wearing plaid pajama pants and a long-sleeved shirt, and a grey fuzzy blanket is pulled around his shoulders.

"Not happening," I say, pushing past him and moving into his kitchen.

"Brought you food," I say and hold up the plastic bag. "And meds. Didn't know what was wrong, so I brought the pharmacy to you."

He sinks down onto the edge of the bed and pulls the blanket closer around him.

"I didn't ask you to come here. I specifically told you *not* to come," he says, and I roll my eyes, filling up a cup of water and bringing it over to him.

He stares at it as if it personally offends him, so I just nudge it against his bottom lip.

"Drink, Theo."

His eyes flash up to mine, and he parts his lips. I tilt the cup a little as he takes small, measured sips.

I know when he's done because he stares angrily at me, his lips clasped shut. I set the water down on the floor and press the back of my hand to his face. He wrenches his head away, but I do it again anyway, feeling his feverish, clammy skin against mine.

"You have a fever."

He coughs a little. "No shit."

"I have Tylenol," I say, moving to the bag and rustling through it, pulling out an unopened bottle. I shake two out and hand them to him.

He stares at them warily, and I just shove my hand closer to his face so he's forced to grab them from me.

He places them in his mouth and swallows them dry. Impressive. I've always wondered how people did that without choking. I tried it once and the pill got lodged in my throat and just dissolved there, creating a putrid, burning sensation until I vomited. My pill-swallowing skills are obviously not up to par with my dick-swallowing skills.

"I have cough drops if you want some and Vicks Vapor Rub. Oh, and some NyQuil."

"Jesus," he says as he flops back on the bed and curls into himself. "You need to leave."

"I'll go after the fever breaks. This could be serious. That smart brain of yours could turn to soup."

And I need a reason to not go see my brother. I'd rather be here.

That makes me a bad person, huh?

Shit.

"Don't want you here," he grunts as he closes his eyes. "Want you gone."

"Too bad," I mutter and lower myself onto the other side of the lumpy bed, crossing my ankles and pulling up a movie on my phone.

He looks over his shoulder at me, his eyes looking tired and almost sad, and he sighs heavily.

"Fine, you can stay, but I'm deducting this from what you owe me."

I ignore him, putting my earbuds in.

Asshole.

I couldn't give two fucks about that. This is me being a semi-decent person, but if it makes him feel better, we can consider this a transaction.

When I look over at him a little while later, he's asleep, his chest rising and falling with even breaths.

I let myself sink further into his mattress and roll onto my side, propping the phone on the mattress between us. It plays some true crime documentary. It will probably give me nightmares, but still, it distracts me enough, so I stop staring at Theo.

I watch the horror unfold on my screen until my eyes close in sleep.

I wake up with Theo pressed against me, his body trembling slightly. It's raining outside, and I can hear it pattering against the windowpane.

"Hey," I mutter softly, and he presses his nose against my side.

"Why the fuck you still here?" he grumbles, his words coming out slurred.

I press my hand against his cheek and can tell he's still burning up. For a moment, I debate calling a doctor and then discard it. There's no way he'd let me cart him around anywhere, and I don't even know if this guy has insurance.

"You're still sick, that's why," I say, and he rolls away from me with a groan.

"Go away," he says, but I don't listen. I stand up and move toward his bathroom.

I can feel his eyes on me as I disappear inside, and they're still on me when I return with a wet washrag in my hand. I press it against his skin, and he lets out a contented sigh. Dude is trying to act all tough when he really just wants someone to take care of him.

"Feels good, huh?" I say and then continue pressing it against his overheated face.

"Mmm."

A cough bursts from his mouth, and I reach over for the glass of water and help him drink.

"Do you have anyone you want me to call? Family?" I ask because I always want my mom when I'm sick. It doesn't matter that I've technically outgrown it, there's just something about her presence that makes it all better.

"You make it sound like I'm dying."

I sweep a strand of hair from his forehead and shake my head. "I just meant that maybe you want your mom here or something. Maybe someone related to you, dunno. Someone other than me."

He glances away, and he covers up the bottom half of his face with the blanket.

"Don't have family," he says, his words mumbled beneath the fabric.

"Oh."

His eyes flash to mine, and then the blanket moves to cover his entire face. I stare down at him and then tug the blanket away. His eyes are closed, but when I stare long enough, they finally pop open.

"Jesus. You still here?"

"Yep. You're stuck with me for now."

He blinks up at me.

"Am I hallucinating? Is this a fever dream?" he asks.

"No," I say, pressing the cool washrag to his cheeks again, and his eyelids flutter shut once more.

"You're being too nice. I hate it."

"Nah, Theo. You love it. Being taken care of."

"Argh. Stop it. Stop being so nice and....and hot." My lips tilt up at his admission and he sighs. "*The* Logan Lewis showed up at my door. How the fuck did that even happen? How is this my life?"

Ah, so the fucker did know who I was. He just pretended like he didn't know when we first met.

Asshole.

"You suck my dick so good," he mutters, and my cock twitches in my pants.

Hell.

He turns over on his other side, tucks his legs into his chest, and drifts off to sleep once more.

I let my fingers trail over his side before pulling them away. I can't start getting ideas like this means something. I'm sure as soon as he wakes up from his delirium, he will be just as prickly and closed off.

Yeah, I really need to take my mind off it.

Maybe I should clean up or something. His apartment is

pretty small, but it's never a bad thing to tidy up a bit. I move around his space, wiping down counters and sweeping up the floor. I even clean out Curie's litter box.

She takes a dump right after too, actually making eye contact with me as she pushes a log out.

Shaking my head at her, I turn my gaze and it lands on his desk where I notice a stack of papers. I press my finger against the top one and lean a little closer. It's an application for a legal name change. Interesting. I wonder why he wants to do that. My eyes slide from those and land on a leather-bound book sitting on top of a stack of textbooks.

I pick it up and flip it open before slamming it shut quickly. Shit, it's his journal. I could tell what it was after my eyes swept over a few lines.

Never was good enough. Am I trying to prove that I am? Why do I still care?

I shouldn't have done that. I should probably hide that journal somewhere so I'm not tempted to read more, because if I do, he'll be pissed. He'll probably ban me from his place and refuse to tutor me anymore.

Or he'll stick his cock in my mouth, which honestly, would be the preferable punishment.

I creep away from his desk like the villain I am and move back to his bed, pressing the cool washcloth to his face once more. He sighs in his sleep, oblivious to the fact that I'm skulking around his apartment, looking at shit I shouldn't.

I just pray he doesn't notice that his stuff has been moved and ask me about it, because I'll blurt out the truth like I always do, and then I'll be banned. Then there will be no hope left for me. I'll be a benched player with nothing left to show for all my hard work. My abs will disappear, and my reputation will be in shambles.

The Logan Lewis will just be a washed-up has-been.

And I won't see Theo anymore.

God, I hope he doesn't find out.

* * *

The next morning, I lie in his bed scrolling through Reddit when Theo rustles next to me. I press my hand to his still overheated skin but don't wake him. He needs to rest some more. I'll just leave a note on his bed and text him, letting him know that I have to go to practice and class but that I'll be back later to make sure he's okay.

To make sure he's eating something and drinking enough water.

Maybe to see if he'll mumble any more secrets for me to hear.

I wouldn't mind a review on how well I jack him off, or maybe some more details about him that he keeps so guarded.

Oh, and I can't forget about Curie. Not that she'd let me. She's a hungry bitch. She meows incessantly until I feed her, then eats exactly two kibbles and glowers at me. Oh, and last night I saw her playing with the toy mouse I bought her. She swatted it right underneath the oven. Not quite sure how to get it out now that it's under there.

She doesn't seem to miss it. Cats are weird.

My phone pings, and when I see my brother's name on the screen, my stomach clenches.

Landon: Finn told me you're being tutored for chem.

My heart stutters in my chest. I don't know why I feel like this. I shouldn't. He's my brother and my best friend, but guilt can eat a person up from the inside out. It's going to destroy us if I let it.

I glance at the text again and sigh.

Fuck Finn for blabbing. I mean, I knew he'd tell Landon. The two of them are close, but still. Some things should remain private.

Me: Yeah, desperate times and all that.
Landon: We have a lot to talk about when we see each other.
Landon: When will that be?
Me: Soon.
Landon: Can't evade me forever, bro. You gotta see me sometime.
Me: Next weekend, I promise.
Landon: You better not ditch. Or I'll have to come to you.

I run a hand over my chest and push myself up off the bed. I know I can't put it off any longer.

I saw my brother right before the fall semester started, so it hasn't technically been *that* long since we've hung out. But it's noticeable because we were always so close growing up. We were inseparable. It's one of the reasons Finn is so close to him too. Everything I did growing up, I did with the two of them.

But then the accident happened, and things got weird.

So yeah, my absence has been noted and Landon knows why, so he's calling me on it—like he should.

I sigh and press the palms of my hands into my eyes. I can't think too much about this, or I'll really stress out. And I can't be late for practice either. I need my head in the game today. I can't be distracted.

I tiptoe out the door and then look over my shoulder once more for good measure.

Fuck, I need to peel my eyes away. He's just an ordinary guy with a big brain and an even bigger dick. Nothing to see here.

I shut the door quietly and jog down the steps. First, practice, then class.

Then on to bigger issues, like how to deal with seeing my brother again and pretending like I'm fine.

* * *

"Want to go hang out with Damon and Xander after class?" Finn asks me, and I shake my head.

"Nah, can't. I'm busy. Plus, you've been a tattletale, so I'm kinda mad at you."

Finn runs a hand through his hair and sighs. "God, I know. I'm sorry, okay? You know I don't keep secrets from Landon. He looks at me all pouty and shit, and I just cave."

"Yeah, but I'm your best friend."

"Yeah, but Landon is...*Landon*."

I eye my best friend suspiciously and see his cheeks flush. Yeah, okay. I know my brother and Finn are close, but what the fuck is going on? Maybe having Theo's dick in my mouth has awakened some kind of sixth sense when it comes to gay shit.

"So, what are you busy with? Why can't you hang?"

I shrug and bite into my breakfast sandwich. "Theo's sick. Gonna make sure he's okay."

"Hold up, the guy who's tutoring you? Why the fuck do you care about him?" Finn asks, looking seriously confused.

Yeah, dude. So am I.

"Dunno, Finn. He's really sick, and I don't think he has anyone around to help him. And we all know how it is to be alone when you feel like shit. I just can't help myself, it seems. Ever since Landon..."

Finn's eyebrows scrunch, and then he nods. "Okay. Yeah, I get it. *I get it.*"

Yeah, he better, because Finn is all gaga over my younger brother. He's always doing all sorts of shit for him all the time. Landon only needs to blink, and Finn is at his side, feeding him grapes and fanning his face. He carried him around for a while there, too.

I thought Finn was bad before the accident. Now he's like ten times worse. I'm surprised Landon can stand it. It's almost overbearing. I mean, as it is, he drives out to see him every weekend that we don't have a game.

"Call me if you need anything."

"I will. Thanks, man."

When I make it back to Theo's apartment, I knock on the door. I probably should have grabbed a key when I'd snuck out this morning, but I didn't want him flying off the handle if he woke up lucid and found them missing.

I don't want him to think I'm a creep. Even though I did

stare creepily at him earlier and Curie caught me. She eyed me like she knew what was going on in my head.

I shooed her away, but she just flaunted her butthole again.

When I hear no commotion on the other side of the wall, I start to worry that maybe he's passed out somewhere and is really hurt, but then the door is flung open. Theo frowns at me, all rumpled and groggy. When he doesn't tell me to go away and just proceeds to scowl at me, I think we're making progress.

"How are you feeling?" I ask, stepping into his space.

"Fine."

I press my hand to his face, and he lets me.

"Still warm," I say, moving into his kitchen. "I brought some tea. It has antioxidants and shit."

"I hate tea," he mutters, but I ignore him, searching through the cabinets for a kettle. When I don't find one, I opt to microwave some water instead.

"Alright, now it's shower time," I say and pull out a bottle of eucalyptus oil.

Theo's eyebrows meet as he stares at the bottle in my hand. "What the hell is that?"

"Some fancy oil. Read about it online. It's supposed to help with your illness."

"I'm not sick," he says, and I just roll my eyes and make my way over to the bathroom. It's small and cluttered with a narrow shower, a small sink, and a toilet.

I uncap the bottle and try and dribble a little on the wall but end up spilling half of it instead. As soon as the warm water hits it, the entire bathroom smells like leaves.

Shit, that's strong. My nose burns.

Theo stares at me from the entrance.

"My *entire* apartment smells like a giant Altoid."

"Just think about koala bears. Pretend you're a koala bear if you need to. Be one with the eucalyptus forest. Just don't lick the shower wall."

He just stares at me in disbelief. Yeah, man, I don't know, it made more sense in my head.

"Strip," I tell him, and he shakes his head.

"No."

I narrow my eyes at him and then push the blanket off his shoulders and wad it up in my arms. He doesn't let go of it without a fight, and I end up cradling it in my arms so tightly he can't wrench it from me. He may be as tall as me, but I have more muscles.

"Get in, wash, and then get out, and you can have your fucking tea," I say, my lungs burning.

I can hear him muttering curses from behind the door as I stomp over to the microwave, tossing the blanket on the bed on my way.

When he reemerges ten minutes later, all wet and freshly clean, I'm holding a cup of tea out for him.

"I almost died in there," he grumbles.

"You're rejuvenated," I counter.

"My eyes are bleeding."

"Don't be so dramatic," I scoff, shoving the mug in his hands. This one has another weird chemistry pun on it that I don't understand. Maybe one day he'll explain it to me.

Theo blows on it and meets my stare.

"You can thank me later," I tell him, and he continues to eye me.

"How many free sessions of tutoring do you want for this? Is that why you're here? Do you want out of our original agreement so badly that you're now playing caretaker?"

I huff out a laugh and fold my arms across my chest. This guy is unbelievable.

"I'm here because I'm a nice guy. I'll still suck your dick for those sessions. Don't worry."

"No," he says with a shake of his head. "It doesn't feel right. Not with you being all...nice." He shudders a little. "Let me think about how many free sessions you'll get."

"Whatever, man," I reply as he sips the tea and grimaces.

"Tastes like bark."

"Bark is good for your health. Everyone should eat more bark. Just drink it and stop complaining," I say and then point to his bed. "Now, I'm going to go wash your sheets because they smell weird." I move toward his bed and start stripping it.

"I can do my own laundry," he mumbles, offering a half-hearted protest.

I ignore him, yanking the sheets off and wadding them in my arms.

"Just let me get this load going, and when it's done, and you've proven you're not going to die, I'll leave."

"A week of free tutoring," he blurts suddenly, and I freeze, looking over my shoulder at him.

"A week?"

"Yes. Seven days. Free tutoring sessions...no sex."

Huh. Why do I feel a little disappointed?

"If that's what you want."

"It is. I don't like being indebted to people. And I most definitely don't like being indebted to you."

"I mean, you wouldn't be indebted—"

"Take the offer," he snaps, and I eye him. I see a smidge of panic in his eyes and then nod.

"Yeah, cool. Whatever works."

He sighs in relief as I make my way out of his apartment and down the creaky stairs to the basement. I throw the sheets in the wash, and when I return to the apartment, the door is cracked open, and Theo is sitting on the edge of the bed, sipping his tea.

"I'm really fine now. This tea worked miracles. So did the oil. You don't need to stay," he says. I think his face is trying for a smile, but he's just awkwardly baring his teeth at me. Yeah, he's lying. I might be dumb, but I'm not an idiot.

"Nah, man, let me just make sure you're okay. I'll worry if you make me leave."

"I just...I don't fucking want you here!" he nearly shouts, and I jump slightly. He exhales shakily. "I just...I just need my space. I need you gone."

"Shit," I mutter, rubbing the back of my neck. "No need to yell."

"I just need...I need you to leave. Please leave, Logan. *Please.*"

That last word, said with a hint of desperation, makes me nod.

"Okay, yeah. Sure. No problem," I mutter. "Your sheets need to be switched to the dryer in like forty-five minutes."

"I can do that."

"Are you sure? Because you may still be weak from the fever...."

He purses his lips and then nods. "Yes. I can do it. I'll see you tomorrow at six."

I shove my hands into my pockets. "Can we do the day after tomorrow, before my practice instead? It's just that I have plans tomorrow night."

Theo's lips tilt down in a frown, and his nostrils flare. "Okay."

I run a hand through my hair and feel the need to explain, "Look, I'm sorry. I know you're busy, and I appreciate you going out of your way to help me, but I told my friend I'd go on a double date with him and some girl he wants me to meet. He's had this planned for weeks."

"You don't need to explain it to me," Theo mutters, staring at the floor, and I sigh.

"I won't fuck her, if that's what you're worried about. I won't fuck anyone until this is over between us. For safety reasons," I add.

He pulls the blanket around his shoulders a little tighter, and turns toward the wall opposite me. "You can do whatever the hell you want, Logan. Just let me know if you decide to do something that could put me at risk."

I shake my head and then move toward the door. When I glance over my shoulder, he's still facing away from me, his gaze trained on the small window, the mug of tea cradled in his hands.

I want to tell him to call me if he needs anything, but I don't. I just leave him alone.

It seems he likes it better that way.

* * *

I'm a grump. The asshole ruined my double date. All I could think about was Theo, wondering if he was okay—if he put his damn sheets in the dryer—and I don't know why I even care. He doesn't give a shit about me.

I'm just a body he can use to get off.

I need to remember that.

I rap softly on his apartment door, adjusting my laptop and textbook in my hands. I fought the urge to bring him breakfast.

He wouldn't appreciate it anyway.

I brought Curie another toy mouse though, and a can of fancy food from Target. They even had a special fridge for this shit. Cost me a bundle too.

Suddenly the door opens, and Theo is standing in front of me. I stare for a moment and just take him in—long legs, rumpled hair, sweatpants hanging off his hips. He looks a lot better than he did. When I step forward, he moves out of my way. Don't worry, man, I won't say anything. Instead, I just hold out the expensive cat food toward him.

"What's this?"

"For Curie," I say.

He examines it for a minute and then shakes his head. "What did I say about buying her things?"

I shrug. "Just thought she might like it. You can keep it or toss it, whatever," I say, moving to our dedicated space on the floor. I lower myself down and Theo shifts on his feet, rolling the can of wet food in his palms.

"Okay," he finally says, moving to put it in the fridge.

"How was your date?" he asks unexpectedly.

I ignore him as best I can, with him looming over me. It's not easy when my eyes are dying to roam over him.

I open my book to the page we'd left off last time, and toss the toy mouse over toward Curie, who just eyes it. She'll probably swat this one under the oven too. The landlord will find a hundred toy mice under there when Theo moves out.

Theo clears his throat. "Did you hear me?"

"Yeah, I heard you," I reply, refusing to meet his gaze. He was the one who wanted this distance between us. "And it was fine."

He sinks down next to me, a pained hiss escaping his lips. And there my resentment goes, right out the window. I never was good at holding onto that.

"What happened?" I ask, concern flooding me as my eyes dart over his body.

Theo shakes his head, a wince marring his features. "Nothing."

"Nah, you hurt yourself."

"I'm fine," he grits out, and I roll my eyes.

"Where does it hurt?" I ask, and he sighs, tugging his shirt up and showing me a large bruise on his side, right below the tattoo.

"God, what happened?"

"I fell."

"You fell?"

"When I went to get the sheets. It doesn't matter...."

I run my thumb over his bruise, and he gasps.

"Shit, sorry. I, uh, have a cream for that. I'll bring it over tomorrow."

He leans back and swats my hand away before grabbing onto the book and setting it on his lap. His chest rises and falls with a deep breath, and his hard, ice-blue eyes soften for just a fraction of a moment.

"Thank you."

My brain stutters, and for a second, I'm confused because what the fuck is he thanking me for?

He must read the confusion on my face because he says, "For the helping me when I was sick."

"Oh, yeah. You don't need to thank me for that. Any decent person would do that for someone else."

"Not many would, Logan. Decent or not."

"You must have had shitty luck then," I say and nudge him with my elbow. "Well, now you have me."

He peeks up at me and then shakes his head. "I don't have you. That's not what this is."

I purse my lips and watch him fidgeting next to me.

He clears his throat and says, "This is me tutoring you and you letting me fuck you. It's just an exchange."

"Well, technically, we haven't fucked."

He rolls his eyes. "My dick was down your throat."

Hm, yeah, that's true. I swallow and rub the back of my neck. My dick is perking up, and I feel nervous all over again. Nah, nervous is the wrong word. Excited. I feel excited.

"You know what? It doesn't matter. Let's just get started," he says and then begins explaining the content to me.

When he twists to grab a bottle of water and winces, my dick is forgotten, and I can't help but envision him falling down the steps the other night.

As my anxiety rises, images of my brother in a hospital

bed invade my mind—his leg in bandages, his face bruised and broken—and I struggle to breathe.

I should have insisted I stay with Theo. I should have made sure he was okay, even if he's stubborn and would have clawed and fought to keep me out of his life.

"Why are you breathing like that?" he asks, and my eyes snap up to his.

Visions of my brother slumped over, blood dripping from his face start to fade away, and I gulp loudly. "Huh?"

"You're breathing like you ran a mile."

I press a hand against my chest, my thumping heart erratic and wild. God, I hate thinking about this shit. It makes me crazy, and don't even get me started on actually *seeing* Landon. The guilt of it is all-consuming.

I run a hand down my face and lean my head back, closing my eyes. "Sorry. Was just thinking...."

"About what?"

"My brother was in a car accident a year ago. Lost a leg. It was kind of traumatic."

Yeah, that's an understatement. It was life-altering. I still have nightmares about it and still can't breathe when my brain decides to conjure it up.

Theo blinks rapidly at me.

"I just...the thought of you falling and hurting yourself just made me think of it. I guess I kind of have a little PTSD over it."

He swallows, his Adam's apple bobbing. "I didn't know."

"Yeah, well, you *would* know because it's not a secret, but you keep everything so professional and shit..." Then a bitter laugh escapes my mouth. "Professional is the wrong word."

Unless sucking someone's dick for tutoring services is considered professional.

"Boundaries aren't a bad thing."

"Pfft," I mutter. "Those aren't boundaries you have. Those are hundred-foot walls with motherfucking space lasers."

He huffs a laugh and then shakes his head. "Dammit, Logan." I nudge him gently. "We should get back to this. I have another student coming in thirty minutes."

"Yeah, okay. Cool."

When we're done, and I'm gathering my stuff, a little kernel of disappointment erupts inside of me. Leaving without sex just feels so unfinished.

I adjust my pants and jog down the stairs.

Six more days, and then we can get back to normal.

four

THEO

I SIT IN THE STANDS, watching the water polo game unfold before me. It's been six days since Logan showed up at my place with soup and a bag of medicine. And that eucalyptus oil. That shit has not dissipated from my shower. I can still smell the remnants of it in my entire apartment.

I hate to admit it, but it kind of helped. It just killed off any remaining sickness I had.

My traitor cat seems attached to him too. It's probably those toy mice and that expensive-ass food he keeps buying her.

She's getting so spoiled.

Why the hell did he have to go and be someone completely different than I'd imagined?

It helps to be here, to remember what kind of man he is. The athlete, the jock. Men like him and I don't mix.

I know. My father *is* one. A very famous one.

I spent the better part of my life despising who he was and yet hating myself for not being more like him. That and protecting myself from the jock bullies who tormented me relentlessly.

Cheers erupt from the stands and it pulls my gaze to where Logan shoots out of the water. Thoughts about how different we are vanish into thin air as visions of his thighs overwhelm me.

God, those thighs. No wonder they're so thick. His entire torso is out of the water right now, his abs flexing as he arches back to throw the ball across the pool.

I've run my hands down those abs.

My cock twitches between my legs, and I shift on the hard metal seat.

I might have an issue with jocks in general, but looking at them…. I run a hand over my mouth. Yes, they're very, *very* nice to look at. Logan, in particular, is delicious.

His face is gorgeous too—so gorgeous, that it almost makes me angry to look at him. His chin-length curly hair is covered up by his swim cap right now, but fuck, I want to run my fingers through it every time he's within five feet of me.

I should have never suggested this asinine plan— tutoring for sex. I don't even know why I blurted that out, but he was standing outside my door looking so damn hot, and my brain just short-circuited.

I didn't actually think he'd agree to it. I was half-joking when I said it. I mean, he's not even gay. The posts about him on Instagram always show him with different women—

beautiful women. I had no idea he'd actually be willing to touch me. I guess I underestimated his desperation.

But fuck, is he good at touching me.

His mouth.

His hands.

I shift again on the seat, and then Logan shoots out of the water again, and my dick is fully erect.

I should get out of here. This was a mistake.

Yet, I stay riveted to my seat, unable to tear my eyes away from him. I watch the entire game until the very end, and when it's over, I sit and watch some more. I try not to drool as Logan pulls himself out of the water, slaps a teammate on the back, and smiles widely. He even has nice teeth. Perfection, that's what he is. Everything about him is flawless.

I need to get up and walk away, but my ass is planted on this seat, and I'm squinting my eyes to make out the shape of his dick under that tiny spandex.

Shit. One more day until I can resort to sexual favors again. I know that without this arrangement, I'd never get the opportunity to see his cock. I've been fantasizing about it. I lie awake at night thinking about it. I felt it against me a couple times and I know what we did got him hard. I wonder if I can make him come, even if he's not physically attracted to me.

It's happened before, a long time ago. Although, that guy did close his eyes a lot. Logan never does. He always watches me carefully.

A small, niggling part of me thinks continuing with this entire thing is a bad idea, but then again, when has that ever stopped me? I usually do what I'm not supposed to. Plus, he's a big boy and he agreed to this. If he really didn't want to suck my dick or jack me off, he could have told me, and I would have let this whole thing go.

But I'm enjoying him a lot more than I thought I would, and I find myself hoping he enjoys it too.

Logan disappears through the locker room door, and I stand up quickly, needing to make my exit.

I get stuck behind people lingering in the stands, and the next thing I know, I hear my name being shouted from across the gym. It echoes off each corner with so much force that people turn to stare.

"Theo!" Logan shouts again.

I freeze, turning slightly, my cheeks flushed.

Fuck.

I point to myself, in case I'm wrong and he's calling out to someone else—there are thousands of Theos in this world— but he just smiles widely and points and yells, "Yeah! You!"

Shit.

I watch in mortification as he jogs over to where I stand. His curly hair is still damp, and hell, he smells like watermelon.

"What are you doing here?" Logan asks, adjusting his duffle bag on his shoulder. "Do you know someone playing tonight?"

No, Logan. I came to see you, against my better judgment.

I swallow roughly and shrug. It's best not to answer, but this guy is more intelligent than I thought because his eyebrows rise, and a slight smirk comes out to play.

"Oh. *Oooh*. Hell yeah. Did you come to see me play?" he asks.

I shake my head. "Never."

My face flames as his lips pull up into a wide grin.

"Knew it. You're a bad liar. What did you think? Impressive, right?"

I shrug and press the back of my cool hand to my hot cheek.

Fuck, I'm embarrassed.

Logan thinks this is fucking funny, too, because he nudges me and waggles his eyebrows like this is all a joke. He has no idea I hate being teased like this by guys like him. It triggers something ugly inside of me.

"You saw my abs the other night and had to see the rest of me, huh?"

"I need to go," I mutter, and his smile slips a little.

"Hey. Hold up, wait a minute," he begins but is interrupted when another man jogs up to us. He's tall and muscular with shaggy brown hair and light brown eyes, and he throws an arm around Logan's shoulders, jostling him slightly.

Logan reaches up and ruffles his hair. "Hey, Finn."

"Hey, Lo. Who's this?" the guy asks, his eyes slipping over me, assessing me. Fuck, I hate this part of meeting people—those initial snap judgments we make about one another. How wrong they usually are.

Case in point—Logan Lewis.

"This is Theo. My tutor."

Finn's eyes widen and then narrow at me. "Oh. I see."

Do you? I fold my arms across my chest, feeling defensive. I eye him right back, hoping my glower will scare him away.

Finn doesn't back down though, and I'm starting to shrink. I hate it when I feel like this. It's something I told myself I'd never subject myself to again, and yet, here I am, melting.

"This was a mistake," I mutter and then turn on my heel, but I don't get far because Logan is following me, nipping at my heels like some kind of eager puppy.

"Hey, don't go. Come out for a celebratory drink with us."

I hadn't noticed that they'd won, honestly. I was too focused on thoughts of him writhing underneath me as I peeled that tiny swimsuit off with my teeth. My mind has gone places these past two weeks that it has no business going.

"I shouldn't. Your friend over there would be unhappy if I showed up."

Not to mention I won't fit in with a bunch of jocks. What the fuck would I even talk about?

Logan flicks his hand in dismissal. "Nah, Finn is cool. He's just worried about me. He's a worrier. It's a problem he needs to deal with."

My eyebrows meet. "Did you tell him about...."

He rubs the back of his neck and peeks over at me. "Yeah, I mean, not the details, but yeah. I told him we had an *arrangement*."

My breath huffs out in a mortified laugh.

"No wonder he was glowering at me."

"Yeah, he does that. He gets a little protective."

I glance over at Logan's friend and shake my head. He's still leaning against the wall, eyeing the two of us curiously.

"Doesn't matter," Logan says, pulling my gaze toward him. "Come out with us. We can have like *one* drink and then go back to study."

I need to turn him down. For self-preservation, mostly.

"I have things I need to get done...."

"Like what?"

I reach up and touch my ear, searching for my pencil, but when I come up empty, I shove my hands in my pockets.

"Like, grocery shopping."

Logan snorts.

"And laundry."

Logan throws his arm around my shoulders, and then he's moving me out of the stands, out the double doors, and toward a group of guys converging on the sidewalk.

"And homework," I tack on as we draw closer and closer.

Oh god. It's hopeless. There's no escaping it now. Logan just continues to usher me toward his teammates as he says, "Hey, guys. This is my friend Theo. He's helping me keep my grades up in chem so I can keep playing."

A chorus of *heys* assaults my ears, and a few move in to high-five me. Never in my life have I *ever* slapped hands with men like this. I'm awkward and clumsy, and I end up folding my arms across my chest to keep them away from me.

I need them all to back the fuck up.

"Alright, alright," Logan says, reading the distress on my face. "Back up. He's like a cat. You gotta give him space." He then turns and swats one of the guys on the ass.

I frown and force my gaze away. Shit, it shouldn't matter. Why does it matter?

"We'll meet you there, yeah?" Logan tells the guys and then gently grabs onto my arm and moves me toward the parking lot.

"Hey, just ride with me. The restaurant is around the corner."

This is a terrible idea, and yet, I still let him lead me to a black muscle car parked a few yards away.

"Hello, carbon emissions," I mutter, and Logan rolls his eyes.

"It's sexy. Admit it. Ms. Chevelle is hot."

It is hot, I want him to fuck me in the backseat, but I'll take that little admission to my grave. Mother Earth is too important to acquiesce to this.

"Get in, Theo, and stop overthinking it. It's just a drink and then back to your place, yeah?"

I stand there frozen because I should not be entertaining this. I need to leave, but then flashes of Logan gently wiping my feverish skin with a washrag infiltrate my mind, and my heart melts a little. Why did he do that? Why did he insist on taking care of me when I'd been nothing but awful to him?

Why does he have to be so fucking perfect when I'm such a hot mess?

When I don't move, Logan rolls his eyes and moves over to where I'm standing. He wrenches the heavy door open and stuffs me inside and I fucking *let* him manhandle me.

When I'm buckled into the seat and Logan has slid into the driver's seat, I ask, "Did you restore this?"

He leans back a little, his big hands running across the steering wheel. Fuck, those hands—the way they stroke me.

"Yep. With my uncle. My dad would have done it, but he'd rather grow his own vegetables and sing to the chickens."

I force my gaze away. "Well, it's very nice. Impressive."

"Yeah, it is. Fucking mint, this is," he brags, then turns the ignition over, and the car starts with a low rumble that vibrates my entire body.

He glances over at me and winks, and my boxers catch fire. They blaze and turn to ash.

Shit.

As we pull out of the parking spot, a few people wave, and I feel utterly ridiculous...and a little bit like a rock star. Because this is Logan Lewis. I'm going out for drinks with one of the most popular guys on campus; the one guy people fawn and faint over.

And I've had my dick in his mouth.

I shift in my seat and glance out the window, trying to keep my wayward thoughts contained, but they flutter like the fall leaves outside.

I'll go back to the way things were once we get back to my place. I need to.

I will not like this man any more than I should. It's too dangerous.

He and I don't mix. Like bleach and vinegar, we're toxic.

five

LOGAN

THEO and I walk into the restaurant side by side, but not before I pulled his car door open and nearly had to pick him up to get him moving. He looked like he was ready to become one with the seat.

"Let's sit here," I say, pointing to two empty chairs at a long table slowly filling with my friends. When he doesn't budge, I pull the chair out and press on his shoulders to get him to sit, but his knees lock, and I have to knock into them gently with my own to get them to bend.

Man, oh, man.

It's obvious he doesn't want to be here. I just don't know why. Everyone has been really friendly. But I saw the way he was when they converged around him, slapping their hands against his. He froze, his body growing rigid. It almost looked like he was afraid.

I'll need to ask him about that later, not that he'll tell me anything. The man is a closed book and every time I get a peek under the cover, he snaps it shut.

"What do you want to drink?" I ask, leaning into him. He smells fresh and sweet, like fruit and that soap he uses. I like it. So does my dick, apparently.

"A shot of vodka."

"Damn," I say with a chuckle. "You're going down swinging."

"Make that a glass of vodka," he amends, and I hold up my hand, getting the waitress's attention.

She comes sauntering over, all hips and boobs, like a fucking hourglass. I eye her a little and she smiles widely. Yeah, she's noticed, and I've noticed. I can't help it. I can admire a work of art.

"This guy will have a shot of vodka, and I'll have an old-fashioned, please."

She winks at me, and I smirk at her. But before I can flirt a little, another woman approaches me. I can tell who it is just by the scent of her perfume.

"Hey, Logan," Tiff says, fluttering her eyelashes at me.

"Hey Tiff," I say, pressing a kiss to her cheek when she leans over to hug me. "Where you been, girl? You ghosting me?"

"Never, I've just been busy. You know how it is. But I'm never too busy for you."

"True. True," I say, laughing.

"Hey, you free after? Maybe we can hang out?"

I eye Theo, who is fidgeting with a discarded straw, his eyes glued to the tabletop.

"Can't do that. I have plans after this, but maybe another time."

She beams at me, one of her plump lips between her teeth, and then flutters away like a pretty little butterfly. I admit I do watch her go. She has a nice round ass.

When she's fully out of sight, I turn my gaze to Theo, who's looking everywhere but at me.

"Hey, man. Sorry about that. You know how it is...."

"No. Actually, I don't."

My eyebrows meet at the venom in his voice. I mean, Theo isn't like...traditionally attractive, but he's hot in his own way. He's tall, lean, and toned with a sweet face and big eyes. If he wasn't scowling all the time and throwing out the "don't come near me" vibe, he'd easily attract more attention.

I can see guys being into him. Hell, my dick is really into him.

"Right, yeah," I say, trying to distract myself from thoughts of Theo naked. "Um, I have some good news. I meant to tell you earlier, but I got sidetracked. I got a C on that chem test you were helping me study for."

His eyes snap up to mine, and he nods. "Good for you."

"Yeah, man. That's all you." I lean over and say quietly, "So glad I decided to suck your dick for tutoring."

His eyes widen slightly, and he glances around, but no one is paying us any attention. It's too loud in here for anyone to hear what I said. Our little secret is still safe. Finn might blab to Landon, but he won't say a word to anyone else. I know that much.

"Hey, Logan," a sweet voice says to my right, interrupting

my conversation with Theo. "Where have you been?"

I look up and smile. "Oh hey, Kierra. Been a while."

"Sure has," she says seductively and tilts a little farther down so I can get a good look at her tits.

"You want to hang out after this?"

"Nah, babe, can't. Got school stuff," I say, and she pouts and then walks away, looking over her shoulder at me. When she catches me looking, she beams and winks.

"Do you remember all of their names?" Theo asks suddenly, and I glance over at him.

"Yeah. I have a thing for names. I don't easily forget them."

"Bet that makes them feel special," he mutters as the waitress appears with our drinks, and Theo wastes no time in throwing his shot back and asking for another.

"Damn," I say. "You may want to slow down. We have to study after this."

Theo rolls his lips between his teeth and taps his fingers on the tabletop. He looks agitated, his jaw working back and forth as his gaze roves over the people surrounding us.

"Hey, man!" Damon, one of my teammates, shouts, stumbling toward me and falling into my lap. He wraps his large arms around my shoulders and presses a sloppy kiss to my temple.

"You were so fucking good today. Kicked ass," he slurs, ruffling my hair.

I chuckle and shove at him because, damn, he's heavy, and my legs are falling asleep under his weight. But he just clings on like the asshole he is, and shit, why the fuck is Theo standing up?

"I'm leaving," Theo mutters, and I just gape as he quickly retreats from the table.

Why the fuck is he leaving? He said one drink. I mean, technically, he had his, but I haven't even had a sip of mine.

I shove Damon off of me, and he lands on his ass, but there's no time to care about the state of his butt because Theo is walking out the door, and I'm jogging after him. I follow him a little too closely, and my toes accidentally hit the heel of his shoe, giving him a flat tire.

"Hey, Theo, what the hell, man? Where are you going?"

"Home," he says, bending down, fixing his shoe, and then continuing his walk down the sidewalk. "I told you; I have things I need to do."

"Come on. Come back in."

"No. Go back to your friends. I don't belong there. You have your adoring fans to keep you company. You don't need me there."

I run a hand along the back of my neck. "Yeah, sorry about that. I don't want to be rude, you know?"

"Logan," he says, stopping abruptly and facing me. "Just leave me alone."

I sigh heavily and then dig my keys out of my pocket. "Alright, let's go."

"No. I'll walk."

"Nah, Theo. Come on. We can go. I should probably study anyway. The C on my test improved my grade, but I still need major help if I want to pass the class."

Theo eyes me and then lets out an aggravated sigh.

"I don't *want* you to come home with me right now. Do I need to spell it out for you? Go the fuck back to your friends."

My eyebrows meet because why is he so angry with me? I haven't done anything wrong.

He starts to walk away, and I watch him for a bit and then jog up toward him again.

"Jesus Christ," he mutters. "Are you dumb? Is that it?"

My head rears back. "Nah."

"Then get the fuck away from me."

He's getting worked up, his cheeks flushed, his eyes wide, and I hold my hands up, feeling my heart sink a little. Because I thought we'd made progress this week, or something.

It seems I was wrong.

"Alright, man. Calm down. I'll back off."

He blows out a breath, running his hands roughly through his hair. He glances at me briefly but his eyes don't reflect his anger, they just look sad. He suddenly turns and jogs down the street, his long legs carrying him away quicker than I thought possible, and before I know it, he's disappeared.

Part of me wants to go after him, but the asshole called me dumb. He's not the first person to do that, but it still kind of hurts my feelings. Especially, coming from someone who's supposed to be helping me learn.

But hell, maybe I am dumb for wanting to be friends with him. I should have just let him be and pretended like I didn't see him in the stands watching me, waiting for me.

Goddammit.

Why do I even care?

I make my way back inside the restaurant and it's like nothing is amiss. No one's noticed Theo's gone. It bothers me more than it should. I drink my old fashioned slowly, making small talk with my friends, but underneath, I'm still simmering in my frustration with Theo.

Needless to say, I take my time showing up at his apartment later that evening. It's a wonder I even bother at all, but my grade in this class means too much to me. I'm not going to let him fuck shit up for me because he has some issues. I've been nothing but nice to him.

It's eight o'clock when I knock on his door, two hours past our meeting time, and I half-expect him not to answer.

When he opens the door though, he looks completely wrecked.

His eyes are bloodshot, and his clothes are rumpled— well, what little clothes he's wearing. He's barely covered in only a pair of short athletic shorts that look too small against his long legs and a sweater that's unzipped and hangs off one shoulder.

"You're late," he mutters.

I shrug. "Yeah, I'm dumb. Couldn't tell time."

Theo eyes me and then opens the door a little more. "Logan—"

"Nah, I know what you meant. Can't take it back now. I'm just a dumb jock, right?" I try for lighthearted but I know it comes out as passive-aggressive.

Yeah, so he for sure hurt my feelings. I'm sensitive like that.

I sink down to the floor in front of his bed and open my textbook, my eyes stinging slightly.

"Better explain it to me like I'm five since my brain isn't as big as yours," I mutter, blinking away the moisture.

"Well, at least now I know what you really think about me."

Theo stands above me, eyeing me, and then runs a hand over his face. "Stop it."

I glower up at him because I'm pissed, but still, my dick twitches in my pants. I've been jacking off to thoughts of him for the past few days and my dick obviously doesn't know how to be mad at him. It still wants him. Stupid dick.

"Nah, don't think I will."

Theo looks away, his jaw clenching.

I run my tongue across my front teeth. "Is that what you think about all jocks, that we're dumb? Is that why you didn't want to hang out with my friends? You think you're better than all of us because you're smarter?"

He refuses to look at me and I kick at his foot.

"Too scared to look at me, huh?" I ask. "You afraid of me now? I *am* bigger than you. I could take you. Maybe you should be scared, I could tear you apart. You're skinny and frail."

His eyes bore into mine. "Shut up."

"Nah."

"Shut. Your fucking mouth."

"Make me."

He steps into my space, and his fingers thread into my hair, and my breath catches as he tugs on it roughly.

"Make me," I gasp, and he pushes his crotch into my face.

My hands grasp onto his hips, my fingers digging into his sides.

"God, I hate men like you," he says, arching into me again.

"And I hate pretentious pricks like you...thinking you're better than everyone else," I mutter, nipping at his hip.

"Pretentious? Big word for a dumb jock," he mutters, and I yank his shorts down roughly until they're stretched over his thighs. His hard cock bobs out in front of me, and I stare at it but don't touch it.

The asshole doesn't deserve it, even though I want it.

He presses the tip of his dick against my mouth, but I lock my lips. I'm going to make him work for it.

"Open."

I shake my head, and he yanks on my hair roughly.

I yelp and open for him, pulling him into me. He drives his dick inside, all the way to the back of my throat and stops. His hands are still gripping my hair, holding my face against his pelvis, his cock lodged in my throat, and drool starts to leak from the side of my mouth. I can smell him, his unique scent, the coarse hairs around his dick tickling my nose.

"That's better," he says gruffly, and then pulls out and pushes all the way back inside again.

My cock is rock hard now, pushing painfully against my track pants as he starts to thrust his hips and fuck my face. I'm needy, desperate...want more.

But then suddenly, the cloud of lust briefly clears and common sense erupts inside of me. What the hell am I doing? He doesn't deserve to have his dick sucked.

I lash out, shoving him off of me. The shorts around his thighs hinder his ability to balance, and he tumbles down onto his ass.

Then there's silence. He just sits there, his cheeks flushed and his chest heaving, as I swipe at my mouth with the back of my hand.

"What the hell?" I say, and he shakes his head, his eyes a little wild.

"I...I'm..." he begins and then shuffles, pulling his pants over himself. "You need to go, Logan."

I shake my head and grasp onto my book, staring at him.

"I'm not leaving until we go over this shit. I paid for my time, and now you owe me for *that*."

He draws his knees up to his chest, leans his head back, and closes his eyes. "Get out," he mutters.

"No."

He opens his eyes, and throws his arm out, pointing to the door. "Out."

"No."

He shuffles over to me and grabs onto my shoulders, his fingers digging into my skin. His mouth opened in a frustrated cry. Curie startles from her nap on the floor in the kitchen and stares at us, she seems just as confused as me.

"Get. The fuck. Out!" he cries, shaking me roughly. The torment and anguish in his eyes disintegrates any anger I was holding onto.

I don't do what he asks because it doesn't feel right, leaving him here like this. I don't know what's wrong with him but he's a mess. I reach out and pull him until his body falls into my lap. Wrapping my arms around him, I hold him tightly against my chest.

"Hey," I say softly, soothing him. "What's up? What's wrong?"

He sags against me, his face pressed into my neck, his

body trembling slightly.

"You should go," he mutters, but there's no conviction in his voice, and I just pull him into me a little further. The way he shakes against me, his breathing stuttered, reminds me of my brother after his accident—the utter pain and torment he was in. The way he'd cry out in the middle of the night and then lash out at Finn and me.

That entire experience broke something inside of me, and I still haven't found a way to piece it back together.

Theo, like me, may seem like he has it all together, but something isn't right.

He has secrets. There has to be a reason he's acting this way.

"Hey," I say, running my hand across his back, up and down his spine, and squeezing the back of his neck. "It's okay, shhh…"

"I'm so sorry," he says softly.

"Nah," I whisper. "It's alright. We're all entitled to our freakouts. I get it."

He's silent for a few minutes, his breath just puffing against my skin, his fingers clutched onto my shirt.

"You're not dumb," he whispers, and hell, my heart cracks a little.

"I am, a little," I say, trying to lighten the mood, and he huffs a small, choked laugh against me.

He clings to the front of my shirt, his lips pressed against my neck. His warm breath strokes my skin.

"You're not. You're smarter than you think," he says.

"I have a GPA of 2.0."

"Intelligence isn't always measured in academics."

"Don't know what that means."

Theo lifts his head and swipes at his eyes. Fuck, was he crying? Now I feel like shit. Shouldn't have shoved him hard like that.

He moves off me and pulls his knees into his chest. "Logan, I need you to do something for me."

"Sure. Anything."

"We need to go back to the way things were," he says, and I wrinkle my brows in confusion. "This can't get complicated between us. Being friends with you or...getting to know you is *complicated*. And I can't do that to myself right now. I'm going through some stuff."

"What stuff?"

"I don't...I'm not sharing that with you."

My chest clenches a little at how reluctant he is to open up. I want to be the one he tells his secrets to. Maybe it has something to do with what his tattoo symbolizes. Shit, now I really want to know.

"Alright. If that's what you want."

I'm not sure that's entirely possible because I'm inexplicably drawn to him, and my dick obsesses over him. But, the truth is, I barely know the guy. I'm not overly attached. It shouldn't be that bad taking a few steps back.

I think.

"Thank you," Theo says, pulling the book from my lap and sniffling a little. "I can do like thirty minutes of tutoring, and then I have other plans."

I nod, and he starts to explain some concepts, and I try my best to pay attention, but mostly I just think about him and his sad eyes.

six

LOGAN

"SHIT, I'm going to be late," I mutter as I tuck my head against my chest and jog toward Theo's apartment complex. Rain hits my exposed skin and slams into puddles on the ground. I pump my legs a little faster just to get inside and up the stairs, and when I finally make it to his door, my heart is pounding out of my chest, more from nerves than exertion. I exhale deeply.

Okay, I can do this. I can see Theo again today without making it weird.

Last night, as I was leaving, I passed another guy who stopped at Theo's door. I don't think it was another student looking for tutoring. He didn't have any books and he looked a little *too* friendly.

I spent the better part of last night obsessing about it—wondering if Theo fucked him and told him all of his secrets.

"Come in," Theo says, and I eyeball him. He's wearing just an oversized green T-shirt, his long, toned legs on display. I run my eyes over them, stopping where the shirt ends. I wonder what he has on underneath.

My fingers itch to slide up this thigh and lift the hem up to see. But I won't do that because today is the first day that everything is supposed to revert back to normal. Not sure what normal is, to be honest. That word doesn't define anything that has gone on between us.

What we're doing is a little fucked up. I can admit that. But I'm not really complaining, either. I don't mind a little weirdness in my life—makes things interesting.

"How are you doing?" I ask, but he doesn't respond. He doesn't even meet my gaze as I take my seat on the floor in front of his bed.

Huh. When he said he wanted things to go back to normal, I kind of expected us to at least be friendly.

He's not being friendly. He's as cold and distant as the first time I laid eyes on him.

Curie is staring at me from across the room and licks her paw with indifference. Even she's not having it.

"Tell me what you want to review today," he says in a clipped voice, and I stare at him in disbelief.

"For real?" I ask.

He flicks his eyes up to mine and then looks away. He's tapping the whiteboard marker on the floor repeatedly, and it's driving me nuts.

"What would you like to go over?"

I sigh and run a hand over my face. If this is how it's gonna be, fine.

"I have a quiz on Tuesday." I hand him a paper and say, "This is what it's on."

He glances down at it and then nods. "Okay."

He starts to go over the concepts, and I try my best to stay focused, but it's hard when my attention is torn. My gaze slides to his legs, and my mind wonders what's underneath the shirt, and then it latches onto the fact that his demeanor is cold as ice. And he might have fucked another dude last night.

Curie makes her way over to me, and I pet her behind her ears, but then she bites me roughly, and I glower at her.

It seems I'm better off just not engaging. Doesn't help that earlier today, I promised my brother I'd visit him this weekend with Finn. So, I'm dealing with the anxiety of that as well.

My mind is royally fucked at the moment. I need to find a way to move past this guilt I have inside of me because there's no changing what happened to Landon. I need to have an actual conversation with him.

Hell. I hate all of this shit.

"Where do you want me?" I ask when Theo suddenly shuts the book, signaling the end of our tutoring session.

He rolls his lips between his teeth and shakes his head. "No payment necessary. I'll continue to meet with you for free."

What the fuck? We had an agreement. We shook hands on it.

"No. No way, man. That's not fair. Why are you being like this? Is it because you fucked that guy last night?"

He won't look at me, and I set the chemistry book on the floor.

"That's it, isn't it?"

"No, no. Nothing happened last night."

My heart lightens slightly. Fuck, I'm relieved.

"Then I'm paying. I don't take free shit from you. So where do you want me?" I ask, folding my arms across my chest.

Theo's jaw is working as he studies the ground. For a minute, I think he's not going to respond, but then he gives a clipped nod.

"Bed. Clothes off."

Ah, so now he wants to fucking play. I knew he did. Tryin' to turn the tables on me.

I stand up and pull my shirt over my head, and Theo watches me from his place on the ground. I drop my shirt to the floor, and then unbutton my jeans.

I'm sliding them down my thighs when he pushes himself up and stands in front of me.

I move slower, giving him a bit of a show, and when my cock finally pops free, he stares at it intently, licking his lips.

"Like what you see?" I ask softly.

He flicks his eyes up to meet mine and then drags them back down to my hardening dick.

"It's fine."

I huff an annoyed laugh and kick my pants off, standing completely naked in front of him.

My hand wraps around my cock, and he shifts on his feet.

"On the bed. Jack off," he says.

I glance down at my dick and arch an eyebrow at him. "Lube?"

He walks into the bathroom and returns a second later with a small bottle. I hold out my hand, and he squirts some onto my palm.

As I'm rubbing it over my dick, I lower myself onto the bed. Theo moves across the apartment, pulling out his desk chair and sitting on it. He leans forward, his elbows on his knees, as I grasp myself tightly.

"You're smaller than I thought you'd be," he mutters. What the fuck? My eyes narrow at him.

"I'm average," I reply. "I've been told that it's a good size for the vaginal canal."

He huffs and then bites down on his bottom lip. "That's what those bitches told you?"

My hand freezes on my dick, and his eyes meet mine. "You talkin' shit, Theo? I bet this cock would fit nice and snug right up your ass."

His cheeks flush, and he swallows.

"Why don't you come over here and we'll see how good it fits," I add defiantly, and his cheeks darken. Yeah, asshole, you're thinking about it now. You know it would fit just fucking fine. There would be no complaints from you.

"Enough," he mutters, wetting his lips. "Hurry up. I have shit to do."

I don't do as I'm told though. I'm feeling just the tiniest bit insecure about my dick now. I mean, it's not small, but it's not enormous like his. So yeah, fuck him.

My dick can't move past the insults he's spouted, and it starts to wilt. My cock is a sensitive soul.

"Maybe I will take you up on that non-payment," I murmur and start to push myself up off the bed.

"Don't. I'm sorry…" I look over at him and his facial expression is soft for the first time today. "Your cock is perfect, Logan. It's just the right size for my ass."

My breath comes out in a whoosh, and I feel my dick hardening again as I stare at him.

"You'd want that?" Theo says. "To take my ass? Bend me over and tunnel up inside of me. I'd take you so good, Logan."

Oh hell. I lay back down and start to fuck my fist. I like his dirty talk. I like it very much. A small whimper escapes my mouth as desire slams through me.

"More, talk more," I grunt, and the chair screeches across the floor as he brings himself closer.

But he doesn't indulge me. Of course, he doesn't. Instead, he just says, "*Faster.*"

"Always bossing me around," I grumble, and he shifts even closer. But that ass of his doesn't move from his chair, it stays planted right where it is.

"Afraid to come over here?" I taunt. "Afraid that ass will sit on my dick if you get too close?"

He huffs, his cheeks pink and his pupils dilated.

"Come on," I say, egging him on. "Come over here. Don't be a pussy."

Theo's chest heaves, and then whatever's holding him back snaps, and he's on me. I barely have time to blink, and he's pressing against me, his shirt riding up his thighs.

And he's not wearing anything underneath it. I knew it. *I fucking knew it.*

My hand lets go of my dick, and I grab onto his bare ass as he rocks into me, our dicks sliding against each other and the sensation only makes me hornier. It feels fucking amazing.

I picture them moving together, all that hard, taut skin just rubbing together, and I have to see it but his oversized shirt is hanging down, hiding it from me, so I grab onto the hem and yank the fabric up.

He looks at me inquisitively with the shirt bunched around his neck.

"I need to see," I pant and then wrench it off over his head, tossing it across the room. I hear a muffled shriek and then a scamper. The shirt must have landed on the cat. Whoops.

I lift my head and glance down at where our thick and throbbing cocks meet, and my heartbeat stutters. A bit of precum has leaked out of his and I brush my thumb across the tip, smearing it onto mine.

"Oh my god," Theo whispers as I clasp us in my hand and squeeze our shafts together.

"Look how big you are," I say and then meet his hooded stare as I slide my hand rhythmically up and down our lengths.

His cheeks are flushed, and his breath comes out in short, desperate pants. His pink lips are parted. What would it be like to taste those mean, pouty lips?

Why the fuck shouldn't I find out? What's stopping me?

Nothing, that's what.

I lean up and smash my mouth to his. His whole body stiffens against me but he doesn't pull away. So, I take that as a green light, and gently grasp his jaw and tilt his face just a little, slipping my tongue inside his warm mouth. Holy fucking hell, he tastes good—like cinnamon and coffee.

I hum my satisfaction and start to pump our dicks more frantically.

He groans, his mouth opening wider for me, his body trembling with each thrust into my hand.

I'm overwhelmed by sensations—the taste of him as I lick my way across his tongue, the smell of our sweat, the sounds of our mouths and bodies grinding against one another, sloppy and depraved.

One of his hands slips into my curls, and he tightens his grip, and I moan loudly.

God, I love this—rough, needy, unfiltered sex.

At this moment, nothing else matters but Theo and I finding release.

I feel my balls draw up, and I groan loudly as my come splatters across my hand and stomach. I feel Theo's body shudder as he follows me over the edge, spilling onto my dick and abdomen. The sight is so hot that my dick refuses to soften.

I look up at Theo and for a brief moment, I see only peace and satisfaction on his face, but it's quickly snatched away as he wrenches himself off of me and stumbles toward the kitchen.

His trembling hands fist his hair, and he begins to pace.

"Oh fuck," he groans, sounding entirely too worked up for that epic of an orgasm. He should be napping right now, not pacing the kitchen.

I lean up on my elbows and watch him as he moves back and forth.

Curie eyes me, and I ask her, "Does he normally do this?"

She just cocks her head, being unhelpful like usual, so I grab some tissues, wipe myself up as best I can, and approach him.

He recoils away from me, like he's afraid. I didn't hurt him, did I? He seemed to enjoy everything. He was kissing me back so enthusiastically.

"Hey," I say, coming to a stop and holding up my hands. "What's up? Why are you so upset?"

"We're not doing that again," he says, his voice shaking. He holds up a finger and then points it at me. "Never again, Logan."

"What part of that aren't we doing again?" I ask because I need him to spell it out for me.

"Kissing. Whatever the fuck that was. Oh, Jesus."

"Why not?"

"We just can't. Oh fuck," he turns away from me, fisting his hair, and I can't help it. I move into his space and wrap my arms around his shaking form. My splayed palms are pressed against his bare stomach as I pull him against me.

"Hey," I say as his back hits my chest. "What did I do wrong?"

He yanks himself from my hold and then spins around, his hands moving to my chest and shoving me back.

"Did I say you could fucking touch me?"

My mouth opens and closes, and then my eyebrows meet.

"Who hurt you?" I ask, and he exhales shakily.

He gestures toward the door angrily. "Get out."

But I don't listen. I just plant myself right in his kitchen and refuse to budge.

"Who hurt you, Theo? Because it sure as fuck wasn't me. What we just did was fucking consensual, and you know it."

His cheeks redden, and he shoves me again. And yeah, his dick might be bigger than mine, but I'm stronger. He can't move me.

"Who hurt you?" I repeat more softly, and he huffs.

"Men like you!" he nearly shouts, and my chest aches. "It's always men like you."

"Men like me?"

"Yes, you heard me. Now get the fuck out of my apartment."

I stand there just staring at him, and he swipes at the back of his mouth like it was an afterthought.

Wiping away my kiss. Asshole. Good luck trying to erase what just happened over there.

"What men?"

Now I'm feeling angry because, yeah, I don't really know the guy, but someone did something to him to make him like this—all cold and detached and mean.

He shakes his head, his eyes nearly wild as he tries to move past me, but I don't let him go. I just pull him against me, and he kicks his leg out, connecting with my shin. Fuck, that's going to bruise, but still, I hold onto him, pressing his back against the wall. Our bodies are touching from our dicks to our chests as we both struggle to breathe.

"Easy," I murmur, and he clutches onto me, his fingers digging into my lower back almost painfully.

"Easy," I repeat, my words brushing against his ear, and he finally sags into me.

"Logan..." I tilt my head so we're eye to eye. "I wish I'd never met you," he whispers, and I see the regret in those depths. "Nothing good will come of this."

I lean forward an inch and press my lips to his.

"Only four more weeks, and then you'll be rid of me," I say, pulling back a little, giving him space. His fingers are no longer bruising my skin as he loosens them.

"I'll be counting down the days."

I step back a bit and he watches me warily.

"I'll see you tomorrow," he says, eyeing the floor.

I run a hand across my jaw and nod. "I'll listen if you ever want to tell me your story, Theo."

He shakes his head, his throat bobbing.

"Sometimes it helps to share it. To not hold it in."

"And what would you know about it?"

I run my tongue over my teeth. "You're not the only one with skeletons in that big-ass closet of yours."

I turn and move toward the bed where my clothes are discarded on the ground. Curie is sitting on my shirt and refuses to move off of it. It's revenge for accidentally smacking her with Theo's shirt. I hold the hem and drag her around the floor for a minute before Theo snatches her up. He's wearing that extra-large shirt again, and I eye his legs.

Fuck, I really like his legs.

"What are your skeletons?" he asks.

"How about...I'll tell you when you're ready to tell me."

I mean, it's only fair, I think as I button up my jeans and run a hand through my hair. I'm not going to open up to this asshole if he's going to remain a mystery. I need a bargaining chip.

"Then I guess we'll never know, will we," he mutters, eyeing me warily.

"I guess," I say, striding over to him and pressing my lips to his once more.

Because I can and because I *want* to.

Theo allows me entry. He even slides his tongue into my mouth for a second.

Then I'm striding out the apartment door, my mind reeling from everything we did together.

But more importantly...what is Theo hiding? And why does he hate the idea of me so much?

seven

THEO

"HEY!" a voice calls from behind me.

I look over my shoulder and see Logan loping toward me, his curls slightly damp from the rain, his broad shoulders filling out his sweater so damn nicely. My hand clutches the umbrella I'm holding over my head and I inhale deeply.

I can do this.

But fuck, my lips tingle and my heart breaks a little at the sight of him. Our kiss still replays endlessly in my head—the best kiss of my life.

From him. Fucking Logan Lewis of all people.

It was so different from the others. So much better.

"Hey, Theo. You walk super-fast," he says when he finally makes it up to me. He nudges me in the side as he ducks down under the umbrella, and suddenly he's entirely too close.

I've managed to make it another four days without kissing him. I've just watched him jack off after our tutoring sessions.

I can't get near him.

Not after kissing him. I lost control in those heated moments and his achingly soft lips did something to me, did something to my heart.

However, watching him writhe and thrust on my bed as he touches himself and not being able to participate is becoming harder and harder. He's a fucking dream and watching him come—his muscles flexing, the sheen of sweat lining his skin, and all that unruly beautiful curly hair—he just looks so angelic. Which is so at odds with how sinful he moans.

The past few days, I've had to physically hold onto the chair to keep myself from jumping on him.

Ugh, why can't he just leave me alone? Why can't I leave him alone? I wish I knew.

"Where you off to?" Logan asks, running a hand through his wet hair.

"I have lab," I say, trying to move away from him, but he keeps invading my space.

"Cool, so, I was going to text you, but saw you instead," he mutters. "I can't meet tonight. I'm actually going to see my brother."

My heart sinks, because as much as I detest what a temptation he is, the thought of not seeing him does horrible things to my stomach.

"I'll be gone the weekend too, so unless you want to like Zoom or some shit, we could just meet again on Monday?"

I swallow and nod, "That's fine."

He eyes me and then clarifies, "Like, do you want to Zoom? Or are you cool with just waiting until Monday?"

"Whatever," I say, and he nudges me slightly.

"Alright, can I text you if I feel like I need it? I don't want to get behind. I feel like I'm doing so good."

I nod and his eyes slip down to my mouth and fuck, my lips are dry. My tongue peeks out to wet them and his pupils dilate.

"Fuck, Theo," he grumbles.

I inhale sharply and force my gaze away, lest I kiss him right here in the middle of campus. God, what would people think? I don't need any attention drawn to myself. No, I much prefer to blend into the background.

"Hey, Theo, hurry up. We got stuff to do!" my lab partner shouts from the doorway as we approach the science building.

I glance at him and then back at Logan.

"I'll see you Monday," I tell him.

Logan eyes Carlos for a minute and then nods. "Alright, Theo. See you in a few days. Don't miss me too much."

He winks at me, and I feel my cheeks heat.

Logan smirks and then jogs away, his grey sweater darkening from the rain. I just stand there in the middle of the walkway and track him until he disappears into a building.

"Who was that?" Carlos asks me.

"That was Logan. I'm tutoring him."

"He looked at you like you do more than just study together," Carlos teases.

I glare at him. But this guy has been my lab partner for years and he lets my scowl just roll right off his back.

Carlos leans into me, his eyes wide behind his glasses. "So, are you two like a thing? Is it this big secret?"

"No," I reply, collapsing my umbrella.

"Pfft. You looked like a thing."

"Jesus, Carlos. Can you leave it alone?"

Of course, he doesn't listen. "You've kissed him, huh? Or done...other things?" His dark eyes hone in on me.

I refuse to answer, but my blushing cheeks tell all.

"Ah, I knew it. Logan Lewis, man. Who knew he was into guys."

I roll my eyes and continue to remain silent. I will not be divulging what Logan and I do behind closed doors.

It's my little secret.

"You're really not going to give me anything? Like an itty-bitty tidbit? I've had your back all these years...."

"Nope," I say, popping the P.

"Damn you," Carlos replies and then nudges me softly. "Alright be all mysterious. Let's get to work."

Thankfully, he doesn't bring it up again, but I know he will eventually. I don't have many friends; Carlos is as good as it gets. I can trust him as much as I trust anyone—which is practically zilch. Trust is just not something I easily give out.

I'm able to put Logan out of my mind for the rest of the day, until I arrive home and the silence overwhelms me. I'm pulling at my hair and pacing, as thoughts of him nag and nag at me.

I'm going stir-crazy.

Jesus, that man needs to fucking leave my head. I have no idea what it is about him that I can't let go of. I've never had this problem before.

I've paused my pacing to get a soda from the fridge and Curie bats something onto my foot. I glance down and see that stupid toy mouse Logan bought her.

Hell, even my cat is reminding me of him.

Suddenly, there's a knock at the door.

As I move to answer it, my stupid heart flutters in anticipation that maybe it's Logan on the other side. But when I wrench the door open my heart sinks—just full-on drowns.

Because it's *him*.

He lifts a hand and I shake my head in disbelief.

"Hey, son," my dad says, and I start to close the door, but just like that first day I met Logan, he stops it with an outstretched hand.

I hate it when men use their strength against me like this. It irks me to no end, and makes me feel so defenseless and exposed.

I swallow roughly. "What are you doing here?" I ask, proud that my voice doesn't break from the stress of it all.

"I was in town...."

Now, I know that's a lie. He lives like six states over. No, this asshole made a purposeful trip here to see me.

What I don't understand is why.

"I don't have time for your lies."

He looks a little bashful, which only makes my heart flip in my chest. He doesn't get to look like this.

No, this fucker doesn't get to change his mind about me twenty-four years later. That's not what happens in the real world. Although for Sutherland Reign, maybe it does, because my dad always gets what he wants. No one says no to him. I learned that the hard way.

But I say no. I will continue to do so until the day he dies.

"I was hoping we could go out for a drink," he says, and my eyebrows meet. Because, what the actual fuck is happening?

"I'm busy."

He nods and looks away and then moves toward me and I start to panic. Guess that's what happens when you're mentally beaten down by your own dad for most of your life.

I've been a disappointment to him from the moment he found out about me and I haven't been able to live up to his expectations, no matter how hard I tried. So, I stopped trying when I was eighteen and moved away from any kind of influence he may have over me.

I've thought about changing my last name but haven't gotten around to it yet. The paperwork is still sitting on my desk, blank.

Just seeing him again revives the urge to fill it out and send it in.

I'll do it soon, I think, as I stare at the man who is my biological father. God, we don't even look alike. Maybe in the color of our hair and the shape of our eyes, but I favor my mom in almost every way. It doesn't matter anyway; he wasn't the one who raised me. That was my mom. My poor fucking mom who died six years ago in a car crash.

Jesus.

"Theo, look, I'm staying at a hotel just down the street

for a few days if you change your mind," he says and holds out a card. "If you want to call or text. I'm free anytime."

I snatch the card from his hand just to get him out of here and then slam the door in his face.

Quickly, I grab Curie, holding her in my arms and sinking onto the bed.

I toss his card onto the table and hope that Curie blesses me by swatting it somewhere I can't reach.

Fuck, why did he have to show up? I was fine letting whatever tethered us together just slip away. After my mom died, I felt like it was severed, but apparently not. Just when I feel like my life is getting back on track, he jumps in and derails me.

Screw him.

I need something to distract me.

I glance at my phone and then pocket it. For a moment, I consider asking Logan to come over and kiss me senseless, but then discard the idea. There is no way in hell I'm calling him and making myself vulnerable like that.

I glance at my phone again and nibble on my bottom lip.

No way.

eight

LOGAN

"YEAH, I'M ON MY WAY," I tell my brother, my phone squished between my shoulder and cheek. "I'm just getting gas."

"So, you'll be here in like two hours?" Landon asks, a note of hope in his voice and dammit, I'm such an asshole. I should have done this sooner.

I don't deserve him. I am the worst big brother on the planet. Ship me off to outer space.

"Yep," I say, hopping out of my car and sliding my card into the gas pump machine.

"Alright," Landon says, sounding excited. "I'll make up the sofa bed."

"Nah, don't bother. I can sleep on the floor. Besides, where will Finn sleep?" I ask because my best friend took off a few hours ago to go hang with Landon. Asshole just couldn't wait a few hours for me to finish my shit so we could carpool.

"You're not sleeping on the floor, and Finn will just sleep with me," Landon says.

Hmm, that's new, right? Or maybe not.

"Cool, bro. I'll be there soon."

He huffs in the receiver and then says, "Really, I'm glad you're coming. It's been too long. We have so much to talk about."

Oh, hell. Because he's right, but I'm just not ready. I should be, but I'm quaking in my metaphorical boots. See? We're all just a bunch of scaredy cats in this family. You should see my dad; he's worse than me when it comes to confrontation.

"Yeah, me too," I say through the lump in my throat, and then I hang up, stuffing my phone in my back pocket.

I sniff a little, my eyes stinging. I need to distract myself before I start weeping openly in the middle of a gas station like a lunatic. Maybe some candy will help. I never have the stuff, so maybe a sugar rush will keep my mind off tonight... and tomorrow, and Sunday.

Shit.

I wait for the tank to fill and then jog into the store.

That's when I see him. Theo is hovering near the chip aisle, his arms full of junk food. Hell, he's a sight, all rumpled, his hair sticking out at odd angles, and I just can't help myself. I duck down and move toward him before popping out into the aisle he's perusing.

"Look at you," I say loudly, and Theo spins around so fast he stumbles into a rack of beef jerky.

"Shit," he mutters when I grab onto his shoulders to steady him.

"Whoa. Didn't mean to scare you," I lie.

Theo adjusts all the snacks, and the bags crinkle in his arms.

"Let go of me," he mutters but makes no move to extricate himself from my grasp. He just continues to face me, his eyes moving across my face and landing on my lips. A slight blush taints his cheeks and I smirk a little.

Caught you looking, Theo. You can't fool me.

"What are you doing here?" I ask, stepping back just slightly, just enough to give him some space.

"I was hungry."

I eye the junk food in his arms and raise an eyebrow.

His neck and the tips of his ears turn an even darker shade of red as he turns on his heels and makes his way to the cashier. But before he can fish out his card, I hold mine out to the woman behind the counter.

"I don't want you to pay for this," he hisses, but I ignore him and so does the cashier. She doesn't have time for our shit—there's a line forming behind us, and she's paid minimum wage.

"Thanks," I tell her, grabbing the bag full of snacks and moving to the front of the store. Theo is helpless to do anything but follow me.

"Logan, give me the bag," he says lowly, and I smirk at him.

"Tell me why the binge? Smoke a little too much?" I tease.

His hand flops to his hip and he sighs. "No. Absolutely not. I just needed a distraction."

I stand up a little straighter and lean toward him a little. Because, me too. Jinx.

"Yeah? Why?"

He reaches out for the bag again. "Just give me the damn bag."

Alright, no need to get grumpy.

I hand it over to him and he opens it, peering inside. But he's not running away from me, which I fully expected him to do. Instead, he just shuffles around nervously and says softly, "My dad showed up at my place."

I move a little closer to him because fuck, he looks kind of vulnerable right now and I'm not sure I like that look on him. It makes me instinctively feel protective.

"Did he hurt you?" I ask, my chest constricting at the thought. Maybe that's why he's always so prickly and defensive.

His eyes snap up to mine. "No, not like that...Jesus. This was a mistake...I shouldn't have said anything."

And yet, we stand, suspended in time, at the entrance to the convenience store just staring at each other.

"I need a distraction too," I admit, and Theo meets my gaze. "I'm going home to visit my brother, as I said."

"And why do you need a distraction from that?"

"I've been avoiding him, kind of. I just..." my voice trails off and I shake my head, trying to gain control of my emotions. "The accident he was in was my fault."

Theo's brows meet and he steps a little closer to me. "Logan."

I swallow and fiddle with the bag hanging off his wrist. "It's hard to see what I did to him, you know? The guilt...."

The sound of cash being exchanged behind us, the voices of customers moving around the store, and the sound of the soda machine dispensing drinks all fade to white noise when Theo reaches out and links his pinkie with mine.

Fuck, he's sweet in his own way. He reminds me of a cold wild animal that snaps at you when you try to pet it, but really, it just wants you to curl up with it and keep it warm.

"Come with me," I blurt. "Come with me this weekend, Theo. I know we don't know each other well, but maybe we can just put that aside and help each other out."

His pinkie slips from mine, and he glances around the store. "I don't think that's a good idea."

"Distract me," I try again. "Distract me and I'll owe you. I'll owe you big time."

He swallows, his eyes flicking from mine to the door, like he's looking to escape. I full-on expect him to dash away and leave me staring after him, but miraculously, he doesn't. He just whispers, "Okay."

It's said so softly, I can barely make it out, but fuck, he actually said okay.

"Yeah?" I say, feeling kind of excited and mostly relieved. The thought of not seeing him this weekend bummed me out more than I cared to admit.

"Sure, I just need...I just need to grab some stuff before we go."

I nod, already pulling him out the door and as I do, I slip my fingers through his. A slight gasp escapes him, and I glance over, squeezing his hand lightly.

"Don't make it weird, Theo."

His eyes flash as he stares at me, his mouth parted slightly.

"People may see," he protests, and I roll my eyes.

"You embarrassed to be seen with me?" I ask and he just stares down at our interlocked hands. Because the truth is, no one has ever been embarrassed to be seen with me.

Although, if anyone would be, it would be Theo. For some reason, this guy wants to keep me a secret.

I'm not sure if I like that. I want someone who will be proud of me.

"A little," he mutters, and I scoff.

"Whatever," I say, walking him through the parking lot. Our hands are still linked, and he makes no move to extract himself from me, so I just hold on a little longer. I don't really know why and I don't bother questioning myself. It is what it is, as my grandma used to say.

"Where's your car?" I ask, not really sure where I'm going. Maybe I'll just walk to my brother's place. We could get there Sunday and then turn around and walk back. Avoid all this nonsense.

"Um, uh...." Theo stumbles on his words, his mouth opening and closing. He keeps staring at our hands.

"Your car?" I remind him.

"Oh, I walked. I walked here."

"Huh. Well, I'll drive you back," I say, tugging him toward Ms. Chevelle.

"I changed my mind," he says, but still makes no move to pull his hand from mine.

I just gently push him until his back is pressed against

my car and I'm standing against him, our mouths so fucking close. I could just lean down and press my lips to his...

"Logan," he whispers as I move closer and closer. I'm just a breath away from his lips, I can feel the heat radiating off of them, but a sudden horn blaring has me jumping back.

Our hands unclasp and I chuckle.

"Shit," I mutter, running a hand through my hair. "Scared me."

Theo blinks and then starts to scoot away from me, but I loop an arm around his middle and wrench my car door open, gently setting him in the seat.

"I can do it. I'm not a child," he mutters as I lean down and buckle him in.

"Mhmm," I reply, but I still don't let him buckle himself in. I don't trust him not to make his escape. I really want that distraction this weekend and Theo is already doing a great job. I haven't even thought of Landon once.

I mean, I'm thinking of him now, but still, the past five minutes were golden. I want Theo to continue to distract me so I don't fall apart when I see my brother.

I don't need Landon consoling me when I should be the one doing that for him. He's lost so much more than I have.

Jogging to the driver's side, I slide in and then I'm twisting the key in the ignition and the rumble vibrates the entire car.

"Sexy, huh? Panties getting all..." My voice trails off. Hmm, that doesn't work. Oh, I know. "Boxers getting all tight?" I ask instead.

He glances over at me and says, "Who says I'm wearing any?"

My eyes swivel down to his crotch and then fly back to his eyes. "For real?"

His lips twitch and then he turns to look out the passenger side window. Damn him. Now I'm going to be wondering.

I watch Theo's ass as he moves around his apartment, feeding Curie and gathering a duffle bag full of clothes for our weekend excursion. He bends over for an extraordinarily long time—probably just to tease me—and the entire time I try to make out an underwear line through his pajama pants, but I can't quite come to a determination.

I might need to peek inside to kill my curiosity.

"I'm ready," he says and then shifts on his feet, watching me. His duffle bag sits on the floor next to him.

"You worried?" I ask, reaching down and grabbing onto it. I'll hold it hostage until he gets into my car. Then it's game over. I'm keeping him.

For the weekend, I mean.

"I'm second guessing my decision to go with you."

"Too late," I say, leaning down to scratch Curie behind her ears. "You promised."

"I did no such thing."

I glance up at him and narrow my eyes. "Get your ass out of this apartment, Theo."

His cheeks flush at my tone but as I watch him, I get a sense he's not annoyed. No, he's something else entirely. I stand up and run a hand up over my chest to my mouth and his eyes follow my fingers as they run gently along my bottom lip.

"Jesus," he mutters, forcing his gaze away and swallowing roughly.

Yeah, don't think I haven't noticed how intensely he watches me while I jack off in front of him. He refuses to kiss me again, but he always stares at my mouth while I fuck my fist. He seems more interested in that than my dick.

I slide the tip of my finger into my mouth and tease it with my tongue and Theo slams his eyes shut.

"Stop it," he mutters, and for a moment I consider ignoring him, forcing him to fucking look at me, but instead I let my hand fall to my side. I don't want to be the reason he wriggles his way out of this weekend. I am giving him zero excuses.

One of his eyes pops open and when he sees that I'm being completely appropriate, he opens the other. A long exhale exits his mouth and then he wets his lips and casts his eyes to the door.

"We should go. Before I change my mind."

"You sure?" I ask, because, you know, if he wanted to stay and mess around first, I think my dick would really appreciate that. It jumps a little in my pants in affirmation.

"Yes, Logan. Let's go."

Yeah, that's a no then. Bummer.

I follow him out of the apartment with his duffle bag swinging over my shoulder.

"I can carry it," Theo says frostily, but I ignore him.

"I know, but I have more muscles," I tell him, and he narrows his eyes at me. But they don't hold any resentment. He's just faking it now. I'm wriggling my way into his heart...

or under his skin, not sure which one. I don't really care; I just want to get inside of him any way I can.

"Are you sure he won't mind me showing up?" Theo asks, his wary eyes meeting mine as Ms. Chevelle makes her way down the street.

"I'm sure," I reply in confidence because I *know* my brother and he's so fucking nice. He'll be happy to meet someone new, and Finn will do whatever Landon wants. He never wants to make him unhappy. And Theo can be kind of...nice-ish...when he wants to be.

"Alright, but if this gets weird, I'm leaving," Theo says, pressing his palm into his thigh, forcing it to stop moving. He has his pencil behind his ear. I saw him grab it before he left, along with his journal, which is currently shoved under his leg.

Damn, that shit is so *tempting*.

I roll my lips and tap my thumbs on the steering wheel. "Yeah, well, it might get a little weird, but not in the way you think," I tease and Theo eyes me warily.

I still can't believe he's in this car with me. Part of me expects him to roll right out of the door and onto the highway. He'd be like D.B. Cooper, but without the parachute.

And the money. I don't have that much on me.

I reach over and lock the doors, just to prevent any mishaps or sudden urges he may have. I've never had someone run away from me before and I'm not looking to start now.

"You locking me in? Do you spend your weekends kidnapping people?" Theo asks and I snort.

"Puhleeze. If I was kidnapping you, you'd be in my trunk. Tied up."

He coughs a little and eyes me. "You're a strange guy, Logan."

I chuckle and then reach over and lightly punch his arm. "I mean, we're all a little strange up in here. Right?"

"You are weirder than I imagined you'd be. I, however, am mostly normal."

That has me wheezing because Theo is fucking whack. He has to know that.

His eyebrows slam together, and he glowers at me. "Why are you laughing at me?"

"Because," I say, swiping at my eyes. "You told me that in order to get tutoring from you, I needed to fuck you."

He clears his throat and glances out the window.

"That's some messed up shit, Theo. Even you have to admit, that's weird with a capital W."

His leg starts bouncing again and suddenly, I feel bad for even bringing it up. I'm always walking on eggshells with this guy. They're just crunching under my feet.

"Not that I'm complaining. I...you know, I kind of like doing it. It's different than what I'm used to."

He doesn't reply. He just silently stares out his window. I, on the other hand, can't stop blabbering and simpering. Someone, please stop me.

"If I really wasn't into it, I would have told you. So don't worry about that. I even bought a dildo...."

Okay, now is the time to zip it, but I can't help it. I keep going. I'm like a runaway motorboat just chugging along through this gator-infested murky water.

"...I stuck it up my ass multiple times. Didn't mind it so much. I even watch gay porn now."

Oh, dear lord, send help.

Theo is staring at me, his eyebrows raised, his mouth agape. I'm sweating a little.

"You know, just in case you wanted to stick that gigantic dick of yours in my ass. I have a little nervous thing about being prepared...I wanted to stretch myself out a bit, ya know? Is that a thing?"

Theo wets his lips and blinks rapidly.

"And what if I, like shit myself or something. I wanted to make sure that didn't happen...you know...."

Oh, Jesus, take the wheel. I slap a hand across my mouth, trying to force my words back inside. I don't need to talk about shitting myself if Theo fucks me. What the hell is wrong with me?

I'm flushed and embarrassed now.

"Logan. I'm not going to fuck you," he says softly, and my eyebrows pinch together. Because why the hell not? Maybe all that poop talk really turned him off.

"You got something against me personally?" I ask, feeling a little defensive.

Theo shakes his head. "I'm not answering that."

"You do, don't you? Did I..." I swallow, my mind going a hundred miles an hour because nothing else makes sense at the moment. "Did I do something to you? Like, did I hurt you or something? Because I didn't mean to."

"No..." Theo says and then shakes his head. "It's...don't worry about it, Logan. Just...your ass is safe from me, okay?"

I don't want it to be safe from him. I want it to be

violated. Trespass, Theo. Stick that big dick right up inside of me.

"But I've been practicing."

"Well, you can stop."

Silence permeates the cab of the car and I tap my fingers on the steering wheel. Light rain has started to fall from the sky, and I turn on the windshield wipers as we both stare out at the road ahead. Fuck. I'm not sure what to talk about now. I kind of want to pester him about it some more.

See, what did I say? Distraction. He's doing a brilliant job. I haven't thought of my brother once, nor the overwhelming guilt I'm going to have seeing him again. This whole weekend is going to be a total clusterfuck.

"Is it because you aren't attracted to me?" I blurt. That's never actually happened to me before, but with Theo, anything seems like a possibility.

"Logan, are you fishing for compliments? Because you know what you look like. I don't need to tell you."

"Yeah, well, I think you should tell me."

"I'm not doing that. You can just look in a mirror and see for yourself."

"What if I told you what I think of you?" I ask. "We could trade."

"Don't do that," he says, almost sounding desperate now. Like I'm going to insult him or some shit. "I don't want to hear what you think of me."

"It's not bad, Theo."

He shakes his head and purses his lips. "Don't. Don't do it."

I sigh and then decide I should change the subject. He's

getting agitated and I don't know why. I was just going to compliment his dick and his legs and those soft lips of his.

So instead, I ask, "Will Curie be okay all alone in the apartment? She seems kind of vindictive."

Theo exhales, seemingly relieved by the change of topic. "She'll be fine, but yeah, I'm sure she'll hold my absence against me. She'll probably piss on my pillow in protest or something."

I chuckle at that. "What a bitch."

Theo is silent for a moment and then glances over at me. "You talking shit about my cat, Logan?"

I chuckle a little at that and then swallow it down because I'm not sure if he's messing with me or not.

"Yeah, no, I mean...kind of?" I let my words trail off and clear my throat, "You can turn on some music if you want." Because shit, I need something to listen to besides the garbage spewing out of my mouth right now. I can't quite seem to stop myself.

He shakes his head. "I'm good."

"That's cool. Just listening to the sound of the rubber meeting the road, huh?"

He peeks over at me. "Very poetic."

"I know, right?" I say with a lopsided smile, and he huffs. Well, what the fuck ever. Not everyone can have such a big brain with a side of giant dick.

"So that guy who was waving at you today, was he a friend?" I ask. Because I'm nosy like that.

"Kind of. A lab partner."

I tap my fingers on the steering wheel. "Have you guys... you know?"

"No, I don't know," Theo replies and now it's my turn to huff in annoyance. Why does he have to make me explain myself? I'd rather he read between the fucking lines. And trust me, I have so many lines. They're spaced out wide too. This isn't rocket science.

"Have you been *together*?" I ask.

"We've been together for three years...as *lab partners*," he tacks on, and I reach over and shove him lightly.

"Come on, man. You know what I'm asking. Don't make me spell it out. I might not get it right," I tease.

Theo huffs a laugh. "No, never. Carlos is straight."

Why do I like the sound of that so much? Yeah, I know the answer to that. I'm not fooling anyone. It's because that makes him mine for the moment, in some small way.

And I don't have to share him.

"Do you have friends?" I blurt and then bite down on my tongue because that came out all wrong. God, I sound like an asshole.

He must think so too because he stiffens a little.

"I didn't mean...fuck, I didn't mean it like that. Sometimes my words come out wrong."

Theo folds his arms across his chest. "I have some friends, but not like you. I'm busy with school. I don't have a lot of time for relationships."

I bob my head. "Makes sense. Makes sense."

Silence once again infiltrates the space between us, and I fidget a little in my seat. Goddamn him, making me all fidgety. I'm drowning here. Throw me a life jacket, Theo. Or maybe he'd rather watch me sink.

"What's your major?" Theo asks suddenly and I exhale in relief.

"Communications."

"Is that so?"

"Yeah. It's an easy major. Or so I was told. And it doesn't really matter anyway. I'm here for water polo."

Theo rolls that pencil between his fingers. "I think you're smarter than you give yourself credit for, Logan."

I clench the steering wheel a little because no one has *ever* referred to me as smart. I've always been the athletic, strong one. *You're a good swimmer. My little fish.* Even my mom, bless her heart, never told me otherwise. And let me tell you a secret, I'd even overheard my grandma once say I was as dumb as a rock.

Maybe the curse is genetic. I was born this way.

"I don't know about that," I reply, clearing my throat.

"You've caught on to everything I've gone over in each session, and what I'm explaining is *not* easy. I think you don't give yourself enough credit."

I clear my throat again because damn, now my eyes sting. No one has ever really believed in this part of me. I've always just laughed it off, even though it hurt a little, but hell, maybe if Theo believes in me, I'm not a total lost cause. Maybe I can have options in life.

A sniffle escapes me and Theo eyes me from his seat.

"Are you...crying?'

"I never cry. I'm a man."

Lies, I cry all the fucking time—just blubber on and on— usually in a locked bathroom with my fist in my mouth, but still.

I'm a crybaby, with muscles.

Theo is silent for a few minutes and then rolls his pencil around in his fingers.

"I almost failed one of my STEM classes my freshman year."

I gape because this guy almost failing at anything is almost unbelievable.

"I almost gave up and changed my major. But I didn't and now I'm getting my doctorate in chemistry."

"I didn't know that."

"Of course, you wouldn't, but my point is, you're trying, Logan. Sometimes people think that because they're not naturally good at something that they shouldn't even try. But the truth is most successes and talents aren't natural, they're won by hard work and persistence. You're trying and you're working hard, despite it all. That's admirable. You're brave, Logan."

I sniffle loudly. No hiding it now. He's making me all emotional.

"You'll pass this class. I'll make sure of it."

I swipe at my eyes. "Thank you."

Theo nods and then returns his attention to the window. I'm not sure what to say after that, so I just turn the radio on —mainly to hide the sniveling I'm doing, but also to distract myself from Theo. See, now I'm doubly distracted. Landon isn't even on my mind, and Theo is scribbling in that journal of his and I'm trying to sneak a peek without driving us off the road.

Is he writing stuff about me? Why is he writing so fast?

Oh my god, I want to read it.

When Theo and I finally walk into Landon's apartment, my mind is a mess. My eyes immediately snag on Finn sitting at the small dining table, fiddling with his phone. As soon as he hears us approaching, he stands up with a big smile on his face.

"Hey, man…" His words taper off when he sees Theo walk in behind me. "Are you serious right now?" he asks me.

I just shrug and ignore him.

Finn narrows his eyes at me and frowns. "I know what you're doing, Logan. You're a fucking glass house; I can see right inside."

Yeah, I know. He doesn't even need to say it; I'm a fucking coward.

I never claimed to be anything else when it comes to my brother. He's my weak spot. I'm like that lion dude from *The Wizard of Oz*, just running away from shit all the time and quaking in my boots.

"Where's Landon?" I ask.

"He was really tired and fell asleep," Finn explains. "He tried to stay up for you, but now I'm glad he didn't."

I run a hand through my hair. "Shit, man. Give me a break. I know what it looks like—"

But Finn interrupts me, "The couch is made up for you. I didn't make up a place for him though. Guess he can sleep on the floor."

Finn gestures toward Theo who is shifting awkwardly on his feet next to me.

"Don't worry about us. We'll make it work," I mutter and Finn scoffs.

"Do better, Logan. Your brother deserves the best parts of

you," he says and then turns on his heels and disappears into the small bedroom. The door shuts with a click and Theo eyes me.

"You didn't tell me Finn was going to be here," he says.

I huff in exasperation. "Yeah, well, he is. Surprise."

Great, now Theo's mad at me too. I don't blame him honestly. I'm feeling a little sorry for myself at the moment. Now I feel guilty *and* I've disappointed everyone.

Theo fiddles with the pencil behind his ear and then sighs. "It's too late to do anything about it now. We should probably just go to sleep. It's been a long day."

I just nod because when I open my mouth, I end up in trouble. "I'll take the floor. You can have the couch."

"There's no need. We can share it," he says, and I eye the small pull-out mattress. We'd have to sleep really close to one another. My heart rate kicks up a notch.

"Fine," I say, trying to sound nonchalant and not overly eager.

I pull my shirt off over my head before Theo can change his mind and then I'm kicking off my pants.

Theo just stands frozen, watching me, his Adam's apple bobbing in his throat.

"Go on. Get undressed," I say and flop down on the bed. It squeaks and moans under my weight and I put my hand up behind my head, watching as Theo eyes me warily.

"Come on. Hurry up. We don't have all night."

I mean, we technically do. Nothing is stopping him from just hovering in the corner like a barn owl until morning, but I'd rather he lie down next to me.

Theo glances around the room and then fiddles with the bottom of his shirt. "Are you sure?"

"I'm so fucking sure," I say and Theo swallows before lowering himself down onto the mattress facing away from me. He's so close to the edge that I worry he's going to fall off.

"Don't be scared," I mutter. "You can get a little closer."

Theo sighs and turns onto his back, then starts slowly sliding toward me. It doesn't look intentional though. My weight is probably propelling him downhill. I snicker as his body presses against mine and he huffs.

"Damn you," he mutters, trying to scoot back to his side, but failing miserably. "You literally tilt the whole bed. You're a behemoth."

"I'm an athlete with sexy muscles."

"You have your own gravitational pull."

The bed shakes with my chuckle and I swear I can feel him smile.

"I won't be able to stay on my side of the bed," he grumbles.

"Don't worry about it," I say. "We can cuddle." I slowly inch my hand over and lay it on top of his. The connection feels electric and my fingers tingle as I stroke my thumb over his palm.

I feel his body tense up and then the silence pulses between us. I turn my head to look at him and can just barely make out his features from the porch light filtering in from the window. He's looking at me too. We're inches away and it's a stare-down now. I glance at his mouth and his tongue peeks out, wetting his lips.

Oh, sweet Jesus. That mouth.

"Theo," I whisper, and he scoots a little closer. His breath puffs against my mouth and I feel myself start to pant. It's been too long since he's kissed me, since he's touched me, and I crave it.

"This is a mistake," he whispers, and every nerve ending in my body is a livewire as he draws closer.

Just before his lips connect with mine, the bedroom door opens and closes.

The two of us freeze, our bodies so fucking close and yet suspended in space.

We hear the bathroom door open and snick shut and Theo sighs, pulling away and turning his back to me.

Fucking Finn, ruining shit for me.

I probably deserve it though.

I run a hand down my face and stare at the ceiling, my dick straining painfully against my boxers. I'll survive. I've survived worse. Landon has too.

Shit.

Landon.

Theo was a good distraction today, but he can't get me out of tomorrow. No, tomorrow is happening whether I want it to or not.

LOGAN

I WAKE up to the sound of Landon's laugh muffled through the walls, and when I pry my eyes open and feel a body pressed against mine, I can't help but smile.

Theo tucked himself right up against me sometime in the middle of the night. His warm breath puffs against my skin, his arm thrown over my stomach.

I lie there for a moment and savor the sensation of him against me. It feels different, waking up with someone. It's not something I've ever really done before, but I think I like it. He feels good, and I don't want to move.

I know I should get my ass up though and say hi to my brother. But I stay planted on the mattress, listening to Theo's soft breathing, until the bedroom door clicks open and I hear Landon and Finn moving about the apartment.

Fuck me silly. It's happening. My stomach clenches and

my breathing grows labored. The guilt and anxiety of this moment creep up on me and I'm nearly breathless from it.

Maybe a distraction wasn't the way to go. I should have just sucked it up and faced my fears, because now I'm dealing with the aftermath, and it won't be pretty.

"Think he's awake?" Landon asks Finn softly.

I hear some shuffling and then Finn says, "I'll go check."

Then my best friend is right there, standing over me, frowning.

"He's awake," Finn tells Landon and a second later, Landon limps his way over to where I'm lying and smiles down at me.

"You made it," he says.

Theo stirs in his sleep next to me as I stare up at my brother.

"Yeah," I breathe.

My eyes move across his lean body and when they land on his prosthetic leg, I lose the ability to function.

"Oh, here he goes again," Finn mutters and then glowers at me. "Get the fuck up, Logan."

"Alright," I say, and yet still, I don't move. I can't. It's physically impossible to move right now. I'm paralyzed.

Theo stirs next to me and wakes with a gasp. He sits up so quickly, that he nearly tumbles off the mattress.

And there it is—the distraction I need.

I'll just ignore the bigger issues in my life until I die.

"Who's your friend?" Landon asks, smirking as he watches me.

"Theo," I say, and Theo just holds the blanket up to his chest, blinking at the audience he suddenly has. He looks shy, and I kind of like it. "He's tutoring me in chemistry," I explain.

Landon's eyes widen slightly and fuck it all. Finn is such a blabber mouth.

"Oh. I see."

Finn eyeballs me and then moves to stand a little closer to Landon.

"I've heard about you, Theo, and how you're helping Logan," Landon says and then reaches across me, holding out his hand. "I'm Logan's brother, Landon. Nice to meet you."

Theo slides his hand into Landon's and Finn narrows his eyes at the point of contact, his arm moving around Landon's waist. It almost seems like a possessive gesture. Interesting.

Part of me really wants to know what the hell is going on between them because it seems pretty obvious at this point. I should ask, but it's not something I can even deal with right now. I'll just file it under *shit to deal with later*, like I do with everything else in my life.

I force my gaze away from the two of them and push myself upright.

"Sorry about that," I mutter and then stand up, pulling my brother into a hug. His arms slide around me, and he presses into me.

And damn, there go my eyeballs, all watery and shit.

"Missed you," Landon whispers, and I sniffle loudly.

"Missed you too," I manage to say back, even though my voice comes out three octaves too high. I sound like I sucked helium.

When we pull apart, I see that my brother's eyes are a little wet too. Runs in the family apparently. I take a good look at him, head to toe. We look similar, although his hair is straighter than mine and cut shorter, and his body is slim, compared to my broad torso. He looks good. Healthy and happy. It makes my eyes water even more and I have to swipe at them.

I'm such a fucking sap.

Finn is watching the two of us closely and as soon as we step away from each other, he sidles himself right back up to Landon again; overprotective, as usual.

"So, what are we doing today?" I ask, trying to lighten the mood.

"I thought we could go to the redwoods. It's not that far away and it's really beautiful this time of year," Landon says and Finn grumbles something under his breath.

"You sure?" I ask, forcing myself not to look at his fucking leg. It's not there anyway.

Goddammit.

"I can walk just fine, Logan. Don't worry," Landon says softly, his eyes on mine. "I really am fine. This new prosthetic is amazing. Finn, tell him."

"It is amazing," Finn tacks on, parroting what Landon said.

I peek down at the new prosthetic and then force my gaze away.

"Sure, we can do whatever you want," I tell him, even though I'll fucking worry the entire time. What if he trips? What if he gets hurt again and it's my fault? Landon doesn't need me hovering. Besides, Finn does enough of that already.

Suddenly, Theo stands up and says, "I've never been. To the redwoods, I mean. And I could really use some coffee."

All of our eyes swivel toward him, and he flushes slightly from the attention.

"Perfect," Landon says with a wide smile. "Let's get ready, Finn, and then we can go."

Landon reaches out and slaps me on the back before clutching my arms tightly in his hands. "We have a lot to catch up on."

I swallow roughly and nod.

Yeah. We fucking do.

We pile into my car and on the way out of town, we stop by a small coffee shop before heading the twenty minutes up to the redwoods. The national park features some of the tallest trees in the world and there are a lot of hiking trails to explore. It's beautiful in the fall and the few times I've been, when I stand at the base of the trees and look up, it makes me realize how very small I am.

I glance over at Theo as I drive and then my eyes slip down to his crotch.

He sort of has a redwood in those pants of his.

I'll have to let him know when we get a moment alone.

I park the car and we all get out, my eyes immediately searching for a trash can to dump our coffee cups.

I see one near the trailhead and start toward it. In the background, I can hear Landon talking to Finn. "You worry too much. We've done this before, remember? And I was fine."

Finn says something I can't make out and when I look back at them, I see Finn walking a little too close to my baby brother.

Jesus, we really need to have a heart-to-heart. Not that I care if they're together, but it sort of hurts to know they may have been together for a while now and haven't told me. Don't they trust me? I guess I haven't really been around much. Maybe they haven't had the right opportunity. That's on me.

I toss the empty cups in the trash and then stand at the trailhead as Theo approaches with Landon and Finn. Movement catches my eye and I see a little squirrel chilling by the trash can.

"Hey there, little dude," I mutter, and it scowls at me.

Well, shit. I thought squirrels were supposed to be friendly.

"Don't need to be so rude," I mutter, and I swear to fucking God that he slashes his tiny hand right across his throat.

Is he threatening me?

"This is a kid-friendly trail," Landon says with a smile as he approaches, and my gaze snaps up. Creepy squirrel not quite forgotten.

Then Landon glances at Theo. "You're going to love it."

I glance back down, but the squirrel has disappeared.

"Did you guys see that?" I ask, feeling a little creeped out. "It's a demonic squirrel, I'm sure of it. He side-eyed me. I think he's plotting something."

They all look at me like I've lost it. Well, they're not too far off.

Landon rolls his eyes. "So dramatic, like always." He turns toward Theo. "He gets that from our dad." He grabs Finn's arm and pulls him forward. And of course, Finn follows. Closely.

I turn to walk behind them as Theo moves to my side.

"There is no such thing as a demonic squirrel."

"You're not a biology major. You don't know that," I mutter.

He laughs and my lips quirk at the sound. I like his laugh, a lot.

"I can't believe you've never been here," I say, nudging him with my arm. I want to wrap it around him, but I don't think he'll let me do that. To be honest, I'm surprised he's still here and didn't steal away in the middle of the night while I was sleeping.

A sound rustles loudly in the bush next to me and I eye it warily. It could be the squirrel. He could have gone back and gotten all his squirrel friends to prepare for an ambush.

"I don't get out much and I'm not from here, actually," Theo says and my thoughts are wrenched solely back to him.

I slow my pace and glance over at him, my stomach full of butterflies.

"Where you from, Theo?" I ask.

"Wisconsin."

"Oh fuck. Cheese. I love cheese."

Theo eyeballs me like I'm insane. I feel like I am. But can you blame me? I'm kind of giddy that he's opening up to me right now.

"I've never been there," I tell him. "I haven't traveled much."

"I haven't traveled much either," he says, tugging on his oversized sweater that nearly hangs down to his knees, covering a good portion of his black skinny jeans.

"Do you miss it?" I ask, forcing my gaze back to his.

He shakes his head. "Sort of, but I have no one there anymore."

"What does that mean?" I ask.

Theo shoves his hands in the sweater pockets. "My mom...passed away."

I stop walking and fully face him. "You're shitting me."

Theo shakes his head. "I wouldn't make that up, Logan."

I run a hand through my hair and then reach out and pull him into me and squeeze him against my chest.

"Oof," he mutters, his face smashed against my shoulder and neck.

I expect him to push away like he normally does, but instead, he just melts into me.

"I'm so sorry to hear that, Theo." I can't even imagine losing my parents. It makes my chest ache. "When was this?"

He turns his face slightly, his lips brushing against the skin of my neck.

"Summer after I graduated high school."

My arms tighten around him, crushing him to me. He wheezes a little and I loosen my hold just a bit.

"Thank you," he says before pushing away and staring at me awkwardly.

"Any time you need a hug, I'm game."

He scuffs his shoe in the dirt. "It's probably better if we didn't do that."

I roll my eyes. "You do realize that saying that shit just makes me want to hug you more, right?"

He grunts in horror, and I chuckle.

"I'm going to hug you all the time now."

He steps a little farther away from me and I follow him.

"All the time, Theo. I'm a hugger."

He shakes his head, but before he can move away from me, the bushes behind me rustle again and I latch onto his arm.

"Did you hear that?" I ask and Theo bites down on his bottom lip like he's holding back a laugh.

"It's the squirrels," he whispers ominously.

"Don't fucking joke about that shit, Theo. It could have rabies, and if I get bitten, I'll have to get a shot. I hate shots. I don't want to have one stuck in my butt."

"It's actually four shots," he clarifies, and I scoot even closer to him.

"Well, that's much, much worse!"

Theo chuckles. "But, contrary to popular belief, squirrels don't carry rabies. So, you can let go of me now."

"Really? Wow, you really are like a walking encyclopedia. Did you—" My words are suddenly cut off when a squirrel leaps out of the leaves and lands directly in front of me.

A squeal of epic proportions bursts from my mouth and Theo doubles over laughing hysterically as I hop and dance away from the tiny possessed creature.

But this isn't fucking funny. It's chasing me around in

circles and trying to nip at my ankles with its sharp, pointy demon teeth.

"Oh. My. God," he cackles, tears streaming down his face as he watches me kick out at the evil fluffball. Finally, it gets the message and scampers away back under the brush. I just stand there and scowl at Theo. He's still laughing so hard he's crying and I try my best not to smile at him because he looks so fucking sexy all happy like that. His eyes are even twinkling.

"That sound you made..." he says as he swipes at his eyes. "Who knew a giant man like you could scream like a seven-year-old girl."

"Well," I huff. "You obviously haven't seen my dad encounter a spider."

Theo takes a deep breath. "Jesus, I haven't laughed like that in ages."

"Well, I'm glad someone enjoyed my near heart attack. I'm never recovering from this, you know."

I nudge him again and the two of us make our way down the trail, my eyes constantly scanning for the squirrel.

I hate the woods. Everything in the woods is just pure nightmare fuel.

When we catch up to Landon and Finn, they're just standing in the middle of the trail staring back at us.

"What's wrong?" I ask as we approach. "Why are we stopping?"

"We were just watching you scream like Dad," Landon says, a smile on his face.

I glance down at his leg and then run a hand through my hair.

"Yeah, well it's not my fault the squirrel had it out for me," I mutter, my eyes still on his leg.

He huffs loudly. "Logan, will you stop staring at my damn prosthetic? I haven't had a leg in a fucking year. I'm used to it by now and I'd really hoped you would be too."

My cheeks heat and my words come out stammered. How can he talk about it so calmly, like it's no big deal? It's huge. My mistake changed his entire life.

"Stop looking at me like that. I hate it," he says and then leans into Finn. "Tell him. Tell him I'm fine."

Finn clears his throat, his arm snaking around Landon's waist.

"He really is fine, Logan. I've told you this."

I swallow roughly and feel my eyes begin to sting again. Goddammit, here I go again. I'm turning into a fountain; kids are going to start making wishes and throwing coins at me.

I feel pressure against my side, and realize Theo is leaning up against me.

"Come on, Logan," he says softly. "I want to see what's up ahead. Plus, we should keep moving in case the squirrel comes back."

I glance over at my brother and see the pity in his eyes. He knows. He so knows why I've been avoiding him.

Shit.

"Landon…" I begin but he just shakes his head.

"It's fine, Logan. Let's just keep going, yeah? I want to be done in time for lunch."

I swallow and nod. Okay, yeah, he doesn't want to ruin the day by rehashing it. I get it. I'm making this weird.

Theo wraps a hand around my wrist and tugs me forward.

This is why I brought Theo with me—to help me cope—and I'm so glad I did.

"You need to talk to him about it," Theo says softly.

I sigh, noting that he hasn't taken his hand off of my arm. I wonder if I could just hold his hand like we did in the parking lot of the gas station.

"I know. I'm just scared to face it," I admit.

Theo's thumb brushes against the inside of my wrist and goosebumps rise along my skin.

"He loves you. I can see it on his face when he looks at you."

"I know."

"Take care of the ones you love while you still have them, Logan. Because one minute they're here and the next, they could be gone."

My chest constricts at his words because I know what he's lost.

"You're right. I know you're right, but fuck," I say, running a hand along my jaw. "Why can't I get past the guilt?"

He bites down on his bottom lip and then shakes his head. "I don't know. If you find out, let me know."

My gait falters. "What do you feel guilty about, Theo?"

He peeks over at me and opens his mouth to say something, but before he can, Landon and Finn move past us.

"Could you two walk any slower?" Landon taunts and then points to his prosthetic. "I'm missing a fucking leg and I can still beat you."

My mouth drops open and I shake my head, a horrified chuckle bursting from me. Goddammit, Landon.

I quicken my pace and Theo follows as we speed-walk the rest of the trail. When we finally make it back to the entrance, we're all short of breath.

"Damn you, Landon," I pant, and he just smiles widely at me.

"I'm tired of you making a big deal of it," he says with a shrug and leans into Finn. "I just want to have fun while you're here. Let's do one more trail and then get some food."

I nod and Finn's hand snakes around Landon's hip *again*.

I eye my best friend, but he averts his gaze.

Yeah, okay. I guess we're all going to continue to pretend this isn't a thing.

* * *

We make it through another short trail in the redwoods and then head to lunch at a small café on the edge of town. After stuffing our faces full of sandwiches and chips, we drive down to the Santa Cruz Boardwalk Amusement Park and spend our afternoon riding rides and eating junk food.

By the time we arrive back at the apartment, Landon is wiped out, and I can tell Finn is itching to get him off of his feet.

"We could watch a movie," Landon says through a yawn, favoring his good leg and leaning heavily into Finn.

"I think they're tired," Finn interjects, pulling Landon closer to him.

My eyes settle on Finn's hands and then I arch an

eyebrow at him, which, of course, goes ignored. "I am pretty tired," I agree.

"Hear that?" he tells Landon and then practically carries him back to the bedroom.

When the door closes with a snick, I turn to Theo.

"You saw that, right?" I ask softly.

He wets his lips and then shrugs. "You mean Finn and your brother?"

I nod. "Yeah."

He rolls his lips between his teeth and then steps toward me. "Would it bother you if they had feelings for each other?"

"Of course not."

He continues to watch me for a moment and then his eyes slip away from mine.

"I'm going to shower."

"Yeah, okay. Good idea. Me too."

Theo bends down to grab a change of clothes from his duffle and I shamelessly ogle his ass.

"I mean, I won't take a shower with you," I add. "You know, unless you want me to?"

Theo straightens and bites down on his bottom lip. "I think it's better if we don't."

I nod but feel the smallest twinge of disappointment as I sit on the bed to wait for him to be done.

When Theo reemerges in just a towel, wet and smelling fantastic, my dick is unbearably hard all through my turn in the shower. Unfortunately, he didn't leave any of his soap for me to use, but it's probably for the best. I totally would have jacked off with it.

I wash as quickly as I can, trying not to acknowledge Landon's shower chair that sits in the corner, and then move out to the living room where Theo is once again scribbling in his journal. He's wearing some sort of fuzzy shorts and no shirt.

"What are you writing?" I ask and he snaps the journal shut.

"Nothing."

I lower myself onto the mattress next to him. "You write a lot."

He slides that journal into his duffle bag and begins fiddling with his pencil.

"I have a lot on my mind."

I inch a little closer to him. "Like what?"

"I'm not telling *you*."

"Why not? We're...friends now."

He pulls his lips between his teeth and my eyes snag on the movement.

God, what is it about this guy?

"Will you tell me what happened?" Theo turns to face me and then whispers. "With your brother."

I swallow roughly, my chest constricting tightly.

"Tell me a secret first."

I know I'm pushing my luck, but it's my only bargaining chip.

Theo hesitates for just a moment and then shifts to face me and leans in. I can feel his warm, hard chest against mine.

"If it's a secret..." he says seductively, and then swings his leg over to straddle my hips. "I need to whisper it."

Jesus.

My hands move to splay across the skin of his waist, and I pull him closer to me. We're groin to groin and chest to chest. His lips are so close to mine, I could just tilt my head up and kiss him. I want to, so fucking bad.

He slides his hands through my hair and roughly pulls me so we're eye to eye, noses brushing. I lick my lips in anticipation, but then he moves his lips to my ear and a tremble vibrates Theo's body. My dick is so hard, pressed up against the fabric of my boxers, begging for him to touch it.

His soft, breathy words hit the shell of my ear, causing my entire body to shudder.

"I know what guilt feels like too. I feel guilty because my mom was on her way to a science fair I was competing in when her car was struck by a truck and she was killed."

My breath catches in my throat and my hands tighten on him.

"She would have been at work, and wouldn't have been on the road that day if I hadn't asked her to come."

"Theo," I whisper, and he shudders once more against me. I can hear his staggered breath in my ear and despite the horror of what he just told me, my body continues to respond to the feel of his body pressed against mine.

"I had to take her off life support. Me. I made that decision alone."

Jesus Christ. I clench onto him tighter, probably bruising him with my fingers, but I don't want to let go.

"Your turn," he says, his lips brushing against my ear as he speaks.

I try to will him to bite down on it. I just want to fuck our guilt away.

"It was last summer," I start, my voice barely audible. I remember it like it was yesterday. My baby brother calling me, his words slurred, the heavy beat of music in the background, and the panic in his voice. "He was at a party late at night and he called me to pick him up."

Theo shifts a little, his lips grazing my neck as he listens.

"I took my parents' car and went to go get him, and when I got there, he was so out of it. He wasn't himself. Come to find out, someone had slipped him something and he was high as a kite."

Theo breathes against me and then asks, "Did you find out who did it?"

I shake my head. "No."

One of my hands slides up his spine, bumping along the ridges, until I reach his neck. I love the feel of his skin. I love touching him.

"When I was driving him back home, he was freaking out and rambling, and I wasn't watching the road like I should have. A deer ran out and I swerved to miss it and drove us right into a fucking tree."

My chest hurts as I relive that night—the crunch of metal, the way Landon had cried out in agony, the red and blue flashing lights of the ambulance as they approached. His cries of pain are forever etched in my brain.

I still dream about that night sometimes. It took me a long while before I could get back into a car, too.

"They got us out, but his leg couldn't be saved. He ran track in high school, and in college too. And now...."

I can't keep going. My words trail off as I let out a long exhale. Shit.

"It wasn't your fault, Logan," Theo says, his words soft against my skin.

"It was, though. I should have done something differently...."

"No, you did nothing wrong. The only person you should blame is the person who spiked his drink."

I swallow, my heart pounding—it feels like it's trying to break right through my chest. All of these emotions mixed with the sensation of him on my lap are overwhelming. I feel overheated and dizzy. I want him inside of me. I want to be inside of him. He's been temping me all day—brushing against me, touching his hand to mine, just fucking looking at me. I can't take it anymore.

"Theo," I whisper, his name floating across his cheek.

He leans up, his eyes boring into mine and that fucking mouth so damn close.

"You did nothing wrong, Logan. Nothing."

Slowly, he lowers his mouth to mine, and when our lips finally touch, I fucking explode. It feels like forever since we've kissed and I feel ravenous. I tilt his head and eat at his mouth like I haven't had a meal in days.

I missed this so much. Why has he been holding back? We should have been doing this after each tutoring session. During it, actually. We should have just skipped all our classes and made out instead. I want to taste him on my tongue forever.

His lips pull away from mine and I whine, but my disappointment is short-lived because he pushes me onto my back and licks and bites his way down my neck and chest. His tongue laps at my nipples and I arch off the bed as he sucks one into his mouth.

Oh my god, I knew it. Nipples. I like my nipples played with. I want to try nipple clamps now. All the clamps. Just clamp them on, Theo.

He tortures me devilishly by latching onto the other one and biting at it. I writhe and pant beneath him as his hands run along the bare skin of my chest.

My desperate and leaking cock strains up toward him. His chest brushes against it and I nearly come from that touch alone. He bites down on my side and I wince in pain, but he kisses and licks at it gently, and then moves his mouth down to the waistband of my boxers.

My breath is ragged, like I just swam miles, as he tugs my boxers down around my thighs.

My cock pops out and Theo nuzzles it with his cheek, his lips pressing against the base of me.

"Theo," I groan so quietly that I swear he can't even hear me. I can barely hear myself. I'm just whispering to the gods now.

Please don't let him stop.

And then all prayers cease when his lips wrap around the head of my cock and I almost blow my load. I grasp the base of my dick and squeeze hard to keep myself from coming, because that would be super embarrassing. He's barely even touched me yet.

He slaps my hand away and starts doing something with his tongue that can't possibly be legal.

I slap a hand over my mouth to keep the moan inside, but I'm unsuccessful. The desperation is barely muffled behind my trembling fingers, and when he slides my entire dick down his throat, I grab onto a pillow and shove it over my face.

This is, by far, the best blow job I've ever had. Nothing can compare. *Nothing*.

How the hell am I supposed to walk around life like normal now, knowing that Theo and his mouth are cruising around out there?

I don't fucking know. I am ruined.

Theo's throat works around me as I tremble beneath him, and hell, this is euphoric, but it's nothing compared to when he starts to move, his head bobbing as he sucks me in and out of his warm, slick mouth. My eyes roll back in my head and my heart rate triples.

My legs shake and drop open even further, and Theo's fingers curl into my thighs.

He moans quietly around me, and I can feel the vibrations travel straight to my balls.

Oh hell, if he does that again I'm going to come.

His finger trails a line right over my balls to my hole and I swear to God, I'm going to need to be hospitalized after this.

This is worse than having a cucumber disappear into my ass.

Death by orgasm—what will the coroner think?

Shit, his finger is pressing against my hole now, and I can't hold back anymore. All thoughts of vegetables and the grim reaper disappear as I unload into his mouth. My orgasm is long and drawn out, my entire body shivering from the force of it.

When the pulses finally stop, my cock slips from his

mouth and he rests his head against my thigh, breathing heavily.

"Jesus, Theo. Come here," I whisper.

He shifts his face, and his eyes meet mine in the dark and then he's crawling up onto my lap, straddling my thighs again.

I waste no time in pulling his cock out and working him over the edge. His back arches and seconds later, come shoots across my chest and even hits my chin.

Oh, Theo. How long have you been storing that up? It's not healthy. I need to make sure you take care of that daily. I volunteer as tribute.

"Goddamn you," he says, flopping down next to me, his breathing ragged. "Why are you so hot?"

"You're not so bad yourself," I chuckle breathlessly as I stare at the ceiling. I need a moment to let what just happened fully process, and as the blissful haze clears, something niggles at the back of my mind.

Shit. Was that a pity blow job?

ten

THEO

I WAKE up pressed against him. How do I know it's him? I've discovered there is this unique scent that is distinctly Logan. There's a faint hint of chlorine and something else I can't quite define. But fuck, it's sweet and musky, and disgustingly wonderful.

I blink my eyes open and realize that I need to move off of him. This isn't appropriate. Somehow, in the middle of the night, I rolled almost completely onto him—my arm thrown over his unbelievably sexy abdomen, my leg tangled with his, and my dick pressed against his hip, hard and needy. I thrust gently against him, remembering the blow job I gave him last night.

The sounds he made, the way he trembled, the taste of him...

Shit, I need to move before my body refuses to detach itself from him.

As I slowly start to remove my arm, I hear a throat being cleared above me.

My gaze snaps up to Finn, who is standing over us, eyeing me with furrowed brows.

His focus slides to Logan's abdomen, and I follow his gaze, noticing the puddles of dried come on Logan's skin.

Oh, Jesus. That's mine. Why the hell didn't he clean himself up before going to sleep? Why didn't I clean him up? Could this possibly be any more mortifying? Then my eyes snag on the two bite marks I'd left on him as I was eating my way across his body.

Fuck. They're completely obvious.

"Are they awake, Finn?" Landon asks softly from the kitchen. I hear him moving toward us, but before he can see the state of his brother, Finn reaches out and slaps a hand over Landon's eyes.

"You don't want to see," he tells him.

"Huh? Why not?" Landon asks, his hand reaching up to pry Finn's hand from his face, and when Landon's eyes land on his still snoozing brother, they widen.

"Oh...*Oh shit*." He chuckles in disbelief and turns toward Finn. "Well, that's not something my eyeballs needed to see. Why did you let me look?"

Finn sighs. "I tried. But when do you ever listen to me?"

Landon's eyes twinkle as he leans down and nudges Logan's sleeping body roughly.

A loud snort escapes him and his eyes pop open. "Wha—?" he mutters, running a hand down his chest, and when his hand catches on some of the dried mess on his skin, he freezes. "Oh, motherfu—."

"Are those bite marks?" Landon asks with a snicker, leaning down a little to get a better look. "Seems *someone* had fun last night...."

I have never been more embarrassed in my life. I blame Logan. It's his fault for being so tempting, in all the best ways. I couldn't help myself last night. I needed him just as much as he needed me. I wanted a piece of him inside of me. But now in the light of day, I have witnesses to the dirty things I've done to him in the darkness of night.

Slowly, I slide beneath the covers. I'll never reemerge. I'll have to cut eye holes in the sheet so I can see enough to escape out the door and call an Uber.

A rough tug wrenches the sheet away from me.

"Stop hiding. It's not a big deal," Logan says. Then he meets his brother's eyes and shrugs. "It was consensual. Best sex of my life."

Oh god, shut up, Logan. And stop lying. That cannot possibly be true.

My face flames as I try and grab the covers from him, but he holds on for dear life.

"Jesus, Logan," I mutter, hanging my head and covering my face with my hands.

"No, we're not hiding and we have nothing to be ashamed of," he says and then gestures to the two of them.

"Now, you two, on the other hand..." Logan begins, but I nudge him roughly.

This is no way to start the day, accusing them of something. It's none of his business what's going on with Finn and Landon and launching accusations never ends well.

"Logan, can I speak with you, in private?" I ask, making my way off the bed quickly, and walking toward the small bathroom.

When he doesn't move right away, I stomp back, grab onto his arm, and tug him with me into the small space.

"What?" he asks as I close the door and lock it. He takes up so much room with his giant, broad body, we're practically on top of each other.

"Do not throw accusations at them. Not now," I say, diverting my attention to more important matters.

"I wasn't accusing. I was being nosy. There's a difference."

My hands itch to touch him. What is it about him that draws me so?

I reach out and slide my finger down his sternum and his breath stutters on an exhale.

"Theo," he whispers, one of his large hands moving to my hip, pulling me closer to him. "You're touching me."

Yes. Yes, I am.

I can't quite seem to stop.

My finger slides down his tight abs, moving over the dry patches of come on his skin. If you take away the utter humiliation of the situation, it's a sexy fucking look on him.

"You have me all over you," I mutter.

"I love it," he says, his eyes hooded.

Outside the door, I can hear Finn and Landon moving about, the two of them chatting about something I can't quite make out, and I'm in no rush to leave the bathroom.

"I owe you a tutoring session for last night," I say and Logan swallows, his eyes fixed on my mouth.

"I don't give a shit about that."

I slip my hand beneath the waistband of his boxers and trail my finger across the tip of his hard length.

"It needs to be fair," I say and Logan gulps as my hand engulfs him.

"Don't care about any of that, Theo," he replies as I pump him once.

"I care."

"Why?" he breathes, and I press my lips against his collarbone, tasting him, smelling him.

"I don't trust men like you," I admit and that's the crux of it.

Men like Logan always end up hurting me. My dad, the boys at school. I didn't enter college unscathed. I have invisible scars from the bullying I was forced to endure.

The things they did to me, to my fragile, naive heart.

You think someone like me would ever be with someone like you? The cruel voice echoes in my head.

"I haven't done anything to hurt you," Logan says as I continue sliding my hand over his cock, my lips move up toward his ear and I bite down on the lobe.

"But you will."

Logan shudders against me, his hips thrusting up as his fingers tighten against me.

"Never," he breathes, but it's all lies. I've heard that before. Guys like Logan do not fall for guys like me. I'm always the one that gets hurt, and Logan wouldn't mean it, but he'd do it all the same.

"Tell me that I *owe* you. Tell me. That's all this is."

He shakes his head as I tighten my grip around him.

"Tell me, Logan."

I'm feeling my control slip and with it my self-preservation.

But instead of answering, he falls to his knees and wrenches my pajama shorts down, pulling me into his mouth without hesitation. All other thoughts evaporate as he sucks me all the way down his throat.

God, what does he want from me? Why is he doing this?

My hands curl into his hair as he bobs his head, his fingers grasping onto my ass, pulling me into him.

A low moan envelops my cock and my balls draw up tightly. I'm not going to last. He's too good—that mouth, the sight of him on his knees for me—everything about him is intoxicating.

One of his hands falls away and I see it moving frantically between his legs.

He's getting off to this. To me.

It's all I need.

I pull him roughly against me and unload on his tongue. He shudders and bucks his hips, spilling onto the floor.

When we pull away from each other, a small line of spit hangs from the tip of my cock to his lips.

Oh shit. He's so hot.

So fucking hot.

Logan swipes at his mouth, his tongue peeking out and licking over his swollen lips.

His shining brown eyes meet mine. "You taste good, Theo."

Oh, my stupid, stupid heart—it cracks, right down the middle, because he looks so sincere, like he really does want me. But he's mistaken. He has to be.

I tug my shorts up and turn away. I'm always shielding myself, but if I look at him, I'll find myself too vulnerable. I don't ever want to be that way again. I learned my lesson the hard way during my senior year of high school. And then again, my freshman year of college.

I'd be remiss to just forget.

Turn around, I don't want to look at you while we do this.

"We should go," I say, my voice cracking.

Logan pushes himself up off the floor and clears his throat.

"I'm going to shower first and clean up," he says, and I nod, my eyes not meeting his.

"Okay."

I leave the bathroom, feeling exposed as Landon and Finn watch me rifle through my duffle bag. I know that they know what just happened in the bathroom. Logan wasn't exactly quiet about it.

Luckily for me, neither of them brings it up.

Small mercies and such.

Instead, Landon cheerfully suggests, "I was thinking we could go to the Mystery Spot and then grab lunch downtown again."

"It's raining," Finn says and Landon nudges him in the side.

"Afraid of a little rain? You live in the water," Landon teases.

"I could do that," I interject before Finn can protest. I

need to get out of this house. I need to breathe, to clear my head. "I've never been to the Mystery Spot."

"Awesome. You're going to love it. Plus, I already bought us all tickets."

Finn reaches out and cups the back of Landon's neck, squeezing it gently.

"I want you to take it easy."

Landon rolls his eyes. "I am. I always take it easy. You won't let me do anything else."

Finn's hand lingers and Landon just leans into him a little.

It's a little awkward watching the two of them together, in their little intimacy bubble, so I avert my gaze. It's not for me to see anyway.

A few minutes later, Logan emerges from the bathroom. He's shirtless and looks like a fucking god.

Ugh, I'm such a sucker for him. Can he see it, my desperation?

"We're going to the Mystery Spot after we grab food," Landon tells him and my eyes snag on his brother.

"Yeah?" Logan asks and pulls on a shirt, slowly hiding away those glorious abs. "Have you been, Theo?"

I clear my throat and shake my head. "No."

"Well, this will be fun then."

"I can be ready in ten," I tell them, moving into the bathroom and closing the door. I lean back against the wall and slam my eyes shut.

I can do this today. I am strong. I can keep my walls up. I've crafted them so carefully; one man cannot possibly knock them down.

eleven

LOGAN

THEO APPEARS out of the bathroom sooner than expected wearing tight jeans and another oversized sweater. It seems to be his outfit of choice—when he's actually fully clothed, that is—and I have to say, it's a hot look on him.

We're left waiting for Landon to get ready. Finn, of course, disappears into his room with him, leaving me alone with Theo.

He moves to the sofa bed and pulls out that damn journal, writing frantically in it. I scoot a little closer to try to sneak a peek.

"What are you doing?" he asks, closing it off from my prying eyes.

"Nothing."

"You were trying to look," Theo says, and I nudge him with my hip.

"Can you blame me? You're all mysterious and shit. What are you writing about in there?"

He tucks the journal away and shakes his head. "Nothing."

"You writing about me?"

Theo's cheeks darken and I reach out and tug on a strand of his hair.

"I'd write about you too, if I had a journal," I admit because I so would. He makes me so curious. I'd just list out all the questions I have about him. They'd take up hundreds of pages.

Theo's eyes snap up to mine and my thumb traces his cheek.

"Don't say that."

"Make me."

He turns his head and snaps my thumb between his teeth. For a second, pain radiates up my hand but then it's replaced by heat as his tongue licks over my sensitive skin.

"Jesus, Theo," I mutter, stepping a little closer to him. I want him to bite me all over. I still have the marks on my skin and I like it.

My dick does too. It's ready to go again, straining toward him. It wants in his mouth, and other places.

But before anything fun can happen, the bedroom door opens, and Theo wrenches his head back and stands abruptly. He strides to the door and opens it, moving outside before I can stop him.

"You ready?" Landon asks, Finn at his side.

"Yep," I say, tucking my sore thumb into my mouth and tasting him on my skin.

We pile into my car—Finn and Landon sitting in the back seat—as I drive us all to breakfast and then to the Mystery Spot. It's some kind of gravitational anomaly in the middle of the redwoods that makes you feel like you're in another dimension. You can walk from one end of the house to the other and feel like you're getting taller. It's fucking weird.

I know Theo will like it. With that big brain of his, I wonder if he'll figure out what makes it this way. Well, maybe not. It's not chemistry, but still, if anyone could figure this out, it would be him.

"You're going to love this," I say, as we hand over our tickets and begin the tour.

The guide is talking about angles and telling us that the farther up we go, the harder it will be to walk, and damn, he's right. I haven't been here in years and I'm feeling my heart rate increase.

Theo leans against the railing and runs a hand over his head.

"You gonna make it?" I ask, coming to a stop next to him.

I glance behind me and see Finn bending down so Landon can hop onto his back.

Hm, good idea, Finn.

"Wanna hop on, Theo?" I ask. "I work out for a reason."

Theo huffs a laugh. "To carry my fat ass around?"

I eye said ass. "It's not fat. It's perfect."

Theo flushes a little and then shakes his head. "No, I don't need that, Logan. I can walk."

I feel a little bummed that he isn't climbing on my back, so I walk a little too close to him the rest of the way.

We all stand around as the tour guide gives his little spiel and does a little trick with a water bottle rolling uphill. He says it has to do with gravitational pull or some shit. Whatever that means.

"Do you know the secret of this place?" I ask softly in Theo's ear.

"No, this is probably more physics related."

"Hmm," I say and then sway a little closer to him. I'll blame it on gravity and angles. Can't mess with the universe, Theo.

"I know what you're doing," Theo mutters, totally onto me, as I link my hand with his.

"It's the gravitational pull. That guy says so. My hand can't help itself. It's drawn to you."

Theo bites down on his bottom lip but doesn't tug his hand away. Nope, he actually tightens his grip on me.

Yeah, Theo, you can blame it on the gravitational pull too. I know how it is. Your secret is safe with me.

When we finally walk into the shack, hand in hand, I notice how everyone is standing sideways, and so I just lean into Theo, putting my arm around him and walking around the space. Theo's eyes are wide, and his brain is working overtime as he processes all of this.

It's fucking weird. I have to admit.

"Crazy, huh?" I say as we walk up an incline and our bodies lean down.

"Yeah," he says, his eyes moving about the space. "This has to be some kind of visual illusion. I don't think there is any science to verify this anomaly."

I stare at his mouth moving and wonder what it would be like to kiss him in this place. Would it be any different?

"This has to be some kind of gravity hill. There's no horizon outside so there is no frame of reference..." Theo continues, moving forward.

Blah, blah, blah. Don't care, Theo. I care about that mouth of yours. I lean a little closer to him.

"The magic circle due to a meteor that the guide talked about has no basis in scientific reasoning..."

God, enough, I think, as I pull him into me and cup his cheek gently.

His breath stutters as his eyes slam into mine. All of his words trail off, probably pulled into outer space from all the weird alien stuff going on around here.

"What are you doing?" he whispers.

"Kissing you," I say and then gently brush my lips against his, and damn, he tastes even better in here. It must be the magic circle shit that guy was talking about.

Theo leans into me and my arms wrap around his waist. He lets me kiss him for a few moments before he pulls away, his eyes wild and cheeks flushed.

"There are kids here," he hisses, pulling the hood of his sweater over his head.

"So?"

He glances around the room. "Logan, you can't just kiss me in public."

My eyes narrow. "And why not?"

Theo tucks his face further into his hood.

He's always hiding from me. I hate it. Theo shouldn't hide from anyone.

"Are you ashamed of me?" I ask, feeling suddenly insecure. I've never felt this way, until Theo, and I don't much like it.

"No, of course not. I just don't go parading my sexuality in front of people I don't know. No one wants to see two strangers making out anyway."

I cock my head a little and just watch him. Sure the Mystery Spot is trippy, but has anyone met Theo Reign? He's a right mindfuck.

"I think there are plenty of people that would pay good money to see us fucking," I say, and Theo disappears right under the hood. I can't even see his face anymore.

"Logan, stop it."

"I'm guessing you're not big on PDA, are you?"

"No, I'm not."

I run a hand along my jaw and then poke him.

"Alright. I'll keep my hands to myself, mostly. You are tempting though."

"I am not."

I roll my eyes and then grab onto the strings of his sweater and pull him a little closer.

"Yes. You fucking are."

His breath hitches beneath the hood and I want to slide it off, but I decide to respect his wishes and take a step back. The guide is leading us back outside anyway, so it's time to go. When I emerge outside, I see Landon and Finn talking, their arms linked.

That could be Theo and me, but instead, I'm here alone. Theo is loitering inside somewhere.

"Alright, ladies," I say, moving toward my brother and

best friend. "How is that so mind-boggling every single time we come here?"

My brother laughs and knocks me with his fist.

"It's crazy, right?"

"So crazy," I repeat."

After a moment, Finn asks, "Where's Theo?"

I tilt my head back to the shack. "Trying to figure out how this place works. He says it's all an illusion."

"He's a smart guy, huh? You like him?" Landon asks and I eye my brother.

Fuck, if this was any other time in our lives, Landon would be the one I'd share this whole thing with. He knows the inner workings of my brain, but it's been a year of radio silence between us. Because of *me*. Because I didn't want to bother him with my woes when he was getting his fucking leg chopped off.

Motherfuck.

"I want to know," Landon says softly. "I want to know these things. Know what's going on with you. You can tell me, Logan."

I swallow and blink rapidly. I want to tell him so badly, but the words get stuck in my throat. I can't fucking do it.

Guilt is a barrier that keeps all the goodness out. It eats you alive while you writhe in agony.

"When I know what's going on, I'll tell you," I mumble.

Landon watches me and then gives me a clipped nod and hell, I almost just let it all spill out right then, about how confused I am about Theo. I clear my throat and stand straighter as the man we've been talking about approaches.

The fucking hood is still over his head; I swear I'm going to cut the damn thing off when he's not looking.

"You ready to go?" Finn asks.

Theo keeps his distance as we make our way back down the hill, but my eyes are on him the entire time. I can't peel my eyes away. When we reach the bottom, the four of us peruse the gift shop. Landon moves away from Finn and suddenly Theo swoops in, tugging Finn into a corner near the mugs and bumper stickers.

I'm surprised Finn let Theo pull him away from Landon. *I* can barely pull Finn away from Landon.

Must be important.

"What are they up to?" I mutter as I watch Theo lean into Finn and hold up a finger. He looks serious, much too serious.

Shit. They're conspiring. I want to know what they're planning, but before I can get close enough, they're pulling apart and Finn is striding back to my brother.

"What was that about?" I ask.

"Nothing."

Only, it's not nothing, because while we're sitting down for lunch, Finn and Theo suddenly get up from the table, leaving Landon and me all alone.

Those motherfuckers.

Oh, Theo, thinking he's so clever. I'm going to throttle him later.

Or kiss him.

Or maybe throttle him while I kiss him.

"They did this on purpose," Landon says, fiddling with

the fork on the tabletop. "I knew something was up because Finn was acting weird."

"Yeah, so was Theo."

Landon meets my wary gaze. "They want us to talk about it."

I gulp. Oh hell.

"Probably should," I squeak out.

Landon takes a sip of his water and I sigh heavily. I should just get it all out there. I can't keep living like this.

"I just feel so guilty," I blurt. "So much guilt, Landon. It's overwhelming, so I ignore it. I think we're good at that... ignoring the things that feel too big."

My brother's eyes grow watery, and he bobs his head. "We are, aren't we? I blame dad. And the family curse."

I just nod, because he's right. My grandma died from a coconut falling on her head while vacationing in the Maldives, my dad's marijuana plants all caught fire three years ago, and my brother lost his leg because of a suicidal deer.

Shit. I could go on and on.

I let out a wobbly laugh and then my voice breaks, "I should have done better this past year. It should have been me there with you, cheering you on. Not Finn."

"No. None of that. You did nothing wrong. And you were there, as much as you could be."

I swipe at my eyes. "Feels like I didn't do enough."

"You did enough," Landon says, trying to reassure me. "And I don't blame you. It happened, and it's over. I have dealt with the trauma in therapy, but listen, Logan. Listen to me..." He reaches out and clutches my hand. "Do you know what I've been talking to my therapist about the last few months?"

I swallow and shake my head. "No."

"You. Losing you. I couldn't give a shit about my leg."

I sniffle and swipe at my eyes. "You haven't lost me. I'm right here."

"But you've changed. Neither of us is the same."

We stare at each other, and my heartbeat thunders in my ears.

"I'd lose all my limbs if I could have you back. Nothing has been more painful."

A tear slips down my cheek and I force my gaze away because I'm going to sob. And I'm not a cute crier, either. I look ugly when I do it.

"I'm sorry," I say and Landon sniffles too.

Yeah, here we go.

"So, stop being so fucking weird around me. I miss you too much."

I nod and grip his hand tighter.

"I'll do better."

"I'll hold you to that," he says, clearing his throat and blinking the tears away.

We stare at each other in silence and then I laugh softly.

"We're doing great so far."

Landon chuckles and leans back in his seat. "We'll give it time. We'll heal eventually. It will be like nothing ever happened."

"I wouldn't go that far," I mutter and then glance to my right and see Theo and Finn outside, pretending not to look at us.

Assholes, trying to be all sneaky about it. They'd make terrible spies.

Finn glances inside and I flip him off. He nudges Theo who turns to look as well. I narrow my eyes at him, and he tugs the hood over his head again.

"So what's up with you and Finn?" I ask, moving my gaze back to Landon. "You look sort of like a...couple. All handsy and shit."

Landon rolls his eyes. "We got close through all of this. He's just clingy. He always was."

"Hm," I say, not sure he's being completely truthful.

Landon scoffs and takes a sip of his drink. "It's not what you think."

I raise an eyebrow at him, and he chucks a straw wrapper at me.

"Knock it off. And besides, I like it—how he is with me. It's nice to have someone fawn all over me."

"You have our parents to do that. You know how mom is, and dad is even worse. You're still the baby."

"Yeah, well, sue me. I'm a sucker when it comes to Finn, okay? He just gets me."

I lean back and run a hand over my chest, eyeing my brother.

"Yeah, okay. I get it." Not that Theo fawns all over me, but I would fawn all over him if he'd let me.

"Here they come," Landon says, and I put on a faux angry face as Theo slides into the booth next to me, but I'm not mad, not at all. Because this is the most normal I've felt around Landon in ages, and it's all because of smart, clever Theo, who conspired against me for the greater good. Lord knows Landon and I would have ignored this for all eternity.

So, I let Theo know how thankful I'm feeling by invading his space the entire time we walk around downtown. I stand under his little umbrella and press my shoulder into his, and I think he lets me because he thinks I'm mad at him for interfering in my life.

Little does he know, that his interfering only makes me like him more. God, this is so far past transactional for me, I don't even know what this is anymore. Who knew that when I showed up at his door that first day, I'd end up feeling like this?

When we finally say goodbye to Finn and Landon a few hours later, and Theo and I are on the road, he taps his pencil nervously against his journal.

"Theo—" I start, but he interrupts me.

"I owe you a tutoring session. How about I review stuff while you drive? Just let me know if you need me to stop and go back over anything you miss."

I sigh as he reaches back and pulls the chemistry book from my backseat and opens it to where we left off.

"Well, hold on," I say. "I need to stop by my parents' house. Just for a bit to say hi. My mom's been bugging me, and my dad gets too emotional if I stay away for too long."

Theo swallows and taps his pencil faster. "Okay."

"Plus, I want them to meet you," I say, even though this guy just wants nothing to do with me.

"Alright," he whispers and then clears his throat, delving into the chemistry concepts until we arrive at my parents' house.

They only live twenty minutes away from Landon; they wanted him to have his independence but still be close enough just in case he needed help.

He obviously doesn't, as evidenced by this weekend and the way Finn hovers.

I shut off the car and turn to face Theo who is thumbing the pages of my chemistry book.

"You can just stay in here, if you want. I won't be long."

He shakes his head. "No. I can go in and meet them."

I have to purse my lips to keep myself from smiling. Asshole wants to meet my parents, even if he won't admit it.

I hop out and then wrench his door open because I know I'll need to physically push him through that front door.

"Don't be nervous," I tell him, pressing against his lower back and leading him up the walkway to my parents' two-story home. They live on a small plot of land right outside of the suburbs that allows my dad to do all his gardening and raise his chickens without complaints from neighbors.

"I'm not nervous," Theo mutters, but he's quieter than normal, and I can feel the nerves radiating from him.

Suddenly the door bursts open and my dad barrels through, tripping slightly on the garden hose.

"Logan!" he cries and picks me up and spins me around. He sniffles loudly and presses a wet kiss to my cheek.

"Come on, dad," I murmur, even though I'm getting a little emotional now, too. I missed them.

"It's been too long."

"It's been a few months."

My dad pulls back and clasps my face in his big hands and squeezes lightly.

"Too long," he repeats and then turns to look at Theo who is shuffling on his feet next to me. "Who's this?" my dad asks and for the first time, I see my dad through someone else's eyes. He's big, bigger than me, with large arms and thick legs and a closely buzzed haircut. We actually look a lot alike, except for my curly hair. I get that hair from my mom.

"This is Theo. He's my…friend."

My dad reaches out his hand and Theo gently shakes it. "Nice to meet you, sir."

"Nice to meet you too. Landon told me you guys went out to visit."

"Yeah, Landon is almost as bad as Mom. They just text and text until you cave."

My dad shuffles us inside. "They are, but hey, do you want to see what I'm growing out back?" I don't even get a chance to reply when he says happily, "Pumpkins! And squash!"

"Awesome, dad."

Theo eyes me as my mom rounds the corner with a big smile.

"Logan!"

"Hey, mom," I say engulfing her in a hug. Her waves of curly hair are pulled back in a messy bun and she stands at least a foot shorter than me.

"So, my nagging texts finally brought you home?"

"Yep," I say and then turn to introduce her to Theo who is fiddling with his hood.

"This is Theo. My friend. He's tutoring me in chemistry."

"Oh, I've heard you work miracles," she says, smiling at him gently. She must sense he needs to be handled with care.

"He can walk on water too," I tease, and Theo blushes.

"Come on guys, let's see my pumpkins. And you can meet the chickens too, Theo," my dad says. "We'll send you home with some eggs."

"He's impatient," my mom explains. "He's feeling competitive with our neighbor, Frank. He wants to grow the bigger pumpkin this year."

"And I will win! I'm a winner!" my dad exclaims as we walk through the house and into the backyard.

The cool air nips at my exposed skin and I pull Theo in a little closer to me, even though he fights it a little.

"Do you like vegetables, Theo?" my dad asks, leading us to the large greenhouse on the far corner of the property.

"They're alright," he says as we make our way inside. My dad plucks a few carrots from the ground.

"Well, you haven't had any fresh, homegrown ones then. I'll send some home with you."

Theo begins to protest, but I squeeze the back of his neck and his mouth snaps shut.

Thirty minutes later, we're getting in my car with a dozen eggs and a large bag of vegetables. When we're back on the road, Theo says softly, "You have a nice family."

"I do."

"You're very lucky."

I watch him fidget with that pencil of his and then he pulls the chemistry book from the backseat and starts going over concepts once more. Again, he blows my mind with how easy he makes it all seem. I listen attentively, for the most part. If I'm distracted, it's because I don't like how distant he's being.

Has this weekend changed nothing? He met my fucking parents. Does that mean nothing to him?

The past two days have changed things for me, that's for sure; everything has changed.

"You don't have to walk me up," Theo blurts as I shift Ms. Chevelle into park in front of his apartment complex. I shut the ignition off and stare at him.

"I'll carry your bag up for you because I'm a gentleman," I tell him, and he wets his lips.

"Fine, but you're not coming inside."

I roll my eyes and push the door open, grab his duffle bag from the trunk, and then slam it closed. I stomp up the stairs to his apartment and Theo follows behind, holding the eggs and vegetables, but he's not close enough. I want him on top of me. All the time.

As soon as he unlocks his apartment door, he turns to face me, his hand outstretched for his bag.

I sigh and hand it to him. Asshole really is reverting back to the way things were, and I hate it more than I care to admit.

"You're really not going to let me in?" I pout.

"No."

I run a hand through my hair and his eyes are drawn to the movement.

"Nothing's changed for you, huh?"

"No. This weekend was a...distraction. Like we said it would be. It has to go back to normal now."

What the fuck is normal? I open my mouth to ask but Theo just closes the door in my face. I stand there staring at it, and I can hear him shuffling around, and then nothing.

Silence.

Why does he always have to push me away? I can't fucking stand it. Maybe it's because I grew up in such an open family where emotions were shared readily, that Theo's reserved nature bothers me.

It's okay to feel, Theo.

I pace the hallway for a few seconds and then make a decision.

I grab onto the door handle and shove the unlocked door open, and it bangs into the wall from the force.

Theo is right there, standing in the middle of the room, that damn pencil between his lips, his eyes following me as I approach.

I kick the door closed behind me and move toward him.

"Get the fuck out," he whispers, the pencil dropping onto the floor.

"I'm not leaving."

I slide my hand around the back of his head and pull him into me, my lips smashing onto his.

He stiffens for a moment but then just melts into me as I tilt my head and lick my way into his mouth. I groan loudly as my dick hardens, and I push my groin up against his.

My hands slide down his back and roughly clutch onto his ass, lifting him. His long legs lock behind my back as I walk us to the bed.

God, he fits perfectly in my arms.

He's simply perfection.

My knees hit the edge of the mattress and the two of us fall onto it, our lips fused.

"Logan," he groans as I arch my hips into his. His cock is

hard and pressing up against mine through the fabric of our pants. He wants me, no matter how hard he fights it. I can feel it, can taste it. He can't hide from me now.

"No more hiding," I mutter, thrusting against him again.

His fingers dig into my back, his breath coming out in short pants.

"Yes," he moans as I bite down on his neck and reach down to pull his pants down as far as I can. I do the same to my own until they're stretched around our thighs as we rut against each other, our cocks starved for friction.

He gasps when I bite down on his neck again, bruising him with my teeth. I like that I'm marking him.

Mine. He's mine.

But then suddenly he's shoving at me.

I lean back our dicks still pulsing against each other, and all I can see is his swollen, wet mouth.

"Fuck me," he breathes, his body trembling. "Fuck me."

I groan loudly as I lean down to kiss him again. God, I've dreamt of this, of what it would feel like to have him clench around me as he comes.

Theo presses on my shoulders and we roll over, our cocks caught between our heaving bodies.

He jumps off of me, grabs a bottle of lube off the nightstand, and then yanks both our pants off in record time. He peels his sweater off over his head and then squirts some gel into his hand, grasping onto my thick length.

"Have you been with anyone else since we started?" he asks, uncertainty in his eyes.

"No. Of course not," I whisper.

"Good," he breathes and then straddles me, his body all lithe with hard angles.

"Tell me I owe you," he says, and I shake my head. This isn't just an arrangement for me anymore. This is me having really awesome sex with a hot guy. With Theo.

My Theo.

"No."

He flexes his hips and my tip slides into his ass and my entire body thrums with need.

Oh. My. God.

"Tell me," Theo moans, sinking down another inch. I can't think or focus on anything besides how his ass feels slowly swallowing up my cock. I cave, giving him what he wants. I'll just take it back later.

I cross my fingers and say, "You owe me."

That seems to reassure him, because he slams himself down, taking my entire cock inside in one fell swoop. My back arches off the bed at the sensation. I've never fucked someone like this before and now I'm wondering why the hell I haven't. Because this is so hot.

"So fucking hot," I gasp. "More. I want more."

Theo's chest heaves above me as he fucks me fast and hard.

My hands dig into his sides as I hold on for dear life. I'm not going to last with him riding me like this. He's wild, like something has been unleashed inside of him.

His eyes are on my face, his hard dick bouncing with each thrust.

I bend my knees, arching my hips up and Theo gasps.

"*Yes.*"

"*Yes.*"

"*Yes.*"

He's chanting now, completely unhinged and I'm so gone for it. I lean up and reach for him, pulling his mouth down onto mine. I want to kiss him and taste his desperation, his need for me.

It's silent in this apartment except for our moans and the slick, slapping sound of me entering his body.

It's filthy and so fucking hot that I'm starting to combust.

"Theo," I say, wrenching my mouth away from him. "Wait."

But he doesn't stop, he just slams his mouth back on mine and rides me until I feel my balls draw up. With one last thrust, my come sprays inside of him, and as I mark him, he releases across my chest, warm and wet until we're both slumped over from exhaustion.

"Theo," I say softly when I've managed to catch my breath. I'm still inside of him, plugging him. I never want to pull out.

"Fuck, Logan," he mutters, swiping at his forehead. "Why is this so good?"

Our eyes meet and the pink tint on his cheeks darkens a bit. He's so damn...*beautiful.*

I reach up and cup his cheek and he leans into it slightly.

"Theo..." I begin, but he cuts me off.

"A free tutoring session," he blurts, and I close my eyes, the moment broken.

"Fine, yeah," I say, over it. My hand flops down to the mattress.

I'm over him always bringing it up.

This was so much more for me, but he's never going to let me in.

I throw an arm over my eyes and breathe deeply as Theo watches me. I know he is because I can feel it, his heavy gaze on me. But I won't look at him. I can't.

My rapidly softening cock slips from his ass as he moves off of me.

I keep my face covered as the bathroom door snicks shut. Then, and only then, do I open my eyes. Curie is watching me from the kitchen counter.

"Don't blame me for this," I mutter, sitting up and looking at the mess on my chest.

I need to leave. I don't want to hear about how much he *owes* me, or what I owe him. I stopped keeping track a long time ago.

I quickly wipe up the mess on me, toss that shit in the trash can, and then pull on my clothes.

As I'm walking out, my phone buzzes and I see my brother's name on the screen, and for the first time in an entire year, I don't ignore it.

Fucking Theo, being so damn perfect and imperfect at the same time.

Infuriating man.

"Hey, Landon," I say, pulling the door closed behind me and shivering slightly. The adrenaline has left my body, leaving me cold.

And alone.

If he would have let me, I would have stayed. I would have held him tightly all night long.

"Did you make it home safe?" Landon asks.

"Yeah, made it home safe. You turning into mom or something?" I ask, jogging down the stairs and toward my car.

"I think Finn is rubbing off on me, actually."

What kind of rubbing, I think, but don't mention it. When they're ready, they'll tell me what's really going on.

Although, I think Finn is more into this than my brother. Landon seems a little clueless, to be honest.

I wrench my car door open and take one last look at the apartment complex that Theo lives in and sigh.

Yeah, Theo. I'll take the hint.

I'll try and leave you alone.

twelve

THEO

LOGAN IS quiet when he enters my apartment two nights later, and I feel the absence of his sunshine immediately. I've grown used to it, his bright energy that lights up the room. And I know that I'm the reason it's been snuffed out. I'm the dark cloud in his life now.

"Hello," I say and fidget with my pencil.

My journal is almost full since meeting him.

I need to buy another one.

"Hey," he says glumly, lowering himself onto the floor in front of my bed.

He didn't show up yesterday and that's when I knew things were wrong. I shouldn't have bailed on him after letting him fuck me, but I needed to.

The way he touched my face, the way he felt beneath me.

That was the best sex of my life.

I am never getting over this man.

He is goodness personified and I am just too broken for someone like him.

"You didn't come by yesterday," I say, hurt lining my words, despite my efforts.

"Yeah, I had plans. I texted you."

Yeah, he did. It was impersonal and so brief that I spent the night under my covers trying to forget him. But my ass and my heart wouldn't let me.

Now here he is, but he's not the same man I left on the bed two nights ago.

"Logan," I say, lowering myself down next to him. Our knees knock and Logan swallows a little before scooting away.

"Please don't be mad at me," I say so softly my words nearly evaporate into the space between us.

"I'm not mad. I'm just...nothing. I feel *nothing*."

My heart clenches at that and I feel my eyes begin to sting. "That's not true."

"Nah. It is, Theo. I got the hint," he says. "You've told me a shit ton of times and I finally get it. This is just transactional. Tutoring for sex. Nothing more."

I wet my lips and his eyes catch on the movement, but then they drop to the floor.

"I think you owe me a free session still," he mutters, handing me the textbook. "So we better get started."

With shaking hands, I open it and start to talk, but I can't get the words out right. What I'm saying makes no sense and Logan catches onto it because his eyebrows meet as he stares at me.

"You okay?" he asks and I swallow roughly. Because I can't stand it, I can't stand seeing him so down.

"My dad is Sutherland Reign," I blurt before I can think better of it. Opening up is so painful and scary. But I want to do it, even if it's just a little.

It takes a minute for that information to register, but Logan's eyes widen.

"No shit. The hockey player?"

"Yes."

Logan sits with that a minute but doesn't ask any more questions and I can see Curie watching us from her perch on my chair.

Yeah, I know. You let me know how you felt last night by biting my toes. I'm working on it.

I swallow and force the next words out. "I was never what he wanted. I mean, just look at me."

Logan's eyes slide over my body, and he purses his lips, but he still says nothing. Jesus, what is going on in that head of his? I want to know what he's thinking. I'm opening up my fucking heart and he seems like he couldn't care less.

Am I too late?

"Was that not enough for you?" I ask. "What the fuck do you want from me?"

Logan chews on his bottom lip and nods. "Nothing, but thank you for sharing, Theo."

I push myself up from the floor and stalk to the kitchen and grab a cup and fill it with water from the sink.

"Fuck," I mutter, taking a long sip. My hands are shaking so badly that I can barely hold the cup in my hand.

Goddamn him.

"You going to come back here and finish what you started," Logan asks, his voice rough.

I glance at him over my shoulder and then set my cup down angrily and stalk back to him. I snap the book open so roughly that I tear a page.

"Fine."

"Don't be mad at me, Theo. This is what you wanted."

My vision blurs and I feel a ringing in my ears.

"I don't know what I fucking want! But I don't want this. You being so cold!" I nearly shout and then start to crawl away because I can't breathe, but he catches onto my ankle and pulls me back to him.

"Don't fucking run away from me," Logan grumbles.

"Let me go," I say, lamely kicking out at him, but he grabs onto my feet and pulls and then yanks me by the arms onto his lap.

My legs fall on either side of his and he holds me in place with his strong hands as he eyes me. My breath is coming out ragged and my stomach twists.

"Tell me."

My mouth opens, and I can't hold the words in any longer. "It wasn't only my dad. I was bullied, Logan. Badly. For so many years."

"By who?"

"By guys like you."

Logan's fingers dig into my sides, and he presses his forehead against mine.

"But I'm not them. I won't hurt you."

Oh, he thinks that, but he will.

Right?

I don't know anymore.

"Popular jocks like you only care about what I can give them. They pretend to like me until they get what they want and then they dispose of me."

"No—"

But I cut him off. "I've been told one too many times that I will *never* be good enough for someone like you."

Logan shakes his head. "You are good enough. If anything, I'm not good enough for you. You're the smartest person I've ever met."

Jesus, what is he saying? He can't mean that.

"My freshman year in college, I tutored a handsome athlete and..." I swallow, looking away from him. "He acted like he was into me so he could use me, so that I would give him my tutoring time and do everything I could to help him pass. He pretended he wanted to be my friend at first, and then he pretended he wanted more. He even fucked me. But then he began to get mean and say things...horrible things... but I was so naïve and into him that I let it go. And when the semester was over, and he had what he wanted, he ended it. He fucking laughed in my face. Told me it was ridiculous and hilarious that I actually believed he could be with someone like me."

"Theo..."

"He used me. And you know the fucked-up thing? That's not even the first time that's happened. I should have learned my lesson in high school. And now you want me to believe that *the* Logan Lewis could ever seriously be into me? No. I won't let myself be vulnerable like that again. You have to understand. Men like you and I don't mix."

Logan sighs, his eyes shutting for a minute.

Curie meows, breaking the silence, and Logan's eyes snap open.

"Yeah, okay. I get it."

I gnaw on my lip as I watch him.

"If you need to keep this transactional or whatever, we can do that. Tutoring for sex. I won't make this more than it is," he says defeatedly.

"Okay." I swallow, my throat bobbing. This is what I want, right? Then why does it feel so awful?

His hands tighten on my waist and then he gently moves me off of him. He hands me the chem book and pulls out his notebook.

"We better get to it."

I peek over at him and feel my heart stutter. God, he's gorgeous and so damn nice. I want to kiss his kind mouth, run my hands through his hair, and feel him inside of me again.

But I don't do any of that.

It's better this way. We're both better off this way, right?

I sit and explain all the concepts in the chapter, and when we're done and he walks out my door, I stand in the middle of my lonely apartment, waiting for him to come back inside.

To take me, to take what he wants.

But he doesn't come back.

And for the first time, I worry that Logan will find someone who won't treat him like a business deal.

And then he won't come back at all.

* * *

I'm walking swiftly through campus, trying to get to my next class, when I see him. I notice him everywhere I go now; it's like my eyes have been calibrated to hone in on him. It's been a week since I confessed my heartbreak to him, and Logan has been infuriatingly kind.

But he hasn't touched me either.

I just watch him get off after every study session, and it's so impersonal that it makes my stomach hurt. I don't even want to do it anymore.

Logan makes no move to stay after. He just cleans himself up, says goodbye to Curie, and leaves.

I miss him.

I spent the entire week obsessing over him, even eating those vegetables his dad gave me until there were none left, and I hate vegetables.

Jesus, I'm messed up.

"Logan, stop!" A feminine voice squeals, and I look over to see a girl perched on his lap, her mouth wide open and laughing.

Is he tickling her?

Jesus.

I force my gaze away from them and pick up my pace. I need to get to class anyway. So what if I'm a little early?

"Theo!" Logan shouts, but I don't turn around; I walk faster. I'll just pretend like I don't hear him. It's better this way.

Better for my heart.

"Hey!" his voice draws closer and then his hand is on my shoulder, pulling me to a stop. "Hey, why are you running?"

"I didn't hear you," I lie, not meeting his eyes.

Logan lets go of me and runs a hand across his chest. "Yeah, okay, if you say so."

We just stand there awkwardly for a minute, visions of the way he kissed me so tenderly weighing heavily on me. I can still feel him inside of me.

"I have to go," I say, and Logan lets out a huff.

"Fine."

"And you have your friends to go back to," I say, looking over his shoulder and seeing a group of people watching us.

"Shit, Theo. Is that what this is about?"

I roll my lips between my teeth and look away.

"I don't fit," I whisper, and Logan reaches out, his hand clasping onto my neck.

"You fit with me just fine. You just don't want to."

God, I want to. But it's not that simple, is it? It can't be.

I swallow, trying not to meet his eyes, but unable to resist the pull.

"I'll see you at six?" I ask and Logan lets go of me and nods.

"Yeah."

And as I walk away, his gaze heavy on me, I feel my heart crumble just a little.

* * *

I make it through class and lab mostly intact, but when I get home to my apartment, the careful façade I've held up all day breaks down a little. Images of Logan jogging back to his friends infiltrate my mind.

How he took his place at their table and that girl just plopped down on his lap again.

He didn't push her off either.

He just wrapped his arms around her.

That could have been me, if I'd been brave enough.

Instead, I'd peeked out from behind a building and watched it all, and then tortured myself by replaying it endlessly in my head after.

I'm such an idiot. When Logan appeared at my apartment looking for tutoring that first day, I should have just told him I'd tutor him for a fee. Not that I needed the cash—I still have the payout from my mom's life insurance policy which easily pays for my living expenses and tuition—but I should have been a little less cocky and not bargained with sex.

But I let my ego win. I wanted the upper hand—the power—when it came to someone like him, and for a few days, it worked. It had felt good having control over the situation, over someone who in the past could have easily hurt me. But now, the only person who has hurt me, is me. I'm so utterly lost and despondent. He's taken over my heart and my mind, and pushing him away like this is tearing me apart little by little.

I'm not sure what will be left of me at the end of this semester.

I know for a fact I won't be whole anymore.

My journal sits next to me on the bed, and I roll the

pencil between my fingers, itching to write it all down. How I'm feeling, how I'm breaking.

How I'm fucking miserable without him.

Curie jumps into my lap, purring gently. She must feel my distress because she's being incredibly sweet.

I pet her soft back and she closes her eyes.

"What am I supposed to do?" I mutter, but Curie has no answer. She's off to dreamland. So I just sit in my apartment, counting down the minutes until Logan arrives, writing endless incoherent sentences until there's a knock on the door.

I lurch to my feet without thinking, Curie making a mad jump off my lap as I stumble toward it.

I wrench the door open and—*what the mother-fucking-fuck?*

"What the hell?" I ask, seeing my dad standing on the other side of my door. "I didn't call you for a reason."

"I know. I know, but I just want to talk," he says, running a hand through his hair. He looks a little thinner than the last time I saw him, and his face looks pale.

"I don't have anything to say to you."

I start to close the door in his face when he blurts, "I'm dying."

My entire body freezes, my hand tightening on the door handle.

"I'm dying, Theo. And I just needed you to know." He runs a hand down his handsome face and meets my wide-eyed stare.

A ringing has started in my ears and the room starts to

tilt, because even though he's been a shit dad, he's still my dad.

Isn't that how it goes? No matter how awful and belittling they are, there is always a sliver of hope living deep inside of you that burns for their love and acceptance.

I've lived with this my whole life.

Hating him and yet yearning for something he'll never give me.

"I know we haven't spoken in years, and that's my fault…" He lets out a long exhale. "But I was hoping we could rectify that with the little time I have left."

"How long?" I choke out, unable to fully comprehend what is being said.

"A few months."

I close my eyes and feel my heart in my throat.

"I can't right now. I can't," I whisper.

"I'm staying in a hotel just down the street. Call me. If you want. I know…" He swallows roughly. "I know I was terrible at being a father. I'm sorry and I know I can't fix it, but I'd like to get to know you."

Oh, my heart.

I clutch at it and nod, slowly closing the door on him.

Because what the fuck am I supposed to do? Accept him into my life, disrupt everything, put aside how awful he was to me my entire life, just because he found out he's out of time? Now that he's dying, he suddenly wants to know me? Wants forgiveness? Forgiveness from all the times he stood me up, all the times he didn't show, all the times he said hurtful, condescending things? Forgiveness for destroying my self-esteem?

I was never good enough for him.

I slide down the door and pull my legs up to my chest, my entire body shaking.

I don't know how long I sit there, time passing in fragments as I escape into my mind.

Suddenly, the door is shoved open, and I'm pushed across the floor. I peek up and see Logan standing above me. When he notices me on the floor, curled up in on myself, he drops to his knees and runs a hand down my cheek.

"Hey," he says, so softly, so gently.

Another tear slips from the corner of my eye as I meet his tender gaze.

"What happened?" he asks, brushing away the wetness.

I open my mouth to respond, but nothing comes out.

"Theo," he groans and then pulls me into him, and I let him hold me.

I press my face into his neck and inhale him, his innate goodness.

He will always be too good for someone like me.

He rocks me gently, pressing his lips to my hair, one of his hands massaging the back of my neck lightly.

"You're okay," he hums.

I'm not, not really, but I let those words settle over me. Maybe if I hear him tell me that enough, I'll believe it.

"I'm sorry," I manage to say, my voice broken and rough.

"Nah, don't be. I cry all the time," he says. "It's healthy."

I let out a wet laugh, but don't move from my spot on his lap. I just want to stay here forever. Safe and cared for.

I have no one now.

I'll be all alone in this big, daunting world when he's gone.

"My dad came by," I say softly, clutching onto the front of his shirt.

"Shit."

"He's dying." The last word comes out broken and ugly and I shudder against Logan's strong body.

He's silent against me.

"He has a few months left. He wants to get to know me, Logan. After all this time."

Logan's grip tightens around me, and he presses his lips to my forehead and lets them settle there for a few seconds.

"He never wanted me. He never loved me and now he wants a part of me. He's so selfish. So fucking selfish. Why can't he just leave me alone?"

"Oh, Theo."

I lean back a little and see Logan's kind, handsome face staring back at me.

"What do I do? Tell me what to do."

He cups my cheek with his big hand, "You do whatever feels right. Whatever's right for you."

"What if I don't know what's right for me?"

His thumb brushes against my damp skin.

"You know, Theo. You know. Just take time to come to terms with it."

My eyes flick down to his lips.

"Logan," I whisper, pressing my lips to his.

His hand moves from my cheek to cup the back of my head as he slants his mouth over mine, licking gently into my mouth and I melt.

I fucking melt into him.

I want him.

Need him.

He abruptly pulls away and I chase his lips.

"Theo, we shouldn't."

My body tenses and I freeze. He doesn't want me. I knew it.

"No. Don't you dare," he mutters, cupping my face in his hands, forcing my gaze to his. "Don't you fucking run away. I'm not turning you down," he says, arching his hips a little, and I can feel his dick, hard and straining against my thigh. "I'm just saying *not yet*. Not right now. Not when you're this upset."

He presses his forehead against mine and I let out a trembling breath.

"Okay."

"Let's go somewhere. Can I take you somewhere?"

"What about tutoring?"

"Later," he says and then presses a kiss to my cheek. "I have something we can do instead."

"Okay, we can deduct…"

His hand presses over my mouth. "Don't you say it. This is me being a friend, Theo. Your friend. It's a thing people do."

Fuck. I don't want to be his friend.

I want to be his everything.

But I don't say that because I don't deserve him. So, I just nod and let him help me stand up.

He adjusts my sweater a little and brushes my hair from my face. And then he leans toward me and kisses me softly.

God, that's not a friendly kiss. Not in the least, but I let him do it anyway.

I have a stupid thing called hope burning eternally inside of me, despite my years of effort to try and snuff it.

"Ready?"

I can only nod as he slips his fingers through mine. And for the first time today, I feel like I'm home.

thirteen

THEO

LOGAN WALKS me to his car through the busy parking lot, his hand in mine. A few stares are garnered from this, but Logan doesn't seem bothered. I mess with my hood, tempted to pull it over my head, but Logan shoots me a murderous stare.

"Don't you fucking think about it."

I feel my cheeks heat but do as he says, and when we arrive at his car, he helps me inside. He even bends over and buckles me in.

And I let him.

It feels nice to be cared for by someone, when for so long, I've been on my own. I'm too weak to fight him; I am just so fucking tired.

When the car rumbles underneath me and he pulls out of campus, I let myself indulge, just this once. I reach out, pluck his hand from the gearshift and thread my fingers through his.

He bites down on his bottom lip as he glances at our entwined fingers and squeezes them lightly.

"Where are we going?" I ask, my heart thunderous in my chest.

"It's a surprise."

I nod and run my thumb across the back of his hand. "I hate surprises."

"Why?" he asks, looking so fucking sincere.

"I've been surprised one too many times in my life, and the outcome has never been good."

Logan groans a little, sympathy in his eyes. "Well, then, let this be your first good surprise, Theo. I promise you'll love it."

I nod, my leg bouncing nervously as we move through traffic.

"You won't just give me a hint?" I ask after a few moments of silence.

"I want you to have a surprise in your life that's good, even if it's small."

I huff and he squeezes my hand again and I just let him hold onto it, his thumb rubbing circles on my skin.

After another moment, he pulls into a dirt parking lot and turns the car off.

"Ready?"

"Going to tell me where we're going?"

"The Swing."

"I think I've heard of it," I say as he gets out of the car and opens my door. He extends his hand again and I latch onto it, still feeling incredibly fragile from earlier and just wanting to be held.

I'll let things go back to normal tomorrow.

Maybe.

As he leads me to the trailhead, we pass a few people who take note of Logan Lewis walking hand in hand with another guy, and I wince slightly, fighting the urge to hide.

"I haven't done much sightseeing while I've lived here, to be honest."

He smiles at me, unbothered by all the attention. "Oh, well, then I'll have to show you all my favorite spots."

I nod my acceptance as I watch him. The sun is starting to go down and the soft light shines through his curly hair, making him look almost ethereal.

"See something you like?" he asks slyly, and I let out another small laugh.

"Yeah. I do."

He stumbles a little and my lips tilt up even more.

"Stop teasing."

I tighten my hand in his and he squeezes it back.

"I have water," he says as we make our way up the steep incline, and for the first time, I notice the bulge in his sweatshirt pocket. "Let me know if you need any."

I nod and we continue our trek up the hill. Words don't need to be spoken in this moment. Instead, I just feel him next to me, listening to his steady breathing as we crest the hill fifteen minutes later.

At the top, a few people are taking turns sitting on a wooden swing overlooking the valley below. The setting sun casts an orange and yellow hue around us, and the sky is turning a light pink.

It's absolutely beautiful up here, and momentarily, all thoughts of my dad are forgotten.

"Want a turn on it?" Logan asks, his voice low in my ear.

"Okay," I say, eyeing the swing in the distance.

As we approach a group of people our age, still holding hands, I squirm but don't let go. I know people are going to recognize him, it's going to happen whether I like it or not.

"Hey, man!" A tall guy with a shaved head is grinning and moving toward us.

I expect Logan to pull away from me, but I only feel his hand grip tighter. He throws his arm around the guy and then nods toward me.

"Hey, Xander, what's up?" Logan asks.

"Not much. Just brought Chloe up here to see the view. You?" he asks, eyeing our interlocked hands for a second.

"Ah, yeah, us too. This is Theo," Logan says. "We came up to take a turn on the swing."

Xander bobs his head and nods at me. "Cool, nice to meet you, man."

I swallow, feeling the urge to disappear, but Logan won't let me go, and I have the feeling he'd wrench my hood off if I tried to pull it over my head.

"Hi."

It's all I can manage. I'm feeling much too fragile for anything more.

"We met the other day. You were at a game of ours, right?" Xander asks, his head tilted in contemplation.

"Yeah. He's the one tutoring me in chem," Logan

offers up.

"Ah, that's right. Cool, man, cool. Well, better get in line for the swing. It's going to rain soon, and you don't want to get caught in that."

"Rain doesn't bother me," Logan replies.

"Right, yeah. You're a motherfucking shark," Xander jokes and then gives us the peace sign before jogging back toward the girl waiting for him.

I watch him go and turn my eyes to Logan.

"He's going to think we're together," I say.

"So?"

"Logan," I begin, but he just tugs me closer to the swing.

"I couldn't give two shits what they think. What other people think doesn't matter. I live for me, not for anyone else."

"But you could have anyone."

"I know."

I roll my eyes at that, at his easy confidence. What would that be like? To be so self-assured in all things?

We move behind a few other people and Logan refuses to let go of my hand, even when two other people come up to chat with him.

He's so easy-going with others and remembers all their names. Everyone loves him. The selfish part of me hates it because his attention is pulled away from me, but I know this is just who he is. I'd initially thought he was an attention whore, but now I realize that he's just a genuinely nice person that people want to be around.

I don't blame people for flocking to him.

I want to flock to him.

I have currently flocked.

Oh my god, I'm a stage-five clinger.

I try to wrench my hand away from his and he lets me steal it away, but then he just wraps an arm around me. As we move closer to the swing, I'm now pressed up against his delicious, warm body and I can smell him. My mouth waters and my entire body lights up, so I try to sidestep and put some space between us.

"Not so fast," he mutters, his lips brushing against my ear. "You're staying right here, next to me."

I huff a breath, giving in and just leaning against him. He fiddles gently with my earlobe while I stare at the ground, avoiding eye contact with curious onlookers, until it's our turn on the swing.

Light rain has started falling from the sky and people begin to disperse, but Logan gestures for me to sit my ass down on the swing and so I do.

His strong hands press against my lower back as he's pushing me on it, and I feel like a child all over again, playing in the park near my house. I used to spend countless hours just pumping my legs as the wind rushed through my hair.

I feel so fucking free.

After a few minutes, the rain suddenly starts coming down harder, soaking my hair and clothes as I swing. I close my eyes and revel in the feeling for a moment and then Logan is grabbing onto me, pulling me off the swing and into his strong chest.

"It's going to get muddy. We should go," he says, and I clutch tightly onto his strong back, watching the raindrops stream down his handsome face.

His breath stutters as his eyes find my mouth and I lick the rain off my lower lip.

"Fuck, Theo," he whispers, and his thumb brushes a trail across my cheek. "We really have to go."

I let out a shaky exhale but neither of us moves; we stand frozen in the middle of a storm, desperately trying not to kiss the other.

I'm the first one to cave, rocking forward and pressing my open mouth to his, swallowing his groan.

I feel his hands in my hair, pulling gently on the strands and I cling to his wet sweatshirt for dear life as he tilts his face and deepens the kiss. My knees are weak and my brain is practically mush, but I know, without a doubt, this is the most romantic moment I've ever experienced. What is it about kissing in the rain?

When we finally pull apart, breathless and soaking wet, Logan looks so damn happy that my heart almost bursts from my chest. I shyly smile back as he takes my hand once more.

"Let's go," he says, tugging me down the hill. We slide a bit on the muddy decline, and halfway down, my legs completely slip out from under me. I fall right on my ass, bringing Logan down with me.

He laughs so loudly and so joyfully, as mud smears across our clothes and we struggle to help each other back up, that I swear to God, my stupid heart just detonates. This sweet, gentle man is going to be the end of me.

We eventually make it back to his car completely soaked and filthy, and he grabs a blanket from the trunk and pulls it around me.

"Gotta keep you warm," he says softly and then proceeds to strip out of his muddy clothes right in the middle of the parking lot, leaving him clad in only his boxers and sneakers.

I just clutch the blanket and stare, everything else is forgotten—my dad, our tutoring arrangement, my resolve to not make this complicated. At this moment, my mind's singular focus is Logan—his smiling face and his flawless body on display for me.

I snap out of my reverie long enough to slide into the car, and he cranks up the heat as we drive back to my apartment in silence. When we arrive and park, he immediately gets out and without asking permission, follows me into my apartment building.

A few people do a double-take at us because of how little he's wearing, but he doesn't even seem to notice. His eyes seem laser-focused on getting into my apartment. He even grabs my hand and pulls me along faster and I have to jog to keep up.

When we stumble in and the door closes behind us, we stand in the quiet space watching each other for a moment. He's so damn beautiful, practically naked and dripping wet, I wonder how I'm even breathing. I slowly let the blanket fall from my shoulders and puddle at my feet.

His breath stutters as I reach up and pull my sweater over my head, and then work my jeans off until we're both standing in our underwear.

His eyes rove over my body and then land on my lips.

"I don't want to push you," he says gently. "But I want you again. I want you so bad."

I can hear the blood pounding in my eardrums and I feel almost light-headed.

"Okay," I whisper and then he's on me, his hard body crashing into mine as he walks us toward the bed.

Our teeth clash in desperation as we slant our mouths to tongue-fuck into them deeper.

His fingers slide into the waistband of my boxers, shoving them down, before doing the same to his own. We fall onto the bed naked, our hard cocks pressed together.

He breaks our kiss, looking into my eyes. "I need you to know, I'm not like those other guys, Theo. I'm not them. You can trust me. I just want you to give me a chance and trust me. I won't hurt you."

My eyes sting and I nod, because I know this. I know it.

"I want to fuck you, but it's for no other reason than I want to. I need to."

I close my eyes and he arches his hips, thrusting against me.

"God, look at you," he says, leaning down to taste my mouth again. "Look at how hot you are."

No man has ever said that about me, but Logan says it like he truly means it. He's slowly stitching my heart back together with his words.

"Fuck me," I say. "Now. Please."

I can't wait any longer and Logan groans at the desperation in my voice. He reaches over and grabs the lube, coating his fingers and dick with it.

I pull my knees up to my chest, exposing myself to him and he groans. He slides two fingers down my taint and slips them right into my hole.

My back arches off of the bed and he leans down to capture my mouth as he scissors me open.

"Goddamn," he grunts into my neck.

He removes his fingers and then they wrap around my dick, slicking it, pumping me tightly and my eyes roll back in my head.

Then I feel him shift his body down and his teeth scrape against my side, right against my tattoo—the tattoo I had gotten years ago, right after James. James had laughed at me the night that he broke up with me. He told me he couldn't even look at me when we fucked, that there was no way in hell he ever actually *liked* me and that I was dumb for believing it. Later, after crying my eyes out, missing my mom, my mind repeated endlessly what my dad had said about me. That I was a disappointment. That I was just an overly emotional, nerdy gay kid who didn't have an athletic bone in my body. My heart broke in two.

I'd gotten the tattoo a few weeks later, a reminder of the torment I'd endured and a promise to myself to never let anyone hurt me like that again.

Now Logan is pressing soft kisses to those words on my skin and fuck, it all feels so raw and I can't stop the tears from running down my cheeks. Logan moves to my face and looks carefully into my eyes. He smiles and softly kisses my lips because somehow, he knows the tears aren't really from sadness.

"I'm going to fuck you," he whispers, brushing the tears away with his thumb. "And then you're going to fuck me. Okay?"

I nod and suddenly his hand is gone, and his cock is

pressing up against my hole. I breathe deeply and try to relax as he breaches me entirely. He's balls deep inside of me, his muscular arms tight with tension as he holds himself above me, and I wrap my legs around his thighs. Then he starts to move.

"Harder," I groan, watching his abs flex as he fucks me.

"Theo," he moans as he pegs my prostate with each thrust, and my cock leaks desperately between us. "You're so fucking hot and so tight, I can't last long."

I run my hands up his broad chest, trying to clutch him to me tighter, but suddenly he's pulling out of me and I'm so fucking empty.

He crawls up my body, straddling my hips, and grabs onto my dick, hovering over me.

"Wha—?" My words are cut off by a violent gasp because my dick is suddenly in Logan's ass. "Jesus fuck," I manage to say as he slams all the way down onto me.

Oh my god, he didn't even edge into it, he just went down full force.

"Told you I've been practicing," he mutters and then begins to fuck himself on me and I can't do anything but let him. My balls are drawing up tightly against me and I feel like I'm going to come with each downward thrust. He pulls off of me before I can, and shifts down to enter my ass again, grabbing onto my legs and swinging them over his shoulders as he rails into me.

What the fuck is happening? I've never done this before.

But of course, sex with Logan would be different. I should have known.

He pounds into me, his body sleek with sweat, and my

muscles are all taut as bowstrings ready to fire. And then he's pulling out again and sitting on my oversensitive dick.

It's torture. Absolute fucking torture. Logan is edging me to death.

"Damn, this feels good," he pants, bouncing on top of me for a minute before pulling off again and entering me with a thrust of his hips.

His hands clench onto my waist roughly and he's arching me up off the bed, fucking into me almost violently and I am helpless to do anything but let him impale me.

"Logan, Logan, Logan," I chant his name and suddenly my ears start to ring, and I swear to God, I am going to black out.

My come shoots across my chest as I clench around his cock, and Logan's eyes roll back into his head as he releases inside of me, his entire body trembling with the aftershock.

"Holy fuck," he says, collapsing down on top of me, his arms bracketed on either side of my head.

I swallow roughly, trying to breathe.

"You're so sexy," he says, pressing his forehead to mine and pressing a kiss to my nose. "So fucking hot."

If only he knew what it was like seeing him above me. He is so out of my league that it's not even funny. What would seventeen-year-old me think if he could see me now?

"Shit," I say, running my hands over his arms as he gently pulls out of me and rolls onto his back.

His chest heaves as he tries to catch his breath and I feel him leaking out of me.

"Logan," I begin and he sighs heavily.

"Yeah, yeah. I know. I know. Give me a minute and I'll

clean us up. Then we can get to tutoring if you want."

My heart sinks a little because that wasn't what I was going to say. I don't want to talk about chemistry when I've just had the best orgasm of my life. I kind of want to be held, to be honest.

But how do I ask for that? What if he turns me down? What if he laughs at me?

Logan turns his head and meets my gaze. He looks so fucking earnest.

What is life, if we don't try?

"Hold me?" I whisper.

He freezes, his eyes widening in shock, and then, without teasing or questioning, he twists and pulls me into his arms and buries his face into my neck.

"Thank fuck. God, I love cuddling."

I chuckle and he presses a kiss to my skin.

"Touch is my love language, I think."

"What the hell is a love language?" I ask, snuggling into him closer and letting myself enjoy this moment.

"It's how you express and need love," he replies, moving my body so I'm half on top of him.

Love? This isn't love.

Is it?

It can't be.

This has to be some kind of infatuation on his end. I can't let myself hope. On my end...I already know it's hopeless. He's chiseled away at my stony heart and it's completely cracked open but I know this thing between us has an end date. He'll get tired of me and then we will part ways.

I have to remember that.

fourteen

LOGAN

MY ASS STINGS from taking Theo's monster cock, but fuck, if that wasn't the hottest, best sex I've ever had. Now he's tucked in my arms, and he's actually letting me hold him.

He even asked me to do it, in that quiet, unsure voice of his.

Hell yes.

This, right here, is what I want. I love snuggling and it feels so natural with Theo.

"You okay, your ass feel good?" I ask, tracing the line of his jaw.

Theo looks up at me as I run my hand through his hair.

"Yeah. Yours?"

"Hurts a bit, but I liked it. I really fucking liked it."

Theo bites down on his lip. "You didn't even take me slow. You just stuffed me right inside."

"Damn right I did. I told you. Practice. My ass has been waiting for this for days. Weeks even."

He plucks at my pebbled nipple and my dick twitches between my legs.

"I'm discovering all sorts of shit. Like, I *really* like my nipples played with. And my ass."

He pinches it harder, and I gasp.

"Dammit, Theo," I grumble because now he's teasing me for real.

His fingers walk over to the other nipple, and he tugs at it roughly, and I grab onto his hand and pull it to my mouth, kissing his fingers.

"Knock it off."

Those pretty blue eyes meet mine and his cheeks flush.

"We can do that again later. Give a man time to recover. I'm not a god."

"I'm sure some people would think you are."

I chuckle because he's right, but I couldn't give two shits what anyone else thinks at the moment. I only care what he thinks. "Do you think I am?"

Theo rolls his eyes. "You're much too full of yourself."

"Well, I have you to bring me back down to earth."

Theo sighs and presses in closer, his hand tracing the line of my hip.

We lie in silence for a minute and then Theo says, "My dad gave me his number."

"Yeah?"

"Yeah, I think I want…I think I should hear him out."

"I think whatever you decide to do will be the right decision. I don't think there is a right or wrong answer in a situation like this."

But I know he wants this, deep down he does. I saw those words in his journal that one day.

Theo blinks up at me and I run my hand through his hair again. I love how unruly it is, sticking up all over the place. He looks thoroughly fucked.

"The phone number was on a little business card, but I think Curie hid it somewhere."

I chuckle because I can definitely see her doing that. "That little shit."

Theo pinches my nipple which only makes my dick perk up a little more.

"That's not a punishment. It's really more of an incentive," I mutter, and Theo laughs a little. "But I'll help you find it. Where do you think she put it?"

Theo squeezes me to him and then gets up, pulling on a pair of his ratty sweats and I tug on my boxers as we move around the apartment looking for the small business card. I'm about to move toward the oven to pull it out and check underneath when I decide to look under the bed and, in the corner, I see a small stash of things in a pile.

I reach under and pull out two pencils, a sock, a toy mouse, and a whiteboard marker.

"I found Curie's stash. Think she'll know it was me who raided it and hold it against me?"

Theo takes the card from my hand as I stand up and brush my hands clean.

"She might," he says and then puts the card on his desk. "Thank you."

"Sure thing," I say and then move toward him and kiss him gently.

"How about we do a little chem review and then I'll leave you alone."

Theo rolls his lips between his teeth and looks everywhere but me. "Okay."

But the way he says it, his eyes so fucking sad that I ask, "Unless you…want me to stay?"

Theo's eyes meet mine and he glances away, nodding. "Okay."

Oh, Jesus. Why does his acceptance of this make my heart flutter? This man is making me work for it.

And I like it.

We lower ourselves onto the bed, both of us on our stomachs as he begins to review concepts with me. He scribbles on the whiteboard a few times and I scoot as close as I can, my fingers tracing over the bumps of his spine with my finger.

"You're so hot when you talk nerdy," I say, tracing a line down to his ass. It's a shame that it's covered with clothes right now. I'd like to run my hands all over it.

He flushes and meets my stare.

"I want you to talk about covalent bonds when you're fucking me."

Theo's cheeks darken. "You are ridiculous."

"You could play with my nipples while you do it too. God, I'd come in two seconds flat."

I'm hard again, because duh, talk about a fantasy of mine. His big brain is so damn sexy to me.

"You need to pay attention first and then, maybe, we can mess around a bit."

"What does *mess around* entail?" I ask as Curie hops on the bed and plops right down on the open chemistry book. "See, even Curie wants us to fuck again. She says *no more studying, you two.*"

Theo huffs out a laugh and grabs my face, kissing the hell out of my mouth and neck. I wrap my arm around his slender body, anchoring him to me, and just take everything he's willing to give until we're both breathless.

"She's a cat. If it fits, she sits," he murmurs, his lips swollen and pink.

I groan as he scoots Curie off of the book and then continues reviewing the concepts. Curie makes her way over to my lower back and sits on my ass.

What a cockblocker.

Maybe she doesn't want me to get laid. Maybe she's tired of seeing us fuck around.

Not that I'd ever get tired of watching that. I'd record it and hit replay.

When he finally closes the book and meets my gaze, my brain is buzzing with new information. I honestly feel like I could stop coming to tutoring and be just fine. Theo is a miracle worker, like everyone said. He's made all of this seem so much easier than the professor had. I'm actually ahead in class at the moment and I know that I could pass the final, no problem.

Not that I'm going to tell him this. I want to keep seeing

him every day. If I tell him that I don't think I need his help anymore, I'm afraid he'll push me away.

I'm not ready for this to be over, not when he's finally opening up to me. So I'll play dumb and pretend like I need him for the rest of the semester.

And I do. I need him, just maybe not in the way he thinks.

"Want to order a pizza and watch a movie?" I ask.

Theo sits up and nods, smoothing down his hair. "Okay, but no pineapple."

"Blasphemy," I joke and pull up the nearest pizza place on my phone.

When it's delivered, I bring it to the bed, sit, and spread my legs a little.

"Sit here, Theo," I tell him when he just stands near the bed eyeing me, and I half-expect a fight, but instead, he crawls between them and rests his head against my chest.

Fuck. I think he wants to be held. He was so fragile today, so needy.

I never want to see him cry again.

I wrap my arms around him as he pulls up a movie on his laptop, and we eat the pizza in silence, our eyes on the screen, my hands resting on his bare stomach.

An hour later, he slips off to sleep in my arms and I just hold him the rest of the night.

I fall asleep a fucking happy man.

I make it to Theo's apartment the next evening with a smile on my face. In my hands are four bags of groceries, because I woke up hungry this morning and his fridge was barebones.

I can't live like that, especially if I stay over again. No, not if. When.

This man needs snacks.

And jelly doesn't count.

Especially after the practices that I've been subjected to. I burn more calories than the average guy. I need sustenance.

"Hey, handsome," I say when Theo opens the door, wearing just that oversized shirt that drives me crazy.

I can't help but wonder what's underneath it again.

He's teasing me by wearing it, I know.

I push past him and set the groceries on the countertop and Theo follows me, looking bashful.

I *did* sneak out for morning practice earlier today and didn't wake him, although I wanted to. I wanted to just slide inside that ass of his and fuck him awake. Instead, I kissed his forehead and slipped out of the apartment quietly.

"Sorry about this morning. Did you get my texts?" I ask as Curie brushes up against my ankles. She thinks she's getting food.

Well, fuck you cat, I *so* brought you treats.

He twirls his pencil and nods. "Yeah. How was...practice and class?"

I start unloading the groceries into the fridge.

"Good, class was boring. And practice was brutal. My legs are on fire. Coach had us doing these jump squats that are totally killer and then he made us swim laps."

Theo's eyes move to my legs, and I waggle my eyebrows a little.

"Tempting huh?"

Theo ignores my little innuendo. Of course he does. He never makes it easy. I have to work for it.

He moves to help me unload the food from the bags. "You don't have to buy me groceries, Logan. I do eat. I just get sidetracked with my life and forget to grab what I need."

"Which is why I brought stuff over. So you can eat and I can eat."

He glances at me for a minute, his hands clenched in front of him, and then blurts, "Come over early tomorrow and I'll make you dinner."

"Yeah?" my heart doing some kind of jig in my chest.

"Yeah, Logan. I'll cook for you. If you want."

"I want. It's a date."

He leans over and presses a tentative kiss to my lips, and I groan, the food forgotten on the counter as I press into him. I love when he kisses me first and I'm never turning him down. I was half hard just seeing him in that shirt and now it's full-blown.

Grabbing onto his ass, my hands slip beneath his shirt, feeling nothing underneath.

He's trying to kill me, trying to slowly torture me to death.

I slant my mouth over his and lift him, setting him on the counter. My hands slide up his thighs, pushing the hem up until his hard cock is on display.

I lick my lips and Theo runs his hand through my hair.

"Didn't know I'd like dick as much as I do, but I'm so here for yours."

He smiles at me gently and I begin to bend down to suck that big cock right into my mouth when Curie meows loudly and bites my ankle hard.

"Jesus fucking Christ," I mutter, glancing down and seeing Curie eyeing me angrily.

"She knows you bought her treats and wants them," Theo tells me, chuckling.

I narrow my eyes because this isn't funny. I want Theo and I want him *now*.

"I told you not to buy shit for her. But did you listen? Nope. Now look at what you've done. You've created a monster."

I huff in annoyance because, apparently, he was right. Curie is a greedy bitch who is totally cockblocking me.

"Fine." I reluctantly lower Theo's shirt and he hops off the counter as I rifle through the bags and pull out another cat toy—which she promptly swats under the oven—and then pull out a few canisters of premium cat food.

She sees it and goes wild, meowing noisily and brushing up against my calves like she didn't just bite the shit out of me.

"Better feed her before she bites you again," Theo says, so I spoon some wet food into her bowl.

That's when she shuts up. She doesn't even say thank you.

"You're so rude," I mutter, petting her back before standing upright.

When I turn around, I find Theo watching me, and then

he leans over and kisses me again. Hell yeah, I love his confidence and how comfortable he is kissing me. I pull him into me, feeling his hard cock pressed up against mine. I rut against him, my hands sneaking up his shirt and palming his ass.

"We need to put the food away," he says, panting against me. "Then you need to study. I have another student coming over after this. We don't have much time."

I glance down where our bodies connect.

"I don't want to study."

"You're not failing this class," he retorts and pulls away from me.

I eye him, his cock jutting out beneath his shirt.

"You gonna put on something else for that tutoring session?" I grumble, feeling a little grumpy at the turn of events.

Theo eyes me.

"You better put on something else," I mutter.

He mulls that over, killing me a little inside, and then nods. "Okay."

I let out a breath and help put away the rest of the groceries. And then we're sitting on the floor and he's going over concepts for a future quiz, but I can't pay attention because I keep eyeing his legs and wanting to eat his dick.

"Logan," Theo says, and I groan.

"I think for this arrangement to work, I need to fuck first. I can't concentrate with you sitting there all sexy. That shirt does things to me."

He rolls his lips between his teeth and then nods. He reaches over, grabs the lube, and then straddles my hips.

"Alright."

God, that was easy. I was expecting more of a fight.

I moan beneath him as he pulls me out and slathers my cock in lube before lowering himself on me entirely.

I don't stop kissing him the entire time, we just eat each other's mouths until we both come. And when we're done, we climb onto the bed naked and sated.

I'm not sure the sex actually helped with my distraction issue though, because he's reviewing chemistry concepts, sounding so smart, and my eyes just hone in on his ass and all I can think about is my come inside of him.

"Did that make sense?" he asks, looking over at me and I just nod. Then I shake my head because I can't lie, not to him.

"I was barely paying attention."

"Jesus," he says, blushing deeply.

"You're naked and talking nerdy and I am hard again. I can't help it."

He looks like he wants to take care of that for me, but a knock on the door has me sitting upright.

"Shit," Theo mutters and I watch as he pulls on a pair of pants and a shirt, and I jog to the bathroom to change. Don't need to scare anyone off.

Not that they'd be scared. Impressed, maybe.

When I come walking out, I see a blonde girl sitting at his desk, leaning over a textbook and I catch Theo's eye.

"Bye," I say, and Theo pulls his bottom lip between his teeth, and I fight the urge to kiss him.

Ah hell, what the fuck ever.

I move into his space and plant one right on his lips.

He freezes slightly, but still, his mouth moves against mine.

When we pull apart a moment later, the girl is blinking up at us, her mouth agape.

Yeah, this will probably get around. Don't mind that one bit.

Theo's mine.

"See you tomorrow," I tell him, my thumb brushing against his cheek and he nods.

"Bye, Logan."

I say bye to Curie and let myself out.

I can't wait for dinner tomorrow night.

THEO

"I'M NERVOUS," I tell Curie as I stir the pasta in the pot. "Like really fucking nervous."

Curie just opens a cabinet and disappears inside. She's tired of hearing about it and I don't blame her. I don't know why I invited him over when I knew I'd feel like this—nervous and excited, and just completely overwhelmed.

But the invitation had just slipped out and he looked so damn happy about it.

The truth is, I'm tired of pushing him away.

So, until the semester ends, I've decided that I'm going to just let it be. I won't bring up the tutoring for sex deal, I'll just let us do what feels natural, and then we can see where this goes.

Part of me thinks he'll set me aside once he doesn't need me anymore, because we all know I've been fooled before. I still cling to that cynicism, like a security blanket. It keeps me safe. But the tiny sliver of hope chants in my head almost incessantly that he'd never do that.

I have to just ride this out and see what he wants from me when the semester is over, because I'm not putting myself out there again.

I can't do that to myself.

The knock on the door has me shutting the burner off and making my way to answer it.

When I open it, my breath leaves me in a whoosh because holy hell, Logan is dressed up. He's wearing clean, fitted dark jeans and a blue button-up shirt.

God, he's sex on a stick. My dick immediately hardens in my pants. I want him all the time now.

I remember the first few times we'd fucked around, I was so nervous I couldn't even get hard. I'd expected him to mock me, to make me feel like shit, like all the men that came before him. But now, my dick is perpetually hard when I'm around him.

"What the fuck are you wearing?" I blurt.

Logan blushes and smirks. "Wanted to look good for our date."

He steps through the door, and I eyeball him, nearly drooling. I want to unbutton him slowly and bend him over the kitchen counter. He liked being fucked, and God help me, I liked it too.

I've never been a top before, and ever since he rode me, I want to do it again.

"You always look good. You just look...even gooder."

I can no longer speak English. He has robbed me of this.

"Aw, that's impossible," Logan croons and then pulls me into him. He makes no comment about what I'm wearing—jeans and a loose T-shirt. I'm a hot mess compared to this guy.

I need to try harder. I make a mental note to try to do better, so I'm comparable to him. I want him to be proud of me.

"I brought dessert," he says, holding up a small bag. "Beignets."

I eye the white bag in his hand. "I've never had those."

"Oh, you're in for a treat. They're like an orgasm in your mouth." He eyes the kitchen and his stomach rumbles. "Perfect timing. I'm starving."

"Yeah," I say, feeling dumb for not having a place for us to actually eat. I should have at least set out a blanket or some shit; pretended this was a picnic.

But Logan doesn't seem to mind that I'm woefully unprepared. He just lowers himself onto the floor where we usually sprawl out and Curie meanders over, looking for a treat.

Of course, Logan doesn't disappoint her, and pulls out some kind of cat snack from his pocket. When he holds it out to her, she sniffs at it, and then gently takes it. He pats her on the head and thanks her for not taking his finger off like last time.

God, my throat gets all thick and my chest squeezes at the sight. I'm half in love with him already.

Turning my head away so he doesn't notice how dumb I'm being, I dish some alfredo pasta into two bowls and hand him one. He eats it like I made him some fancy Michelin star meal, moaning and smacking his lips.

"Wow, I was hungry," he says, scraping the bottom of his bowl and sliding the spoon between his lips. "That was hella good, Theo. Thanks."

My cheeks immediately burn, simpering and blushing over the littlest praise. Why am I like this around him?

Logan sets the bowl onto the ground and Curie saunters over and tentatively licks at it.

"You're a good kitty, Curie," he says, patting her as she licks up the alfredo sauce. "Deep down, you're a good girl, huh?"

Jesus Christ.

"I called my dad," I blurt, and his eyes snap up to meet mine.

"Yeah?"

"Yeah. I'm going to meet him on Sunday."

Logan runs a hand across his stomach and cocks his head. "Will you be okay to go alone?"

I swallow and don't respond because I don't know. My dad has always made me feel so small and I'm not sure that this time will be any different. But he had sounded so sincere on the phone, so I thought I owed myself this.

If it ends badly, then I'll know it wasn't meant to be.

"Want me to come?" Logan asks softly.

Oh god. He would offer. Why is he so sweet? He's killing me.

"Can I think about it?" I ask, because I want to say yes, but I don't want to make any rash decisions just because he's being nice to me.

"Yeah, of course. And speaking of," he says and then stands up, moving to the kitchen and grabbing the small white bag with dessert inside. He shakes it a little and says, "You're coming home with me for Thanksgiving."

I shake my head quickly. "Logan," I begin to protest.

"Do you have other plans?" he asks, cutting me off. "Because I'm pretty sure you don't have any other plans."

I shake my head again and Logan sits down next to me, reaching into the bag and pulling out what looks like a square donut covered in powdered sugar.

White powder sprinkles across his dark pants and over mine as he tries to hand it to me.

"Well, then you're coming with me. I already told my mom and dad. And we can come back here on Sunday to see your dad."

I gape at him and when I don't take the beignet, he presses it into my mouth, forcing me to take a bite.

As the greasy sugar coats my tongue, I groan.

Damn, that's good. Where did he get these and why have I gone my entire life without them?

"Good, right?" he asks and then slowly feeds me the rest of it, eyeing my mouth the entire time, like he wants to be the one inside of it.

When I swallow my last bite, he kisses the powdered sugar off of my lips.

"You taste good," he says.

"The beignets taste good," I counter, but Logan isn't listening. He's just kissing his way down my neck, biting my oversensitive skin.

"I'll go with you. To your parents. If you really don't mind."

Logan grunts, his teeth scraping against my jaw. "I knew you'd change your mind. I know you don't want to be away from this for too long."

He's right. I'd miss him.

"My parents are going to be so happy to have you," he says, pulling me onto his lap and rubbing circles against my back.

I blink at him and then turn my head so I'm resting my cheek on his shoulder. The truth is, I would have spent the holiday alone, eating cranberry jelly from a can and watching reruns of *The Twilight Zone.*

It doesn't get more depressing than that.

"You can bring Curie too. My dad loves animals."

Of course he does, he named his chickens. He even cried a little when he gave us the eggs. He probably names his vegetables too. His family is the reason Logan is who he is. He's fucking amazing.

I'm desperately trying to shield my heart and here he is pushing his way past all my defenses.

"Okay."

Logan bites down on my ear and sighs contentedly against me.

"It's a mini-vacay. This is getting serious, Theo."

I roll my eyes at how ridiculous he is, but my heart secretly thunders in my chest.

He presses a kiss to the back of my neck. "It's going to be so fun."

sixteen

LOGAN

"ARE you sure you want me to go?" Theo asks, shifting from one foot to the other in the middle of his apartment and looking so unsure. He's wearing jeans that look brand new and an oversized green sweater, and his hair is combed nicely. He looks hella good today.

I grab onto his duffle bag and Curie's cat carrier and nod.

"Hell yes."

Curie meows despondently and I roll my eyes.

"She's being just as dramatic as you." I glance inside and see the yellow of Curie's eyes as she scowls at me.

"Stop being so ridiculous." Then I look at Theo. "And you, too."

Theo grabs onto his journal and the litter box and follows me down the apartment complex stairs.

"Will Finn be there?" he asks as we get into my car.

"Of course. He can't be parted from Landon for too long. If those two don't end up married, I'll be fucking shocked."

Theo buckles in as I start Ms. Chevelle. Curie has ceased her cries for a few minutes, and I arch an eyebrow at Theo.

"Why do you ask?"

"Do you think he'll tell your parents that we...what we..."

"Of course not. And neither will Landon. That's our business."

Theo seems to deflate a little. "Okay."

"You'll just be my friend while we're there."

Theo glances out the window, his journal in his lap, his pencil tapping a rhythm on it.

"Okay."

"Probably shouldn't have sex in my parents' house, right?"

"Yeah."

"Unless, you know...you want to."

Theo eyes me. "We'll see."

God, I hope he sees very clearly that we *should* be having sex. I'm not sure I can make it three days without it. But if we do decide to sneak around and stick our dicks in holes, I need to be really quiet. Which might be tough, because I can be really loud.

Hmm.

My dick perks up as we drive down the freeway.

Yeah, I'll just have to find a way to be quiet about it.

Maybe we can fuck in my dad's greenhouse while everyone is asleep.

Hmm.

"What are you humming about?" Theo asks and I shrug.

"Just picturing fucking you in the vegetable garden.

"Oh Jesus," he mutters, running a hand down his face, and I chuckle. Curie begins meowing again and I roll my eyes.

These two.

Honestly.

We arrive at my parents' house in a little under three hours due to Thanksgiving traffic and as soon as my car shuts off, my brother is out the front door with Finn at his side.

"You made it. Traffic was shit, huh?" Landon asks, smiling

"Of course," I say, pulling him into a hug and feeling like things are mostly normal again. I do eyeball his leg, but that feeling of guilt, while still there, isn't over-powering.

It's all thanks to Theo. This dude has literally changed my life.

"Hey, Theo, how are you?" Landon gives him a hand-shake. Finn just eyes us both, obviously not happy about my guest—and let me tell you, I heard all about it earlier on the phone. He went on and on about how he didn't think Theo should come, but then I'd mentioned his hands all over Landon and asked what the hell that was all about, and he zipped his lips. Yeah, fucker, that's what I thought. Let's just stay out of each other's business.

Landon nudges Finn and he nods to Theo.

"Glad you could make it," Finn mutters.

"Thank you."

Landon throws his arm around Finn's shoulders and

smiles at us. "Alright, Dad is going crazy inside, cooking up a storm. Mom is about to pull her hair out."

"Is he micromanaging again?" I ask with a chuckle.

"Yep," Landon replies and then smirks. "Got all emotional that we're all going to be here, and he wants it to be perfect so he keeps bossing Mom around."

"Is she threatening to have him sleep in the greenhouse?"

"Yep. Said *you'll be sleeping with the radishes if you keep talking shit.*"

I sure hope she doesn't make good on that because I have plans for Theo later.

I grab our stuff from the trunk and Theo grabs Curie from the backseat and the litter box and then we head into the house.

"Where should I put her?" Theo asks as my mom rounds the corner, wiping her hands on a kitchen towel.

"Oh, hi!" she says with a bright smile and then glances at the cat carrier. "Oh, hello there, cutie."

Curie meows her disgruntled greeting and my mom laughs. "Dad is going to go nuts over her, you know that right? You may leave here without a cat."

Theo holds the cage a little closer to his side and I chuckle, nudging Theo with my elbow.

"He's not really going to keep her. Relax. Let's go let her out in my room."

I hug my mom and she hugs Theo, and then I lead him up the stairs to my bedroom.

Theo eyes the space—the queen size bed, the small writing desk, and then his eyes land on the trophies lining a shelf on one of my walls.

"Shit," he says, taking them all in. He seems frozen in place, Curie and the litter box just dangling in his hands. I take Curie's carrier from him and let her out. She mews angrily and scurries under the bed as I set the litter box in the corner of the room.

"There are so many," he says, eyeing me.

"I am the motherfucking best. Told you so."

He swallows and shakes his head. "You apparently are."

I nudge him a little. "And I bet you have trophies somewhere for that big brain of yours."

He just scowls at me.

"You do, don't you?" I would be completely surprised if he *didn't* have any.

"In a box in my closet, just some science fair awards. But nothing like this."

I run my fingers through his hair, cupping the back of his head.

"Theo, you're amazing. You know that, right? I don't know if you know that."

When he doesn't answer, I add, "You're famous. Everyone knows that if they want to pass chemistry, they need to go to you. We joke about *the* Logan Lewis, but you're *the* Theo Reign, one of the smartest guys on campus."

He gulps a little and then pulls away, moving to the other side of my room. He touches the tops of the frames that show off my family and friends and then he opens the top drawer of my dresser and looks inside.

"Nothing fun in there. All the good stuff is at my place."

Theo's eyebrows raise and I smirk.

"I bought more toys. Seems you made me want to experiment." I lower my voice. "I bought nipple clamps. I have them in my bag."

He closes the drawer and steps toward me, clutching onto the front of my shirt and pressing his groin into mine.

"We are not having sex here."

"Yeah, we are."

"You're too loud."

"I can put a pillow over my face."

He looks toward the door and then presses his lips to mine before pulling away quickly.

"No, and I mean it, Logan. *No.*"

Huh, that doesn't seem promising. I just spent a good three hours on the way here coming up with all of these ideas. It would be a pity to scrap them.

"Why not?" I ask, and he glances over at me.

"Because I don't want your parents to think poorly of me."

"Not going to happen. My dad already named a chicken after you."

"Jesus Christ," Theo says, pinching the bridge of his nose. Then suddenly he's opening the door and leaving my room. Why's he running?

I move toward him, trying to catch him, but his long legs always move faster than I think and he's down in the kitchen before I can pull him into me.

"How can I help?" he blurts loudly as he skids into the room and my mom turns to beam at him. She likes him. I know it.

"I think we got it all under control, Theo," she says and then eyes my dad who is poking at some potatoes boiling in a pot while simultaneously stirring something in another.

"Why don't you show Theo his namesake, Logan," my mom offers because she knows that if we stay my dad is going to get all weird.

I smirk at Theo, and he blushes.

Finn and Landon appear from the garage, each holding a beer in hand and my eyes narrow a bit. Yeah, my baby brother is too young to be drinking. He's only twenty. But I don't say anything. I'm sure Finn already bugged him about it. Like it even matters—Landon does whatever he wants, apparently.

"Ah, that's right. You got a chicken named after you," Landon tells Theo. "Finn has one too."

My dad waggles the fork with a potato hanging off of it. "He's had *several*. They keep dying."

"Well, that's ominous," Theo mutters and I chuckle a little, pulling him into me.

He stiffens and I reluctantly let him go. That's right, *friends*. We're just friends right now. Friends, who may or may not have sex in the greenhouse later.

"Come on," I say, pulling Theo out the backdoor and toward the chicken coop. Landon and Finn stroll out behind us and we all converge around the small hen house my dad made five years ago. It's painted a deep red with white window trim. It looks like a little barn.

My dad was so fucking proud of it.

"Okay, that one is yours," I say, picking out a chicken that's sitting in the corner, sleeping. I cock my head. "Kind of acts like you too."

Theo nudges me and I chuckle.

"He's quiet, anti-social," I lean into him. "And probably asks the rooster for a fuck in exchange for—"

Theo presses a hand over my mouth, stopping the inappropriate—yet, oh so accurate—flow of words.

Landon and Finn laugh behind me and I waggle my eyebrows at them. Landon takes a sip of his beer and leans into Finn.

"They're cute together, huh?" he asks Finn who just rolls his eyes at me. But my best friend's hand is around my brother's hip, so he has no right to judge. You don't see me rolling my eyes at the two of them...much.

"So, I was thinking since Dad is a maniac and totally distracted...we should go smoke."

Theo's eyes widen slightly.

I chuckle and lick a sloppy line across the palm of his hand that's still planted over my mouth. He quickly pulls it away and wipes it on his pants.

"Never smoked before?" I ask.

Theo shakes his head. "Never."

Finn's lips twitch at that. "A virgin then. This will be fun."

"My dad grows his own weed." I explain and Theo shakes his head in disbelief. I mean, come on, is he really that surprised? Has he looked at where we live?

"It's the good stuff. Super chill. Good for your first time."

"Oh, good lord," Theo mutters as I lead him across the backyard and toward a shed on the far end of the property.

"In here?" he asks when I hold the door open and the smell of soil and stale weed wafts out.

"Yep."

Landon and Finn pile in behind us and we all just momentarily stop and stare at the small space. There are only two camping chairs in here, an old desk, and a cabinet that houses all of the marijuana.

"Our parents are such hippie motherfuckers," I say and grin at Landon.

"I can totally see Mom in here smoking a bowl while Dad munches on a head of broccoli," he adds.

Theo giggles and I eye him in surprise.

Shit, is he getting high off the fumes in here? He's a total lightweight. Tonight should be interesting...can't fucking wait. I get horny when I'm high, maybe he will too. Damn, I hope so.

"Let's light up before they find us," Landon says, guiding Finn to a chair. He pushes him down and then sits right on his lap.

I bite my tongue before I say something inappropriate and then lower myself onto the other chair and wrap my arms around Theo's waist. He plops down on my lap without a fight, and I nuzzle my face into the side of his neck.

He doesn't even protest. He's opening up to me, letting me in, one small act at a time.

A haze of smoke suddenly envelopes the space and I look over and see Finn inhaling deeply. He holds it in and then Landon turns his face and Finn blows the smoke right into his mouth.

Well, fuck if that isn't sexual.

They're totally fucking.

Why haven't they told me? Do they think I'm a bigot or something?

"Are we supposed to do that?" Theo whispers and I bite down on his earlobe.

"Hell yeah." Because I want near that smart mouth of his all the time.

Finn hands me the blunt and I take a deep drag. I tilt Theo's head so he's facing me, he parts those sexy lips, and I exhale the smoke right into his waiting mouth.

He inhales right before violent coughs rack his body. His cheeks redden and his eyes water.

I just rub at his back as laughter erupts around us.

"We're not laughing at you, Theo," I whisper because I know he's sensitive about this. "We're just remembering what our first time was like. We all did that. You gotta practice more."

"Yeah, man, you'll get used to it," Landon says, taking a hit from the blunt I passed him, and he blows the smoke right into Finn's mouth again, their lips brushing slightly as they do so.

I take the blunt back and do the same to Theo, and back and forth we go until it's all gone and we're just sitting in the shed high as fuck.

Theo is melted against me, his eyes drooping. He's like cooked spaghetti.

"Did you know that cannabis has over four hundred chemical entities and most have opposing effects?" he suddenly blurts.

"What the fuck is he talking about?" Finn mutters, his hand moving under Landon's shirt.

Goddamn, he's bold. And hell, if he can do that, so can I.

I slip my hand under Theo's oversized sweater and splay my hand on the warm skin of his stomach. He shivers against me, a small groan slipping from his lips, and I pull him in a little closer.

Yep, I'm totally fucking him later.

Or he's fucking me.

Preferably me.

Stick that cock right up my ass, Theo. Don't tempt me with the zucchini.

"The chemical compounds that are in opposition are..." He rattles off a list of long-ass names that I can't even pronounce. But it gets my dick hard. I told you that all he had to do was open up that mouth of his and spout some chemistry shit and I'm done for.

"Wow, you're smart," Landon says, his eyes bloodshot, his head leaning back against Finn's shoulder. "Say those long words again."

Theo mutters them once more and Landon turns his head to eye Finn, his lips brushing against Finn's cheek.

"My brother's boyfriend is a smart dude, huh?"

"He's average," Finn mutters and I roll my eyes. Jealous motherfucker.

I feel Theo's body stiffen slightly against me, and I rub slow circles on his belly to calm him, not sure whether he's reacting to the 'boyfriend' or the 'average' comment.

Suddenly the shed door opens and my dad bursts through.

"Oh, you assholes!" he shouts. "Why didn't you invite me? You know how I hate being left out."

I anticipate Theo will try and move off my lap, but instead, he just wiggles around nervously on my hard dick, making me fucking miserable.

Like I said, I get horny when I'm high.

Theo eyes my dad and then says, "I heard you grow your own cannabis. Did you know that some farmers are feeding chickens cannabis instead of injecting them with antibiotics?"

My dad ponders that for a moment and then nods. "Huh, you don't say? Interesting."

Theo shifts on my lap again. "It's revolutionary with regards to providing meat and eggs that are not full of hormones and antibiotics."

"No shit?" my dad says, moving to a cabinet on the wall and pulling down a box.

He rolls a joint as Theo prattles on and then lights up, more smoke wafting around the space.

"Tell me more about this, Theo," he says between puffs.

We all relax as Theo rambles on and on about cannabis and its effects on free-range farming and then goes on to talk about which vegetables will grow well with cannabis. How the fuck does he know all of this? What do vegetables have to do with chemistry?

And why does my dad pretend like he knows what Theo is talking about? Theo is using big words that I'm pretty sure my dad has never heard before. He's just faking it right now.

Asshole. All a bunch of fakers.

But I don't dwell on it too much because we're all high as fuck with not a care in the world. As proven by my hand, which is still up Theo's shirt, and I wonder for a minute if I can stick it down his pants. Would anyone really notice? Would they even care?

"Hey, where's mom?" Landon asks and my dad shrugs. Both of Finn's hands are up Landon's shirt now and no one is saying a word.

Jesus Christ.

Always trying to one-up me.

"Dunno," my dad says, inhaling deeply and letting out a long, exasperated exhale. "She was pissed at me. Told me not to micromanage her potatoes."

He starts to sniffle a little and swipes at his eyes. He gets very emotional when he's high.

Theo glances at me. "You all cry a lot for such manly men...and you're all *extremely hot*. What is up with that?"

My dad puffs up at that and Landon grins widely.

"We may have the family curse, but we also have the best genetics, am I right?" my dad says, and Landon and I mutter our agreement. Because, yeah, it's true.

"But I'm the hottest, right?" I whisper and Theo eyeballs me, then slides his gaze to Landon, Finn, and then my dad.

Hell, I'd rather he wasn't so honest. He's hurting my feelings. I should be first pick.

"I'd say they've given you a run for your money," Theo replies and I pinch his hip a little.

He just grinds his ass down around on my lap and I bite back a low moan.

He turns his head a little and his warm breath hits my ear. "But you're the only one I want, Logan."

Oh, hell. That does it.

I'm about to break all the rules right now, but I don't get

a chance, because Mom suddenly shows up in the doorway, a frown on her face.

"Boys," she reprimands and we all groan, because we know we're in trouble. We should have invited her.

"You seriously left me to finish up inside to come smoke with them?" she says, her eyes homing in on my dad sprawled out on the floor.

My dad looks a little bashful and shrugs. "You were getting mad. It was self-preservation."

My mom rolls her eyes and sets her hands on her hips.

"Basil Lewis, get your ass inside and help me finish dinner."

My dad scrambles to his feet and Theo chuckles quietly.

"He's named after an herb."

"Hell yeah, he is," I say as my dad disappears and my mom eyes us. She takes in Theo sitting on my lap and doesn't even blink an eye.

Hmm, maybe I'm gayer than I thought if this doesn't even surprise her.

And does she already know about Finn and Landon? Because she's not batting an eye over them either.

If those assholes told her something and didn't tell me, I may cry.

"Ten minutes and then dinner is served, and I expect you all to eat a shit ton with how much you smoked," she says and then disappears, letting the door shut behind her.

"How did the two of you end up with normal names?" Theo asks, shifting on my lap a little.

"We almost didn't. Dad wanted to name me Sage," I tell him.

"And me Oakley," Landon says. "Although neither are bad names. We'd fit right in up here."

"Hell yeah, we would," I say, and then shoot an air gun at my brother.

We sit in silence for a few more minutes, just trying to get our bearings, when suddenly Finn says, "Well, we better get inside." His hands slowly escape the confines of my brother's shirt and settle on his hips, gently helping push my brother up.

Theo also stands up slowly, wobbling a little on his legs, and then they take off for the house, leaving me to walk behind them with my best friend.

"What's up with you and Landon?" I ask because the weed has loosened my tongue, and I'm so damn curious.

"Nothing," Finn replies softly.

"You were groping my baby brother in front of me. You two a thing?" Finn's cheeks darken and I nudge him. "You know I'd be happy about it, right? My two favorite people in the world...I just don't get why you're not telling me shit."

"You don't tell me anything, either."

"Well, damn." He's right. I don't really deserve an answer, not when I've kept everything hidden.

"Fine. Theo and I are fucking. Like, legit fucking, not an arrangement. And I like him. A lot."

That about sums it up.

Finn's mouth is hanging open and he runs a hand through his shaggy hair.

"Shit, Lo."

"It's hot...being with another man."

I eyeball him, wanting him to tell me if he's doing something similar, but he just shakes his head.

"We're not a thing. Just leave it. We're just best friends."

"Best friends who grope each other and practically kiss?"

He shakes his head again and jogs forward, wrapping an arm around Landon, who just leans into him once again.

Well, they both say it's nothing, but clearly, it's something. I'm too high for this shit.

I sigh heavily and move inside the house.

Time to fucking eat.

I'll process all of this later.

seventeen

THEO

I'VE NEVER FELT this out of my mind in my entire life...or this horny. Is that a thing that happens when you smoke pot?

Because ever since I took a hit, Logan grew ten times hotter and more delicious than the apple pie I'm currently eating. Why do I want to slather this in mashed potatoes and season it with pepper?

Why does that sound so good?

I eye Logan who is licking his spoon sensually and our eyes catch. Goddamn. The things I want him to do to me with his tongue.

His parents have to know what's going on between us. I was on his lap and his hand was up my shirt and now I can't stop staring at him. I'm drooling and I'm so fucking *hungry*.

I always knew weed would lower my inhibitions, but I always thought I'd be able to remain logical.

I am so past logic that I'm in another dimension entirely.

"What's your major?" his mom asks me, and I swallow the pie down, averting my gaze from Logan. It's difficult because my eyeballs want to keep ogling him.

"Chemistry. I'm getting my doctorate."

"Oh, wow, so you're incredibly smart."

"He told me all about the chemical makeup of cannabis, Jeanette," Basil says, his hand moving down my cat's back. He ran upstairs right before dinner to let her out of Logan's room because, and I quote, "pretty kitties deserve Thanksgiving too". So, now she's perched on his lap, fawning all over him and eating tiny bites of turkey off his plate. I don't think his mom was wrong. I may be leaving this place without Curie.

Logan throws an arm across the back of my chair and nods like he's proud of me. "He is hella smart. He single-handedly saved my ass this semester. I'm so far ahead at this point that I don't even need his help anymore."

What the fuck?

"What?" I ask, my eyebrows meeting, my heart sputtering in my chest.

"Huh?" Logan asks, his cheeks coloring.

Oh, he fucking knows. What a goddamn liar.

"You don't need my help anymore?" I choke out, feeling my spirits sink.

Because if he doesn't need my help anymore, then it's over.

Finito.

"Nah, I uh, I still need it," he replies, but he shifts on his seat guiltily.

Has he just been keeping me around? For what? Why?

If he couldn't just be honest with me, his reasoning can't be anything good.

Is he using me?

I scoot my chair back and stand up, feeling a little nauseous. I smoked too much, ate too much, *felt* too much.

"I...excuse me," I mumble and then make my way outside. The cool air hits my overheated face as I pace to the other side of the large yard.

Of course, Logan follows me because he can't just give me space. I'm not sure whether I love it or hate it, him chasing me around all the time.

"Hey, why did you leave?"

I keep moving until we're out of earshot of the house and then I turn to face him. I'm too high to do this now, and yet it all comes tumbling out anyway.

I poke him in the chest, my eyes narrowing on him. "You don't need tutoring anymore."

"Uh...yeah, I do. Don't listen to me. I'm high as fuck."

"You're lying."

"Not really. The review is helpful. I need help. I always need help. Have you met me?"

I eyeball him and part of me wants to push back, to make him tell me the truth, the whole truth, so help me God, but I'm not sure I want it. Not now. Not yet.

"Are you sure?" I ask, my voice breaking. "Because it's okay, Logan. It's okay if you don't want to keep seeing me."

He rubs the back of his neck and meets my gaze. "Yeah,

Theo. I'm sure. We have two more weeks. Don't rob me of this."

I sag in relief, and he pulls me into his strong chest. He smells like brown sugar and weed, and I want to gobble him up. "Thank you."

Oh hell, now I'm getting all emotional. I'm never going to smoke again. I'm too vulnerable right now. I hate feeling like this. And yet, I've felt a little like this ever since he walked into my life.

"Nah, no worries. Let's just go back inside. We're all going to veg out and watch a movie and then later…" He lowers his voice, and his lips brush my earlobe. "When everyone is asleep, we're going to sneak into the greenhouse and you're going to do dirty things to me, Theo."

Jesus. If he pulls out the nipple clamps, I'm not sure I'll survive.

I have never met a more ridiculous and sexy man in my entire life.

"What kinds of toys did you buy, Logan?" I ask, curious now, my focus shifting like the wind. It's so weird being high.

"Uhhh," he mutters and shifts on his feet. "Want a list or some shit?"

"Oh my god," I say. "How many did you get?"

"I went a little crazy. Like I said, you unlocked something inside of me. Didn't really know what I liked until I met you."

I step closer to him, and he reaches out and pulls me into his chest.

"I think you're just really fucking high," I mutter into his shirt.

"Nah, I feel this way all the time around you, Theo. You make me feel high, too."

"Impossible," I whisper, and he bends down, grabs onto my ass, and picks me up—just fucking lifts me right off the ground—and walks around the side of the house. I link my ankles together behind his back and tuck my face into his neck.

Then I feel the hard press of siding against my back, and I pull my face away from his skin to see his bloodshot eyes and his messy, curly hair. My fingers run through it as he grasps me tighter.

"Don't know what those guys did to you, Theo, but you've done something to *me.* And I'm not saying this because I'm high."

"Logan," I begin to protest, but he just presses into me further.

"Don't you fucking feel it?"

I feel something, all right. But part of me can't believe he's saying this. It has to be the drugs. It has to be.

"I can't," I say.

He presses his nose to mine and his breath puffs against my mouth.

"You can, you just don't want to. Always pushing me away. Why can't you just let it fucking be?"

My breaths are coming out shaky and my chest aches.

"I won't hurt you, Theo."

"You don't know that. I always end up hurt."

His lips settle on mine, so soft and sweet.

"I think at the end of this, if anyone ends up broken, it

will be me," Logan mutters against my mouth and then just buries his face in my neck.

Oh, sweet Logan, how would that even be possible?

Have the tables turned so much?

I unlink my ankles from around his back and just let him press against me until we hear our names being called from the porch.

"We should go back," he says and steps away, eyeing me warily.

Then he extends his hand and I am helpless to do anything, but link my fingers through his.

* * *

We spend the afternoon lounging around and snacking, and then we take a short walk around the block. Logan holds my hand the entire time, like we're together...like this is a totally normal thing we do now.

I'm not sure exactly when everything changed. But it has. It's flipped my world upside down.

When we make it back from the walk, I hole up in Logan's room, scribbling on the last few pages of my journal, trying to get it all out as Logan, Landon, and Finn leave to see a movie at the local theatre.

I flaked and said I didn't feel well, when in reality, I was feeling too much.

I just need a few hours alone to process everything and figure out how I need to proceed with Logan.

A knock on the bedroom door has me setting my journal

down and pulling it open. Standing on the other side is Logan's dad with a backpack over his shoulders.

Basil turns a little, showing me a content Curie licking her paw and ignoring me completely.

My god, is that a Petpod? Is he carrying Curie around on his back now?

The little brat is getting spoiled to death. First Logan with his incessant gifts, and now she's being toted around like she's Cleopatra.

She'll never want to come home with me now. I won't be able to find her to get her in the carrier on Sunday.

"It has a built-in fan too," he tells me, and my eyes widen in disbelief.

Jesus Christ. Who are these people?

"I just came to see if you wanted to help me in the greenhouse. Thought Curie would like it."

I eye him, completely flabbergasted. Do I want to go pull up veggies in the greenhouse? No, not really. But do I want to see if this man will give me any insight into Logan? Hell yes, I do.

"Sure, let me grab my shoes," I say.

I quickly toe them on and follow Basil down the stairs, outside, and into the large windowed greenhouse. When we enter, the humidity hits me immediately, and Basil pulls the backpack off his shoulder and opens the pod so Curie can hop out.

"She's a great cat," he tells me.

"She is," I say. I rescued her shortly after my mom died. I just needed company, and someone to snuggle with...not that she ever really lets me snuggle with her.

But those times, in the middle of the night, when my grief was too much and sobs would rack my body, she'd curl up next to my head and purr.

She has her own way of comforting me. Most of the time though, she just ignores me or yells at me for not feeding her twelve times a day.

Basil runs a hand across his broad chest and smiles dopily at me. I'm fifty percent sure he's still high. I saw him eating brownies earlier and I think they were laced with something.

"How about you help me pull some carrots and onions?"

"Um, sure," I say, moving to his side.

"You know, I want to buy a house with more land and have a real farm. Cows, sheep, and rows and rows of corn. We could really live off the land, like *Little House on the Prairie*. Although, those books were kind of sad. Not sure I could kill a cow for meat. I'd get too attached."

I can totally imagine that scenario—Basil happily chugging away on a tractor, feeding baby sheep, and carting miniature goats around in his Petpod.

"Anyway, sorry, got a little sidetracked. I have so many dreams, you know?" he mutters and we both stare as Curie hops on top of a row of planters and walks through the plants.

"Is that okay?" I ask.

Basil nods. "Hell yeah. Look at her, smelling the strawberries."

She is, in fact, smelling them. Jesus, is she eating one?

Can cats eat strawberries?

I glance up at Basil, but he seems unconcerned by it.

Instead, he's moving toward a planter farthest from the door.

"Here are the carrots. Let me show you how to pull them up," he says, kneeling down, his knees cracking loudly.

We spend the next few minutes gently tugging the orange root vegetables from the dirt. It feels cathartic and I lose myself in it for a moment.

"Logan really likes you," Basil says suddenly, and I peek over at him. "He told us how you said he was smart."

"He is."

Basil swallows a little and leans back on his heels.

"Thank you for giving him a chance. For believing in him."

Jesus, I feel like a total shithead. If he knew what I'd made his son do in exchange for tutoring, he'd hate me. He'd kick my ass straight out of the house.

When Logan had first shown up at my door, I'd only bargained with sex thinking he'd tell me to go to hell. I generally try to stay away from the popular jock crowd and since he wasn't taking no for an answer, I figured he'd be repulsed by my suggestion and leave me alone. But when he'd actually agreed, I felt compelled to follow through. I'm a stubborn ass sometimes and I didn't want to back down. I wanted to feel in control.

The truth is, I used Logan. I'm no better than James and those other boys who used me and treated me like dirt.

Fuck, I'm a terrible person. And here I am, pulling up carrots with his dad who's sniffling and thinking I'm some great friend to his son.

My stomach clenches with shame, and I feel like I'm going to be sick.

I want to run away and hide.

"Sorry," Basil says when I've been silent too long. "Logan just speaks so highly of you. He told us what you did for him and Landon, too—how you got them to work out their issues. Their mom and I really appreciate that. It's important to us that our boys have a good relationship."

My heart stutters and I feel dizzy. That was nothing. Logan deserves more. He deserves so much better.

"They were always so close. Then the accident...Logan burdens himself sometimes, unnecessarily. I'm glad you were able to get through to him. None of us have the balls to take a stand. We're all a bit non-confrontational in this family."

"I really didn't do all that much."

But Basil waves me off and moves over to the onions. He shows me how to pull them from the soil without damaging the bulb. I mimic him, the two of us working in silence until Basil says, "I see the way he looks at you. It's the same way Finn looks at Landon..."

My chest aches and I close my eyes, focusing on taking a few deep breaths.

I turn to him and say softly, "Logan is wonderful. But we're just...we're friends."

"Nah, you can't fool me. It's more than that," he says and wipes at his eyes, dirt smearing across his handsome face. "My boys...all grown up...falling in love."

I can't stand it anymore. I pull my hood up over my head

so it shields my face, and focus on plucking the bulbs from the soil.

"Nothing to be ashamed of," he says gently, mistaking my hiding for shame.

"I'm not ashamed," I mutter. *Lies, all lies.* I am ashamed, but not in the way that he thinks.

Basil reaches out and squeezes my arm and my eyes begin to sting.

"Logan and I didn't meet under...ideal circumstances," I admit, blinking rapidly and trying to focus on the soil.

"We all thrive on weird up in here. If you had told me it all started normally, I'd be surprised," Basil says, and I peek over at him.

He still has a dopey smile on his face and seems so happy in this moment, I don't want to ruin it. I don't want to admit who I really am.

"Doesn't matter how it happened. Just know that Logan is happy. The happiest I've seen him since before the accident," Basil replies, wiping his hands on his jeans.

Isn't Logan always pretty happy, though? He's like a big, goofy ball of sunshine.

But I don't say anything else, I just stew in my guilt until Basil gathers Curie and leaves me alone inside the greenhouse.

Logan finds me a half hour later behind a coffee tree, my fingers running across the leaves and my mind a complete mess.

"Hey," he says, with a grin.

"How was the movie?" I ask, unable to meet his eyes.

"Good, wish you had come, though. Landon and Finn were all cuddly and I was like the third fucking wheel."

I watch him approach and move back a little.

"Do you feel better?" he asks, concern lacing his tone.

"No. I think it's contagious," I reply and Logan's eyebrows meet.

He reaches out to touch my forehead, but I bat his hand away.

"Wait," I say. "I'm fine. I feel fine...physically, at least. I just...we need to clear the air."

"Clear it? From what?" Logan asks.

I swallow and tug on my hood. "I think we need to end things."

He looks completely shocked. "Um, hell no."

Jesus, of course he won't make this easy.

"I will tutor you the rest of the semester. If you even need it..."

"I need it," he says, moving toward me, his eyes flashing.

"But no more sex."

He folds his arms across his large chest and glowers at me. "And why the hell not?"

"Because..." I throw my hand up in the air and knock it against a hanging plant. "Shit," I say, rubbing my smarting fingers. "Because your dad thinks I'm some kind of saint for helping tutor you, but little does he know, I told you that you needed to fuck me to get any of my help..."

I run a hand through my hair and start pacing.

"So, I'm basically a terrible person. I'm no better than the bullies that fucked around with me. I am a bully. Fuck, Logan. I was awful to you. I used you."

"Nah, Theo," Logan says, but I shake my head so hard my brain rattles in my skull. "I liked it. I liked everything we did."

"So? That doesn't make it right! I'm not good for you." I'm panting now, my eyes brimming with unshed tears.

"Come here, Theo," Logan says, his voice gruff. He opens his arms wide and takes a step forward. "Come here."

When I don't move, he comes to me slowly, as if approaching a wild animal. He stops right in front of where I'm standing and gently wraps his arms around me, gathering me against him.

I can feel his warm breath on my ear as he murmurs, "I don't care about what happened then or how this all started. I only care that we're here right now and I like where we are."

My eyes flutter closed, my heartbeat pounding in my skull. My entire body is trembling and the desire to sink into him is overwhelming.

"Theo, listen. I'm glad it happened this way. Sure, it wasn't perfect in the beginning, but you were just the kick in the ass that I needed to figure stuff out. I've learned so much about myself since meeting you, Theo. And I don't regret a second of it. So, stop beating yourself up over it."

My eyelids open and I stare into his beautiful, kind eyes. He cups my cheek and smiles devilishly.

"Seriously, dude. Stop being so dramatic about it. I'm over here living my best life, fucking a super-hot guy while getting to know the mysterious genius side of him, and you're all up in your head about it."

I let out a choked laugh because he's right. He's just

chilling and I'm over here panicking and overthinking everything.

I dab at my eyes with my sleeve and sniffle. "Are you sure?"

"Yeah, I'm fucking sure, Theo."

"You're right. You're right. I'm sorry," I say.

He eyes me and smirks. "I know a way you can make it up to me."

eighteen

LOGAN

WE SNEAK out after everyone is asleep. It's colder in the evenings and I shiver as I pull him toward our destination.

He's been quiet since we left the greenhouse earlier and went back inside, overthinking shit as usual. Maybe that's what happens when you're ridiculously smart. You just analyze things to death.

I don't want him to question this anymore.

I mean, did we start off weird? Yeah.

But does that mean I don't like it and want to quit? Nope.

I want him all the time, and I'm planning on showing him that as frequently as I can.

Starting with tonight...preferably bent over the strawberry bushes.

I open the greenhouse door and we sneak inside, shutting it quietly. The only light is from the soft glow of the moon as it casts shadows throughout the open space.

"This is creepy," Theo says, and I chuckle as I lead him to the back corner where we're cloaked in darkness. Just in case my dad decides he needs to water the asparagus at one o'clock in the morning, I don't need him to see me getting railed.

"I heard that you helped my dad pick veggies earlier," I say, as I pull him into me and kiss my way across his jaw.

"Yep."

"He says you have a green thumb."

He softens against me, his response lost as I lazily explore his mouth.

I love this...love kissing him.

I'm so ready for him. I prepped already and everything while he was downstairs chatting with my mom. He can just slide himself right inside. He doesn't even need to stretch me.

My hands slide down to his tight ass and I groan into his mouth as I yank his sweatpants down until his cock pops free.

He's so damn big and thick, I'll never get tired of seeing it.

My fingers barely touch when I wrap my hand around him and stroke him torturously slow. He moans lowly and his fingers tremble as he tries to undo my pants.

I help him pop the button and when I'm finally free, I kick them off and wrench my mouth from his.

"I'm ready for you."

Theo's Adam's apple bobs and he looks a little uncertain. Well, that's not a look I want him to wear.

Maybe he doesn't want to fuck me.

"I've never…" he shakes his head. "I've never done this. Except for that one time. I don't want to hurt you."

"Do you not want to do it?" I ask.

"No…I mean, yes, I do. I definitely do," he stutters.

Okay, I can work with that.

I reach up to my collar and pull my shirt off and then turn and bend over, grabbing onto a large, raised planter.

"You won't hurt me. Just stick it in, Theo. I've been waiting weeks for this. I'm ready for you."

He shuffles behind me and then I feel his hands on my ass cheeks. He kneads them gently and then spreads me open.

"Are you sure?"

"Stop overthinking, Theo, and get that big cock in me."

Theo is quiet for a moment, and I wonder if he's going to leave me hanging, but then suddenly, there's pressure on my hole, and he pushes forward, entering me slowly.

Holy fuck, this is as good as I remember.

And last time was fucking epic.

"Good?" he rasps, and I just nod, my hands tightening on the wood beneath them as my ass stretches wide for him.

"More?"

I pant and thrust back in response, unable to form words.

Theo sets his trembling hands on my hips and tightens his hold on me as he impales me completely.

"You feel good," he breathes. "So fucking good, Logan. And you look so hot bent over for me."

"Mmm." I push myself up on shaking arms, wanting his mouth on mine.

He must read my mind because he leans forward, his hand in my hair, his cock thrusting into me as our mouths meet in a wet mess of tongues and teeth.

I'm not going to last.

I lean forward again, grabbing onto the planter for dear life.

"Go on. Wreck my ass, Theo."

He lets out a shuddering breath, pulls his hips back, and pounds into me. The space fills with loud slapping sounds as his groin hits my ass repeatedly and it may be the sexiest and most filthy thing I've ever heard.

I didn't know he had it in him, but fuck, I'm dying. I've gone straight to heaven. My groans echo off the glass walls and I swear to God, the neighbors can hear me as I take it. Everyone on the block will know what a big dick Theo has and what a slut I am for it.

His hand fists roughly in my hair as he pumps into me.

"Jesus, this feels so fucking good," he moans.

He leans over me again, his thrusts short and quick as he bites his way across my shoulders.

"Not going to last," I cry out as he pegs my prostate over and over.

"Me either," he huffs and then pushes up and fucks me so deep my eyes cross. I spit in my hand and stroke the head of my cock until suddenly my come spills from me, hitting the floor as Theo releases inside of me. His orgasm goes on for a while as he shakes and trembles and groans behind me.

Then he slumps over me, his cock still inside, his cheek pressed against my sweaty back.

"Oh. My. God."

"Yes. Yeah. That was...hella good."

His lips brush my spine, and he gently slips from me.

I just rest my forehead on my arm, trying to catch my breath, trying not to pass out.

"You okay?" he asks, pulling his pants up and brushing a hand across my lower back.

"I just need a minute. A little lightheaded."

"Want me to grab you some water?"

I glance up at him and shake my head, a smile forming on my lips. "Nah."

His lips twitch a little and he runs a finger up my side.

"You didn't bring the clamps."

"Shit," I mutter. I'd forgotten them in all the excitement to get out here.

Theo bends down, swipes up my discarded pants, and holds them out to me. I take them, standing up on shaky legs.

"We're doing that again. But with the clamps," I say.

He shuffles before me and I frown. "Did you like it? Really?"

"I did. I really did, I swear. I just...I just still can't believe you let me," Theo says.

I reach out and stroke his cheek softly and then bring my lips to his for a tender kiss.

"I will always let you. I want to do everything with you."

He takes my other hand in his and brings it to his mouth, kissing it softly. He doesn't say anything, but the way he's looking at me, like maybe he adores me, makes my heart skip. Yeah, Theo, I knew you felt it too. If only I could get you to admit it.

I suddenly feel very tired; I guess amazing sex will do that. I pull on my shirt, quickly wipe up the mess I made and tug him toward the greenhouse door.

I just want to spend the rest of the night tucked in bed with him.

"Do you think your parents heard?" he whispers.

"Who the fuck cares?"

Little does he know, I've heard the shit they've done. They even have a sex playlist. I'm traumatized for life. Any time I hear "Whole Lotta Love" by Led Zeppelin, I run from the room screaming.

Well, payback is a bitch.

Theo tucks himself further into me as we make our way upstairs, the wood creaking beneath our feet, and then we climb into bed together. He doesn't even fight it. He lets me hold him snug against me, and I'm pretty sure the smile is still on my face when I fall asleep.

* * *

We spend the rest of the weekend together, hanging out with Finn, my brother, and my parents, and Theo seemed to fit right in. He even helped my dad with weeding the vegetable patch and feeding the chickens. One evening, he showed us all a few chemistry experiments with stuff from the kitchen—something called non-Newtonian liquid—that my dad went wild for. One of them exploded everywhere, and even Finn cracked a smile

Theo positively beamed. I could tell he was happy to win everyone over.

Not that he had to try that hard. When he takes down all those prickly guards of his, he's sweet and irresistible. I want to eat him up, in every possible way.

Friday morning, my dad convinced Theo to go to a 4-H fair to look at the livestock. Theo had been reluctant at first, but I'd basically pushed him out the door. The guy needs to get out more and socialize.

I don't know how the socializing went but they did come home with a pygmy goat.

My dad named him Vincent.

He is a cute motherfucker. My mom was pissed, but I still caught her talking to him like a baby. She can't fool me. She's just as much of a softie as my dad.

But my favorite part about this weekend was nighttime, when the house was completely quiet, I'd pull Theo into me, holding him against my naked chest. We didn't fuck again after that time in the greenhouse, but I sure as hell kissed him, long and desperate until we both fell asleep, horny and needy.

We never did get to use the clamps, much to my disappointment. But later. We'll do that later.

I have plans for us.

When Saturday evening rolled around, we packed our bags and got ready to leave.

Half of that process involved chasing Curie around the

whole damn house. She did *not* want to leave, and she yowled in protest the entire way home.

My dad cried a bit when we said goodbye and made Theo promise to bring her to visit again. He then proceeded to squeeze Theo so tightly that his ribs made popping sounds.

I may have gotten a little defensive, because I don't want anyone to actually hurt him, so I pulled him away from my dad and tucked him into my side.

He wrapped his arm around my waist and nestled into me, like he belonged there.

I had a hard time driving us home when all I wanted to do was pull him against me. It really made me rethink those bucket seats in my car; I should have gone with a bench so Theo could plaster himself to me.

"Thank you," Theo says, pulling my thoughts back to him.

I'm idling in a parking spot outside his apartment. We spent the whole drive home with our fingers interlocked.

"You're welcome. They all loved you, you know?"

His eyes are glassy and he looks out the windshield.

"I haven't been around family in so long."

"Well, then I'm glad you came. I think they like you better than me at this point. My parents practically adopted you."

"Don't say that," he whispers, shaking his head. "Don't say that, Logan."

"Why not?" My eyebrows meet and I'm genuinely confused.

He's silent for a moment, like he's considering whether or not to answer me. Finally, he murmurs, "Don't dangle something like that in front of me, if there's a chance it will be taken away."

He sniffs, dabbing under his eyes with his sleeve, and I tighten my hold on his hand.

"Never."

"You can't promise that."

I shake my head, cupping the side of his face and forcing him to turn to look at me. But I don't think words will convince him. I need to show him.

"Want me to come upstairs? We can face tomorrow together?" I ask as Theo gnaws on his bottom lip.

"You shouldn't."

"I should," I say sternly.

His eyelids close and he nods. "Okay."

Curie bellows loudly from her crate, breaking the moment.

Alright then, Theo. You don't need to say much. I've got it.

I'm staying.

nineteen

THEO

I WAKE the next morning entangled with Logan, my arm thrown around him, my leg tucked between the two of his, and his face smooshed into my neck. As I lie there reveling in the feel of his soft puffs of breath against my skin, the memory of last night comes back to me in fragments and my entire body starts to heat.

The way he'd kissed me so gently as soon as the apartment door clicked shut.

How he'd carried me to the bed, stripping off my clothes, like he was unwrapping a present.

How he'd laid on top of me, propped on his forearms, his cock entering me slowly.

The way he kissed and touched me so affectionately as he thrust into me.

It felt like making love—or what I thought making love

would feel like.

Is that what we are now? Is that what he wants? God, I hope that's what he wants. What am I going to do if that's not what he wants? Fuck, I am so screwed.

"Morning," he croaks into my neck. I jump slightly at the abruptness, and he pulls his head back so I can see his sleep-rumpled face. Damn, he's even more gorgeous when he's scruffy and disheveled. Blinking up at me, he rasps, "How long have you been awake?"

"Not very long."

"Liar. You were laying here overthinking last night, weren't you?"

I reach over and twist his nipple.

He gasps and I chuckle.

"You're evil," he mutters.

"You asked for it," I say, smiling.

He grins and runs a hand across my jaw so tenderly and smacks a chaste kiss on my lips.

"You going to be okay today?"

Oh shit. It completely slipped my mind that I'm meeting my dad for coffee this morning. We're going to *talk*.

"Yeah, I'll be fine," I lie and then sit up on the bed, running a hand through my tousled hair. Curie is asleep between Logan's ankles, looking like a loaf of bread.

"You sure you don't want me to come?" he asks while rubbing my back, and I debate it, seriously wondering if I should bring him into this. Ultimately, I decide that I'm going to. I want him there. I *need* him there.

I nod. "Please."

Logan sighs contentedly. "Fuck yeah. You're letting me

in, Theo. Just you wait. I'm gonna show you, you can trust me."

My throat feels thick so I just nod again and stand up to take a shower. When I see my sleepy eyes in the bathroom mirror, I tell myself to steel my heart and to hang on tight to the last remaining shred of doubt, because it's my only protection against getting hurt.

But it's a farce. When I look deep inside of myself, I realize there's not even a shred left. My doubt is gone, and the truth is, I do trust Logan. I trust that he won't intentionally hurt me. But I still don't know how he feels about me, about us, and if what we have can last.

All I do know is: there is no steeling my heart. It's already thawed, completely melted, and at his mercy.

* * *

When I walk into the coffee shop, my hand in Logan's, I immediately catch sight of my father. He looks thin and pale, like the last time I'd seen him. He's definitely not well. That much is obvious.

He stands from his seat as we approach and Logan squeezes my hand briefly in reassurance.

He's here. I'm not alone.

"Hi," I say weakly, leaning a little into Logan's side for support.

"Hey," my dad says, his brows furrowing as he takes in Logan. He never was okay with my sexuality, but instead of saying anything this time, he just averts his gaze and gestures for us to sit.

"Want any coffee?" Logan asks me, his voice low.

But I can't drink anything. My stomach hurts. I'm afraid if I do, I'll vomit.

"No, but you go ahead."

Logan eyes my dad warily and I reassure him. "Go on. I'm fine."

He moves away from me reluctantly and then I'm left alone with my father.

"Theo," he says, his hands cupped around the coffee mug in front of him. "I wasn't sure you'd show up."

"Me either."

He glances over at Logan who is ordering while watching me intently.

"Your boyfriend?" he asks.

"No," I say, and it's the truth because I don't know what we are. I know we're no longer just friends and I know what I want us to be. But we haven't actually talked about it. I'm too chicken to bring it up, and I don't know what Logan wants. Until then, I can't speak for him.

My dad spins that mug around and around and I blurt out, "What do you have?"

He seems to know what I'm referring to because he replies, "Pancreatic cancer."

My stomach churns and I nod lamely. "I'm sorry."

He nods but doesn't say anything as Logan approaches us, sits down next to me, and pulls my chair as close as he possibly can to his.

"I'm Logan," he says.

"Sutherland."

"Nice to meet you," Logan says, his hand resting on my lap.

I link my fingers with his and let out a sigh of relief.

This isn't going terribly, so far.

"Will you be moving out here?" I ask. "Or commuting?"

"That depends on you," he says. "If you want to spend time with me, I'll stay."

My breath leaves my chest in a whoosh. That's a big commitment and I'm speechless. Am I supposed to just watch him die? Will I be his caretaker?

Will I have to make the choice to take him off life support like I had to do with my mom?

I'm not sure I can do that again.

My vision starts to narrow, and I clench onto Logan's hand tighter.

He seems to read my distress because he says, "What would that entail? Because Theo is busy with school. He can't be at your side 24-7."

I glance over at him, my eyes stinging, my throat sore.

Fuck. This guy. How is he so perfect all the time?

"I would hire hospice near the end. I would just hope to see you when you're free...whenever you want."

"Why?" I ask.

The question hangs between us, and my dad looks away, swallowing roughly.

"Dying puts things into perspective."

It seems so, since he's here, meeting with me and looking remorseful.

"Okay," I whisper. "We'll see how it goes."

Shit. Now my dad looks happy, his eyes lighting up.

I blame Logan for this, for softening my hard heart. There's no going back to the way I was.

We spend the next thirty minutes chatting. Mostly, it's my dad asking about how I'm doing in school. I'm glad he keeps it superficial; I'm not sure I could handle anything else at the moment.

When we're done, I feel completely wrung out.

"You okay?" Logan asks as we walk to his car.

"Yeah. I will be."

He pulls me into his chest, hugging me tightly, his soft lips against my neck. He said he was a hugger and it's true. It's all he seems to do now that I've given him the green light to touch me whenever he wants.

I wrap my arms around his back and don't let go.

I'm just going to hold on for a little longer.

twenty

LOGAN

"MY CHEM FINAL IS TOMORROW," I tell Theo. He shifts between my legs, glancing up at me, the chemistry book open on his lap. Look at those pretty fucking eyes. I remember thinking they were eerie at first, but now I know how wrong I was. They are stunning and I am obsessed.

I can't help myself. I press my lips to his.

It's been two weeks since Thanksgiving, and I've seen Theo every day. It's similar to how it was before, except most nights I sleep over and we stay up late talking. He's told me all about how it was growing up with Sutherland as a dad, how much disappointment he's faced in his life, and despite it all, how amazing and supportive his mom was.

He's also mentioned the bullying a few times and he keeps it pretty vague, but it's still enough to make my blood boil.

I just hold him a little tighter when those tidbits come tumbling out.

It's no wonder he was so bitter and distrustful when we met. I honestly don't know how he came out of all that intact.

But I feel super lucky that he's softening around me. He smiles more and just generally seems more content and relaxed. Like right now, he's wedged between my legs, letting me hold him. Part of me expects him to start purring.

"You will do great," he says, his voice a little sad.

Actually, come to think of it, he has seemed particularly anxious and a little down the past two days. I think it must be because of his dad.

It has to be hard to lose someone like that. Even though, from what I can make out, Sutherland was shit at being a father.

I rest my chin on his shoulder as Theo turns his gaze back to the book and continues to review chapters with me.

When we finish later that evening and I get up to leave to go meet Finn for dinner, Theo kisses me long and deep, his eyes a little watery, and he's reluctant to let me go. I feel bad leaving him when he's obviously feeling low, but I have to get some sleep for tomorrow's test and I know that if I stay, I'll be up all night touching him. I can't keep my hands off of him.

"Hey, I'll be over tomorrow afternoon. Then we can celebrate."

He looks away and nods, his bottom lip clenched between his teeth.

I just cup his jaw and run my thumb along his cheek.

"And thank you, Theo, for believing in me," I say and he nods again and then turns around completely, facing the window. "Do you need me to stay? 'Cause I will…"

"No, it's okay. You need to go, I get it. I'll see you later, yeah?" He sounds like he's okay but he still won't look at me. Strange.

"Alright then. Goodnight." I close the door behind me and make my way to my car. I'll figure out what's bothering him tomorrow. Right now, I need to focus on passing this bitch of a final.

* * *

I blink and then blink again. I rub at my eyes and then look again at the score on my computer just to make sure I'm not hallucinating.

Holy shit.

I passed!

Not only did I pass, but I got a motherfucking A.

I stand up so quickly that the chair hits the wall and I trip over my feet, but I barely notice. I'm fumbling with my phone and sending a quick text to Theo.

Me: I passed! I got an A.

Minutes pass and then he replies.

Theo: I knew you would.
Me: Fuck yeah!

My eyes get a little teary and I know when I see him again, I'm going to kiss him senseless. I'm going to strip him naked and then celebrate by fucking the daylights out of him.

But first, I need to tell my parents the good news. Oh, and Landon and Finn. My fingers fly across the screen as I send off messages, and they all respond back within minutes.

I'm so excited, I want to take Theo out to dinner to celebrate, so I send him a bunch of texts asking if he can meet me at the Italian restaurant later but after twenty minutes, he still hasn't responded. Why isn't he texting me back? I try calling but he doesn't pick up.

He probably just got busy with school shit. Or Curie swatted his phone under the oven.

That's a more likely scenario. I'll just head over there and ask him in person.

I walk outside my building, staring at my phone, but my gaze is wrenched up when I hear my name called.

"Yo, Logan. Grab a bite with us!" Xander says as he throws an arm over my shoulder.

I glance down at my phone once more and when I don't see any more messages, I just shove it into my back pocket.

I'll grab lunch with my friends and then I'll head over to see Theo.

A few hours later, my knuckles rap on the door and I shift on my feet. I need to convince Theo to give me a key so I don't have to wait like this. I'm too antsy. I want to see him.

The door swings open, and Theo is standing there looking like hell. He's shirtless, in his baggy joggers, his pencil stuck behind his ear, and his eyes are red-rimmed. His hair looks like he's been running his hands through it all day.

"Hey," I say gently, stepping toward him, and taking his face in my hands. "Hey, what happened? Was it your dad?"

He shakes his head.

"No. Nothing. I'm fine...I'm just tired."

My lips turn down and I examine him closely. I mean, he probably is tired. He was busy studying for his finals, and I can't imagine what those even look like. Hell, just thinking about what he must have to memorize makes my head hurt.

"You sure?" I ask as I feel Curie brush against my ankles.

I reach into my pocket and pull out a treat, handing it to her.

When I stand back up, Theo is blinking rapidly.

"Yeah, I'm fine. Congratulations on your test," he says, moving away from me.

I follow him into the kitchen and lean against the counter.

"That was all you, Theo. I got a fucking A. Me! Can you believe it? I don't think I've ever gotten an A...except maybe in kindergarten."

He grabs a glass from the cabinet and fills it with water, gulping it down.

"Yeah, I can believe it, Logan. And no, that was all you. You worked hard and you deserve it."

I itch to pull him into me, but he looks like he needs his space, so I just fold my arms across my chest and watch him.

He'll come around. Pretty soon he'll walk right into my

arms and pull me against him, like he's done every night for the past few weeks.

Then we'll fuck. I want celebratory sex, and I want it bad.

"So..." He begins not meeting my gaze. "It's over then."

"Thank God," I mutter with a smile. I am never taking another science class for the rest of my life.

The glass in Theo's hand trembles, water sloshing over the sides, and he sets it down roughly onto the counter.

"Yeah, okay, I get it."

"Yeah, shit. I know. Never again," I mutter and laugh a little.

But Theo isn't laughing, his body is stiff and unmoving.

"You can go," he whispers.

Those three broken words make my entire body freeze. For a moment, I think my brain misheard. "What?"

"It's okay. It's done. You can go, Logan," he repeats a little louder, and I frown. Is he for real? After everything we've been through. Is he...is he asking me to leave?

"Are you shitting me right now?" I ask, frustration welling up inside of me. "Are you kicking me out? Why?"

"It's the end of the semester," he says, swallowing roughly, his eyes on the floor. "So, the deal between us is done."

I push away from the counter and step toward him.

"What the fuck are you even talking about?" I ask. Because I want him to spell it out for me.

Shit, did this mean more to me than it did for him?

He closes his eyes and rolls his lips between his teeth, but doesn't answer.

"Look at me, Theo. Do you really want me to go?"

He glances at me briefly, blinking rapidly, and then turns away from me again.

"Oh, hell no," I say, stomping out of the kitchen, irritation rolling inside of me. I was going to invite him to Christmas. I wanted to spend the holidays with him. I wanted to fuck under the mistletoe.

Does he not want me anymore?

Does he just need a little space?

What the hell is even happening?

My thoughts are running rampant and I don't know what else to do, so I move toward the front door and grab the doorknob, but I suddenly stop, take a deep breath in and out, and turn around. I see Theo crawling under the covers of his bed, pulling them over his head, and my heart just cracks.

I'm not fucking leaving. Not yet.

He needs to tell me to go.

I stomp over to the bed, wrenching the covers off of him and tossing them onto the ground.

"Do you want me?" I blurt.

Theo blinks up at me.

"Tell me!"

He swallows and nods. "Of course I do, but I don't want you to feel like—"

I don't let him finish. I just pull him up into my arms, crushing him to my chest.

"Then don't fucking push me away. I'm not through with you. I don't think I'll ever be through with you."

His body trembles against me and a sob erupts out of him, and all that lingering frustration is expelled in a breath.

"Fuck. I'm not leaving, and you're spending motherfucking Christmas with me. And the new year. And next Christmas, too. And the rest of our time on earth, really."

Theo lets out a wet laugh and clutches onto me, his fingers digging into my back.

"Okay," he mutters.

"Better be okay, asshole. Don't scare me like that, ever again," I mutter and he looks up at me, his eyelashes wet, his lips trembling.

"You really mean it? You're sure you want to be with me?"

"Hell yes, I do. Pack your shit. We're leaving tomorrow."

THEO

It's raining buckets when we leave my apartment the next day.

After holding onto me for hours, Logan went back to his place to pack and then returned with his stuff. We spent the night inside of each other, fucking in the moonlight before waking up and driving out of town.

My hand is currently tucked into his as we make our way down the highway.

I thought I'd lost him yesterday, but it was all just a horrible misunderstanding.

My past came back to haunt me. My stupid brain convinced me that because we hadn't talked yet, hadn't made anything official, that we were still just messing around and he was planning on ending things. And when he got that amazing grade, I was sure he was over me now that he had what he wanted.

Turns out, all he really wanted was *me*.

I'm so glad, he didn't leave.

What would have happened if he'd walked away? My heart clenches in my chest at the thought.

"What do we tell your parents…about us?" I ask, glancing over at Logan.

God, he's so handsome, so fucking beautiful.

Logan shrugs, eyeing me. "Uh, what do *you* want to tell them?"

I glance out the window, not even letting myself hope.

"Get out of that big brain of yours and tell me, Theo. What do you want this to be?" he asks firmly.

Fuck, is he going to make me say it? I can't.

Logan grunts and sighs heavily. "Jesus, Theo. We're boyfriends. Okay? That's what we're going to tell them. Repeat after me, *boyfriends*."

I gape at him and my heart skips a beat.

"Are you sure?"

He grumbles under his breath.

"I'm fucking sure. You're mine. Good luck getting rid of me."

"I don't want to get rid of you. I just…I've never had a boyfriend before."

"Me either…" He looks at me and his lips twitch. "You're my first."

My lips break into a smile and my heart throbs in my chest.

"Okay. Boyfriends then."

"Boyfriends."

Curie meows loudly from the backseat.

"Think she approves?"

I glance back and she just blinks at me.

"Yeah, I think she does."

* * *

We make it to his parents' house and I'm nervous all over again.

But I have nothing to be worried about because when Logan tells his parents that we're together now, his dad full-on sobs and even his mom gets a little teary-eyed.

Logan gets a little sniffly too.

Curie cries out in solidarity.

That's when I see it. A large carpet-covered cat tree in the corner.

My god. Who are these people?

I let Curie out and she walks casually toward it, like she hadn't just spent the last two hours bitching about being in the carrier.

She hops on and makes her way to the very top and then looks down on us like we're her loyal subjects.

Honestly, she's not too far off.

I glance over at Logan and he's hugging his brother and chuckling.

I don't know how I got so lucky as to land *the* Logan Lewis, but I am going to spend the rest of however much time we have together being grateful as shit.

Hell, I may even start buying lottery tickets.

epilogue

HE'S GONE. *My dad. He died in hospice four months after moving to be closer to me. I was holding his hand when he passed. It wasn't perfect in the end, but it was peaceful. And, really, is any ending truly happy?*

Logan was there with me, his arms wrapped around my waist, his chin on my shoulder.

He's always there. Holding me, cherishing me, caring for me.

I've grown used to it. This sensitive man.

When my dad passed, he probably cried more than I did. I had no tears left to shed.

But I am resolved in this: I'm glad I decided to get to know him, to forgive him. And I'm a better person for it. Logan deserves the best parts of me.

I want to be better for him.

It's summer now. We're on our way to Oregon. We plan on spending some time in the forests and then making our way along the coast. Logan says we will fuck our way through every town we stop at.

I'm sure I'll be a willing participant.

I still can't believe that he wants me like he does.

So damn lucky.

Logan is trying to peek over and see what I'm writing. He can't help himself.

But he already knows.

Because yesterday I told him I loved him. I was brave and just blurted it out.

Logan sniffled and held me, whispering that he loved me too.

Who knew that when he showed up at my door all those months ago that this was how it would all turn out?

Who knew he'd be the one to help me heal? Who knew he'd be the perfect person for me?

Not me.

It was never me, until him.

I wrote this book because I had terrible writer's block while working on Lex's book. So I had to step away.

I started writing *Until Him* to help me move past that. And then, I ended up falling in love with the characters.

It wasn't until halfway through that I decided to publish it.

I hope you enjoyed it.

And, yes, I am pretty sure Landon and Finn will have their own book because I fell in love with them along the way.

If you want to see what happens with the nipple clamps click here.

acknowledgments

First, I would like to thank my editor, Angela O'Connell, for all of your hard work on this book. You all don't realize how much she does to make this readable. I can get a little ridiculous.

Also, thank you to my alpha readers Nicole Dykes, Corinne Rochelle and Lark Taylor for taking time out of your busy schedules to read this and encourage me through the panic.

And Lark, thank you for shouting at me when I said I shouldn't publish this. This is all your fault!

Margaret Neal thank you for beta reading this and picking out the lingering mistakes we all missed. You are amazing.

And last, but not least, thank you to all the readers who reached out to me with words of encouragement (see the dedication). They mean everything and keep me writing.

about the author

Cora Rose loves any kind of romance and consumes way too many books each year. She currently lives in the U.S. and spends her days daydreaming about the characters inside her head.

You can reach her on her website or email her at Cora-RoseRomance@gmail.com